UNDER
A BROKEN
SKY

Also by Kris Calvin

Emma Lawson books

All That Fall

UNDER A BROKEN SKY

A THRILLER

KRIS CALVIN

CROOKED
LANE

NEW YORK

Published in the United States by Crooked Lane Books, an imprint of The Quick Brown Fox & Company LLC.

Crooked Lane Books and its logo are trademarks of The Quick Brown Fox & Company LLC.

Library of Congress Catalog-in-Publication data available upon request.

ISBN (hardcover): 978-1-64385-904-0
ISBN (ebook): 978-1-64385-905-7

Cover design by Meghan Deist

Printed in the United States.

www.crookedlanebooks.com

Crooked Lane Books
34 West 27th St., 10th Floor
New York, NY 10001

First Edition: July 2022

10 9 8 7 6 5 4 3 2 1

For Lori

Tuesday, February 2

FOLSOM LAKE IN early February is icy cold. Cold enough to cause a man who suddenly finds himself immersed over his head to gasp heartily from the shock of it, drawing the bracing river water that feeds the lake from above deep into his lungs.

But the solitary figure responsible for Johnny Hill's death thought it unlikely Johnny had felt the cold as he choked on the water's involuntary flow. Surely if he had, he would have fought back with flailing arms and thrashing legs against nature taking its course. They say it takes a grown man breathing water forty seconds to drown.

Ten minutes later, anyone who happened to see the figure sitting cross-legged on a rocky outcrop gazing at the shore might have assumed he was meditating, inwardly focused despite the majesty of the red-orange sun cresting the horizon on this first day in weeks without rain. Except the man who killed Johnny Hill was not practicing mindfulness. He was thinking how nice it would be to ride Johnny's bike back to Sacramento through the cottonwood, valley oak, and willow trees that bordered the American River. He'd be able to hear the bird songs and raucous calls of warblers and scrub jay. A horned owl might swoop overhead.

Yes, it would be nice. But it wouldn't be smart, and the man knew the value of smart choices. So he left Johnny's bike in the campsite propped against the side of an abandoned tent, where along with the empty whiskey and pill bottles it would tell a story that would sadden but not surprise those who heard it.

The man had never killed before. As he climbed down from the rocks, he prodded his conscience.

He found no guilt there.

Perhaps a touch of melancholy, which he did not mind.

FIVE WEEKS LATER
WEDNESDAY, MARCH 10

1

New City Hall

A LIBI MORNING SUN turned his back on the good book and
comfortable armchair that called to him from the living
room of his modest ninth-floor apartment in the Bridge District
of West Sacramento and made his way downtown.

It wasn't light out yet, but he hadn't been able to sleep. He
reasoned that if he was one of the first to arrive at work, he might
clear his in-box before the distractions of the day began.

He was still getting used to his new office. It was the third
he'd been assigned in as many years.

When first promoted from homicide detective to head of
major crimes in the investigative division of the Sacramento Police
Department, he'd worked out of an overheated room previously
occupied by his predecessor in the joint sprawling police and fire
headquarters. Funds had come through for a massive renovation
of that site, and Alibi and key members of his team had been tem-
porarily moved to the top floor of a downtown steel-and-glass sky-
scraper the state had picked up for a song when a hedge fund had
gone bust.

Though luxurious, Alibi had never been comfortable there—
it had seemed an odd place from which to coordinate the pursuit
of those suspected of significant criminal activity.

So he'd been happy last month when he'd been moved again, this time to the fourth floor of the modern building known to locals as New City Hall. Built in the early 2000s, it was only a few dozen yards from the pre–World War I historic city headquarters with its century-old clock tower, a downtown landmark. The two structures together accommodated the principal functions of government for Sacramento's five hundred thousand residents.

Alibi found lots to like about his new office. In addition to ample space for a good-sized desk and a couch long enough to accommodate his six-foot frame when he stretched out for forty winks, there was room for a small conference table and a rolling whiteboard, his preferred tool for thinking through a complex case alone or with colleagues. He'd learned that if he created a visual record of key points and posted it in his line of sight, it helped ideas and threads to percolate in his subconscious, even when he wasn't actively considering them. Best of all, his west-facing window overlooked Cesar Chavez Park, a tree-lined public square. In the late 1800s, it had hosted circuses complete with elephants and now frequently held lively concerts and the farmers' market, creating a fiesta-like atmosphere. Its vibrancy made Alibi feel connected to the city and the people he served.

Some in his position wouldn't like being located so near to the mayor, whose chambers were on the next floor up. But Alibi found the Honorable Melissa Ruiz to be reasonable, at least in terms of the demands she put on his time. She didn't use proximity as an excuse to pop in for frequent updates but instead relied on Breno Silva, a bright young communications specialist whose responsibilities had recently been expanded to include serving as liaison between Alibi and the mayor's office on issues of public safety.

Breno and Alibi got along well. They were both international football fans, and despite Breno supporting the men's Brazilian team and Alibi the Italians, they'd found common ground cheering for Team USA in women's soccer. They also empathized with each other regarding the frequency with which they had to explain the origin of their names.

At fifteen, Alibi had overheard his aunt telling his uncle that the timing of his birth had cleared his father of a murder rap. Upon holding his newborn son for the first time, his father had reportedly exclaimed, "Oh, my beautiful alibi." The rest, as they say, was history. As far as his surname, Alibi had been unable to find any other relatives who went by Morning Sun. He'd concluded that the type of criminal activity that had led to the murder charge had caused his father to invent a false moniker. How better to avoid identification and culpability, pre-Internet, than through a difficult-to-track pseudonym?

Breno had only one unusual name to contend with, and even that wouldn't have been the case had he lived in Brazil, where its Portuguese origin and meaning—"king"—were well known. But in the United States in the year Breno was born, only 10 in 1 million babies shared his name.

When Alibi was offered a promotion to management, he'd underestimated the hours of administrative tasks that would come with it. As he sat down at his computer to engage with the jumble of windows and threads and pings that lay in wait there, he wondered, not for the first time, whether the career move had been wise.

Three years ago, about to turn forty, he'd thought taking on new challenges was a good idea. Plus there'd been the promise of a significantly higher paycheck. Now, still single, still living in his comfortable one-bedroom apartment, and still happily driving his old Chevy pickup when off duty, Alibi was having trouble figuring out what to spend the added money on. Maybe he should take a trip somewhere exotic or relaxing.

After skimming several emails with limited retention of what he'd read, he longed for an infusion of caffeine. He decided he'd walk to Second Chance Café as soon as it opened and pick up a large, fresh-brewed, dark-roast coffee to go. In addition to increasing his productivity, he might run into Emma there—the popular spot was under a mile from her office, and it had happened before.

How long had it been since he'd seen her, a month?

Then he remembered Breno and Kate's party. He was sure Emma would attend. He checked his calendar and confirmed the invitation was for tonight.

We're ENGAGED!
Open House: March 10th Wednesday 5–8pm
Drop by for tapas and drinks. Help us celebrate!
Kate and Breno

Alibi hadn't closed his office door—he hadn't thought anyone would be around this early. Sensing someone there, he glanced up to find Breno standing in the open doorway.

Breno Silva was a fit, dark-haired, handsome young man with strong features. At work he wore conservatively cut suits with a plain dress shirt, collar open, unless he was called to speak to the press, at which point he added one of the many silk ties he kept in his top desk drawer. He had a habit of frequently pushing his gold-rimmed glasses firmly up onto the bridge of his nose.

From the look on Breno's face, Alibi gathered he wasn't there to discuss the latest striker the Brazil national football team had acquired or his engagement party this evening. He must be bringing a message from the mayor.

No surprise that the Honorable Melissa Ruiz was in already. The woman worked as hard from her executive chambers as any union pipelayer hell-bent on getting every possible hour of overtime that Alibi had ever met.

Born to Brazilian parents and raised in Brooklyn, Breno spoke fluent Portuguese and English, both with a New York accent. Despite the cultural stereotypes of New Yorkers as fast talkers and Brazilians as outgoing, he had a cautious and quiet manner. Alibi assumed he was thinking now about how best to frame what he'd come to say.

When Breno finally did speak, it was carefully and in a measured tone. "The mayor asked if you might be free to see her this morning. She'll call down when she's available."

So much for a trip to Second Chance.

Still, Melissa Ruiz was rarely without a cup of coffee in her hand. She'd almost certainly offer him one.

"Of course," Alibi told Breno. "Can you tell me what this is about?"

Breno hesitated. "There is now some question as to whether Johnny Hill's drowning at Folsom Lake last month was an accident."

CHAPTER

2

Clad Corp Ideal Storage

Across town, the hulking silhouette of the self-storage facility was impossible for Emma and Luke to miss, despite the
moonless sky and the absence of streetlights on the frontage road.
With the convertible top down, a rich, earthy scent and the sound
of countless buzzing insects was a reminder the Sacramento River
was less than a mile away.

"Should I turn around?" Luke asked, having slowed the car to
a near crawl.

"No," Emma said. "That might be a way in."

She pointed to an unmarked gravel drive ahead on the right,
barely visible, flanked on either side by dense stands of eucalyptus
trees. Luke made the turn, and in a matter of minutes they emerged
onto paved asphalt. He pulled to a stop behind the building. The
back door was shrouded in darkness, the security lights above it
either broken or not turned on. A sign declaring PROPERTY OF
CLAD CORP was obscured by illegible graffiti in a looping script of
bright-red paint, fresh against the faded gray stucco of the exterior
wall.

"Let's drive to the front," Emma said.

They rounded the structure, and across the empty lot a dimly
lit public entrance to the several blocks-long, five-stories tall

building came into view. Luke smoothly braked and parked opposite a wide ramp leading up to double glass doors. At sixteen, he
was a surprisingly good driver, and one of only two people Emma
permitted to take the wheel of her white-bodied, black-topped
1967 Mustang convertible.

When he hopped out to retrieve his bike from the back seat,
Emma could see his breath, a wisp of white in the predawn air.

She called after him, "We can put the top up and lock the car."

"It's okay, I've got it," Luke said.

Little of the Irish accent of his early childhood remained.
With ease, he lifted the older-model Schwinn with its peeling
green paint onto the ground.

It had been two weeks since Emma had promised Kate—her
best friend and Luke's mother—that she'd pick up the folding
tables from storage before Kate and Breno's engagement party that
night. Yet time had passed, as it always seemed to, without Emma
making anything other than her current investigation at the
Hayden Commission a priority.

Fortunately, Luke had agreed to help. When they were done,
he'd ride his bike along the riverside path, busy with joggers and
dog walkers even at this early hour, to get to his before-school jazz
band practice on time.

Emma pressed the white, plastic key card Kate had given her
against a metal panel next to the exterior doors. They unlocked
with a click. Once inside, she commandeered a flatbed cart while
Luke secured the Schwinn to the railing at the top of an open
stairwell.

They took the freight elevator to the fourth floor, where they
emerged into a long, windowless hallway lined with wide metal
doors painted an industrial green. The occasional clunk and whir
of something mechanical echoed in the empty space. Perhaps it
was a heater—though if that was the case, it seemed to Emma the
thermostat was set for working conditions in a morgue.

Emma had memorized the simple combination to open the
padlock that secured Kate's storage space. The two tables they'd
come for leaned against the back wall, easy enough to get to
since a center aisle had been left clear between furniture and
stacks of boxes neatly lined up on either side. Emma would have
expected nothing less from Kate, who she was pretty sure rivaled

multimillionaire "tidying expert" Marie Kondo in her organizational skills.

Standing at opposite ends, Emma and Luke had hoisted up the first table when there was the unmistakable whoosh of an elevator door opening, followed by the sound of heavy footsteps headed in their direction. Luke stiffened. Emma felt her heartbeat steadily climb. While it was almost certainly someone else getting a predawn start on a household task, as though by agreement they silently lowered the table to the ground.

After the perilous circumstances they'd found themselves in last summer, on the outside chance a storage-facility-stalking, ax-wielding madman was approaching, neither Emma nor Luke wanted to be caught flat-footed, trapped among furniture and boxes with their backs against the wall. Still, Emma was surprised when Luke lifted a heavy brass lamp from the top of a file cabinet and, gripping its stem like a baseball bat, stood poised to swing, his eyes on the open door.

Not going to happen, Emma thought. Luke might be a head taller and quite a bit stronger than she was now, but last she'd checked, she was still the adult in the room. She moved in front of him, blocking his way, and stepped out into the hall.

The source of the footsteps was a pair of work boots worn by a man in khaki pants and a matching shirt, DANIEL embroidered above IDEAL STORAGE on the front pocket. His face was lined with age, his hair thinning and gray, but he appeared straight-backed and strong as he effortlessly pushed a cart larger than the one Emma and Luke had.

"Good morning," he said, his voice rich and low. "Can I help you with anything?"

Emma thanked him and said they could manage, then turned back into the unit.

As Luke replaced the lamp on top of the cabinet, his eyes met hers sheepishly, as though he was embarrassed. He needn't have worried. Emma understood all too well his impulse to seize the initiative rather than hope someone else would save the day. Having lost both parents when she was eleven, she'd stopped trusting others to ensure the safety of her world long ago.

The tables secured, Luke guided the cart from behind and Emma steadied the load from in front. They moved quickly up the hall until they reached a unit with an open door. Inside, boxes without lids teetered on top of one another while a scratched platform bed served as a graveyard for a mass of ancient-looking computer equipment—cords frayed, wires exposed—along with dozens of black garbage bags stuffed nearly to bursting, contents unknown. The Ideal Storage employee who had greeted them earlier stood, hands on hips, facing the chaos.

Emma imagined it must get lonely working in here, hour after hour, with no one to talk to. "Any chance there are gold coins or a rolled-up Renoir in one of those bags?" she asked him.

The man smiled. "I doubt it, but we'll know soon enough. This unit is being cleared for nonpayment so we can rent it again."

Emma was surprised when Luke spoke up.

"Do you have to go through it all now?" he asked.

Luke used to be curious about everything, but he'd become much quieter over recent months. Emma was glad to see that this, of all things—the internal functioning of a storage facility— seemed to have sparked his interest.

"No. I take it down to the basement," the employee said. "It'll sit there until management decides what's worth selling, which usually isn't much. The rest gets recycled or goes to the dump."

"Wow, that will take a lot of trips," Luke said.

"Keeps me young," the man said, lifting two of the bags in each hand and hoisting them onto his cart as he winked at Luke, clearly realizing how that must sound coming from "an old man" to a teen.

When Emma and Luke reached the main floor and exited the facility, Emma shivered, despite the turtleneck sweater and jeans she wore. Early March clung stubbornly to an unusually harsh Northern California winter. But the sky had lightened to a deep gray, the sun would soon rise, and by noon it would be pleasant enough.

They positioned the tables securely in the back seat of the open Mustang so they wouldn't shift around when Emma drove them to Kate's. That accomplished, Luke slung one leg over his bike.

He paused before taking off. "See you at two?"

That can't be right, Emma thought. *Kate's engagement party isn't until hours after that.*

"My community service requirement. Interning at the commission? It starts today," Luke said.

"Of course," Emma said, annoyed with herself for not remembering. She knew it was important to him, and it was important to her too.

With affection, she watched as Luke pedaled at full speed out of the lot toward the river until he was out of sight.

She had just opened the door to her Mustang to get in when the silence of the morning was shattered by a horrendous boom, and the glass on the heavy front doors to the Ideal Storage building rattled loudly.

CHAPTER

3

Having lived in California all her life, Emma Lawson's first
thought was *Earthquake!* But the worn asphalt surface of the
parking lot was steady, and the sound seemed to have come from
inside. For a split second, she considered whether it might be a
bomb, then decided that was absurd—an isolated, uninhabited
storage facility made no sense as a terrorist target. Perhaps a gas
line to the heater had ruptured, or there'd been a massive short in
the electrical system.

Then she remembered the employee on the fourth floor who
had offered his help. Though he'd appeared fit, he was older, and
regardless of his age, something heavy in that chaotic unit could
have fallen on him when the building shook.

Maybe he's injured and can't get out, she thought.

She ran back inside.

She didn't want to take the elevator—the last thing she needed
was to be stuck if there was some kind of electrical malfunction.
She located stairs behind a doorway and, fueled by a rush of
adrenaline, raced up the four flights.

Out of breath, she pictured the man's name above his pocket
on his shirt. She called out, "Daniel, are you okay?" There was no
answer.

His cart was no longer in the hall. When she got to the unit
where he'd been working, many of the items were gone. Then she

recalled he'd said he would take everything to the basement. She turned and ran back down the stairs.

When she passed below the main floor, the smell of smoke hit her—not the sweet, wood-burning scent of a home hearth but something pungent and acrid. The hairs on the back of Emma's neck stood up.

She reached the bottom level. The overhead lights were off, but a reflected glow from beneath a raised wide metal door a good twenty yards to her left pierced the darkness. She hurried toward it, then stopped abruptly when she reached the threshold.

It was a massive space. But what had Emma transfixed was the twenty-foot-high wall of flames, leaping and charging as it made its way forward from the far end, eating through boxes and furniture, melting bicycles and electronics in its path. Trembling, she experienced a moment of pure terror. She wanted nothing more than to turn back, take the stairs two at a time and get outside to safety.

Then she saw him. The man lay crumpled on the floor near his cart, the back of his head dark with blood, more pooled beneath it.

Her eyes stung, and her throat ached as she crossed to him. She raised her voice over the sharp crackling and heavy thuds of items burning and toppling as the fire continued its unrelenting progress toward them. She did her best to block the threat from her mind.

"Can you hear me? Are you okay?"

He lay so still. A feeling of dread overtook her.

She shoved everything off the cart and dragged him up onto it as gently as she could. Then she wheeled him the few steps into the hall, where she was greeted by a thick, dark haze—the smoke had gotten there before her.

She was able to make out a door at the far end. She didn't dare run full tilt. He might slip off onto the floor. She race-walked, and even that made her chest hurt.

The door opened onto a paved drive that led up to a side lot of the facility. Emma didn't stop moving until they were well away from the building. She fumbled for her phone in her pocket and tapped the emergency icon.

"There's a fire, it's out of control," she said, gasping. "And a man . . ." She hoped her next words would capture the worst of it, that he wasn't beyond help. "A man has been badly hurt."

The emergency services operator told her to stay calm, that first responders were on their way. But Emma didn't know if there was time.

She dropped the phone, knelt beside the cart, and administered CPR, or her best impression of it. She'd been trained in the lifesaving technique when she was a summer lifeguard years ago in college, but she'd never before had to use it.

The Hayden Commission

EMMA CROSSED TO her desk and gingerly lowered herself onto her chair. Her thighs and calves ached, a painful reminder that sprinting up and down stairs put different demands on those muscles than her daily lap swim. Worse yet, when she reached to power up her computer, her hand visibly shook. Her mind had shifted to work, but the fight-or-flight response of her body to the morning's traumatic events had refused to extinguish, its echoes haunting her every move.

It felt as though minutes, not hours, had passed since she'd knelt over Daniel Baptiste, covering his mouth with hers, counting the seconds between each breath and chest compression.

She'd been so intent on her task that the screaming sirens of several fire engines and multiple ambulances signaling their arrival had not been enough for her to stop. It had taken a paramedic at Emma's side, gently pulling her back and guiding her away from the injured man to give those with real skill the room they needed to do their work.

She couldn't recall being helped into one of the ambulances. Her next memory was of Sutter Medical Center's emergency department, where she'd been pronounced stable and told to call if her shortness of breath got worse.

So she hadn't been there to see what exactly the emergency responders had done at the site, or what the outcome of those efforts had been. But before she left the hospital, Dr. Nelson Branco had informed her that the Ideal Storage employee was expected to not only survive but to recover, despite having suffered a mild heart attack and a concussion when he'd collapsed and hit his head. Dr. Branco also told Emma that her prompt application of CPR had undoubtedly played a role in bringing sixty-seven-year-old Daniel Baptiste back from the brink of death. She wished she could remember the name of the college swimming coach who had taught her the lifesaving skills, but she said a silent thank-you anyway.

Though she'd known taking the day off from work was an option, it held no appeal for her. When she'd gotten home, she'd showered, washing her shoulder-length, dark-auburn hair with shampoo she typically used after swimming to strip off the odor of chlorine. Then she'd dressed quickly in a rose-colored linen suit and slipped into a blush-tone pair of ballet-style flats. The one concession she'd made to the unusual circumstances of the morning was to drive rather than walk the two miles from her home in Midtown to the Hayden Commission headquarters downtown.

Rising stiffly from behind her desk, she moved to the bar against the far wall, retrieved a bottle of Tylenol, and filled a glass with water from the filtered tap. Given that her body and her clothes were clean, she decided it must be her imagination that caused her to still smell the fire's acrid, industrial-tinged smoke. She hadn't thought about it then, but she wondered now whether the strange odor, like rotten eggs, meant anything about the origin of the fire or if it had been the result of the varied composition of the materials in the path of the towering, white-hot blaze.

She glanced at her watch. She had an appointment in ten minutes with a graduate student from the University of Amsterdam who was enrolled for a quarter in a collaborative program in ethics and government at the University of California at Davis.

Emma had considered rescheduling, but she'd put the young woman off once already, and she wasn't so far from her own college days that she wasn't able to remember what it was like to try to get access to "important people" for educational purposes.

As she swallowed the pills with some difficulty, her throat still sore, she took in the state of the prized corner office she'd been given upon her promotion a year and a half ago. It was hard for her to believe it had been that long since she'd left the analysts' crowded bullpen downstairs for the hallowed corridors of the third floor.

With the budget provided by the commission to new executives, she'd furnished her suite with estate-sale and thrift-shop midcentury furniture, Mad Men style. In addition to her favorite piece, the turquoise, vinyl-fronted bar where she stood, there was a slim-line, avocado-green sofa, a 1960s blond desk, and a pristine ivory-and-chrome dinette set complete with a U-shaped, wrap-around vinyl booth that she used for additional work space or to conduct one-on-one interviews and meetings.

With care, she crossed the room and slid into the booth, her lower back joining her leg muscles in a chorus of protest, since lifting an unconscious man onto a storage facility cart was also not part of her daily exercise routine.

For a beat, she regretted having turned down the prescription painkillers offered to her in the emergency room—though having lived with her grandmother's alcoholism, she was leery of anything that came with a high risk of addiction. Besides, those pills would have made her feel too foggy and sleepy to come in to work, and there was nowhere she'd rather be right now.

It was more than the vintage furnishings that made Emma's office stand out from those of her colleagues. Two of its walls were covered in colorful poster-size sheets filled with her scribbled notes on her investigation into the new San Francisco–Oakland train crossing, a massive $30 billion underwater tunnel set to open in four months.

She'd gotten the idea when she'd met Alibi at his office one day for coffee and had seen how he used his whiteboard, though she preferred something that endured for the life of a project, nothing erased along the way.

There was only one personal item in Emma's office: a small framed sketch on the wall behind her desk. In shades of black and gray, it depicted a flowering tree in the foreground, while a shadowy train streaked past in the distance.

When her father, Atticus, had given it to her on her tenth birthday, his drawing had evoked memories of the many times they'd walked together to San Francisco's Fourth Street Amtrak station, only a few blocks from where they lived. The stories he'd invented on the spot for Emma and her younger sister, Jasmine, had transformed ordinary passengers into mysterious strangers swallowed by gargantuan metal beasts that screeched and hooted as they departed for far-flung, magical places.

But the next year, Emma had found her mother collapsed on the floor of their apartment, the pain of a massive heart attack evident in her eyes. Two days later, following a private cremation only he'd attended, her father had disappeared without warning or explanation. She hadn't seen or heard from Atticus since. In college, she'd hired a private detective she'd found online to try to locate him, but he'd come up empty-handed.

She kept the drawing on her office wall as a reminder that she'd survived the pain of abandonment, not by outrunning it but by outworking it—substituting the satisfactions of a meaningful career for the fickle affections of people. She'd been guided by that mantra until Kate and Luke had come into her life, and she'd learned that the friends she chose didn't carry the same risks to her heart as the family members she'd been assigned at birth.

There was a knock on her door. Knowing it must be the graduate student for the interview, Emma prepared herself to project professionalism, despite her aches and pains from the morning. "Come in," she called out, her voice clear and welcoming. But when the door opened, though she rarely found herself speechless, Emma was at a loss for words. Expectations are a powerful thing, and it took hers a beat to adjust.

The young woman looked like she was in high school, no older than "sweet sixteen." Achingly thin, she had large, round, blue eyes. Her hair, a silvery ash blond, was short, parted to the side, and flat, like a little boy's first professional cut, though her full, pale mouth and the long arch of her neck were anything but childlike. She wore snug, faded Levi's 501 jeans and a loose white T-shirt, no jewelry or makeup. A heavy, old-fashioned camera hung from a thick leather strap around her neck.

Emma glanced at the schedule her assistant, Hailey, had prepared for her.

"Are you Daphne VerStrate, here for the ethics and government interview?"

Daphne hesitated, then said in a quiet voice, "I am."

She had a pronounced Dutch accent. Some might not have identified it, but Emma's mother had been of Dutch descent.

"I'm Emma Lawson. Please, join me." Emma gestured to the place across from her in the booth.

As Daphne sat down, she appeared a bit dazzled by the eclectic vintage furnishings and Emma's lengthy, handwritten notes on the train project, highlighted in bright red and yellow, though she seemed most interested in Atticus's drawing. Her gaze rested there, and Emma saw what appeared to be recognition in the young woman's eyes. Likely she'd seen an artist with a similar style, or maybe Atticus's image of the train had evoked a memory of her own.

Emma decided Daphne VerStrate was older than she'd first thought. Something in her eyes spoke to experience, to a broader life lived than she what she could have gotten in high school.

Daphne lifted her large camera with strong, slim hands and tested sight lines around the room. "Would it be all right if we start with a few photos? I'll be doing a slide presentation for my class on the findings of my paper. It would be nice to feature a shot of you." Not letting the camera fall, she gestured with her chin to the area by the bar. "Over there the light is best."

Emma moved to stand where Daphne had indicated. She was glad she'd worn her rose-colored suit. She'd been photographed in it before and was comfortable with how it looked.

Daphne moved back and forth in a half circle around Emma, her camera shutter clicking rapidly as she captured her from various angles.

5

New City Hall

AFTER BRENO LEFT, Alibi accessed the internal files on Johnny Hill's death to supplement what he remembered from the extensive news coverage at the time. Press interest had been heightened because Johnny was the only son of Frances Hill, chief of staff to the powerful Hayden Government Ethics Commission and a former mayor of nearby San Francisco. Her résumé of past political positions made her a frequently discussed potential successor to Sacramento's congressperson, who had indicated he would not run for reelection next year.

Johnny's death at age twenty-four was ruled an accidental drowning, though there had been questions regarding suicide, since sleeping pills and alcohol had been found in his system.

Alibi uncapped a black marker and created a timeline on his whiteboard:

JONATHAN (JOHNNY) HILL

- DROWNED ON OR ABOUT FEB 1
- AUTOPSY FEB 3. TOX: ZOLPIDEM, ALCOHOL
- SUICIDE CONSIDERED. DISMISSED FOR LACK OF EVIDENCE

- RULED ACCIDENTAL DEATH FEB 4
- BODY RELEASED TO FAMILY FEB 5
- CREMATION FEB 7
- MEMORIAL SERVICE FEB 13
- MAYOR RAISES CONCERNS MAR 10-37 DAYS AFTER JOHNNY'S DEATH

The dismissed suicide theory jumped out at Alibi. If something had caused it to gain new life, that could explain the mayor wanting to speak to him today. His phone pinged. Perhaps that was her. Alibi smiled when he saw it was an auto reminder to pick up his dry cleaning.

Outside his window in Cesar Chavez Plaza, vendors were setting up for the weekly Wednesday farmers' market. He could see booths with farm-fresh produce, flowers, and hand-milled soaps. There was one with a green banner for Bondolio olive oil, produced locally. Alibi planned to pick some up later if there was time.

The morning's major crimes briefing had been relatively quiet. There were no new murders on the docket, though the day was young.

There had been an odd incident at a gallery in Old Sacramento the night before, a violent altercation at a reception for an out-of-town artist. The details were hazy, but someone in the crowd had evidently thrown a glass of red wine at the featured work, ruining it, at which point the artist had assaulted the perpetrator. Alibi had asked for an update once the value of the damage and the seriousness of any injuries were known.

Predawn, there'd been a fire at the storage facility near the river, but it was an old building and the blaze could easily have been sparked by an electrical problem. Even if it turned out to be suspicious, it wouldn't come to Alibi's unit—it would land with the arson investigation officers in the fire department.

There was a knock on Alibi's door.

"Come in."

The door opened to reveal Dr. Jackie Oliver—known to friends and colleagues as Jackie O—a PhD sociologist on a federally funded fellowship to provide advice to the department on gang-related crime. Next to her stood Carlos Sifuentes, a likable junior officer who could turn any sentence into a paragraph. Carlos and his husband had a three-year-old son and were expecting to finalize adoption of six-month-old twin girls any day now. Alibi wondered whether Carlos's kids would grow up to be champion talkers like Carlos, or if they'd develop an early and lifelong appreciation of silence.

Unsurprisingly, Carlos spoke first and without preamble. "We received an update on the fire at the storage facility. Several propane canisters were the source of the powerful blast. Maybe someone found a sale and decided to buy them in bulk for a household generator and boxed and illegally kept them in their storage unit. Or the canisters might have been put there with the intent of blowing up the place. It was the propane gas that gave off a nauseating smell like rotten eggs, but the mechanism to start the fire appears to have been an amateur Molotov cocktail–style beer bottle stuffed with a rag soaked with gasoline. The fire department's arson investigation unit has officers working the scene. That's who sent over the report, and—"

Alibi felt it necessary to perform an intervention, or Carlos might go on all day. "Was there anything actionable for our team?"

"Yes. There was a fatality as a result of this morning's fire, and—"

"The man in the hospital? The employee?" Alibi asked. "I thought he was expected to recover."

"No, not him. A body was found in the fire. Or maybe a body isn't the right term. The remains of a human were found. Arson said it's not possible to identify anything about them yet, given their proximity to the origin of the blast. But if the fire was not an accident—"

Alibi finished Carlos's sentence for him. "Then that would make our arsonist a killer."

6

The Hayden Commission

EMMA HAD FOUND Daphne VerStrate's questions on point, with one notable exception that occurred well into the interview.

Daphne had begun by asking what exactly a government ethics commission did. Emma had answered that the Hayden Commission was charged by the California legislature with promoting the ethical functioning of government; to that end, the commission examined and investigated public sector entities to see where systems fell short in terms of being ethical. Then Daphne had wanted to know how "ethical behavior" was defined for government. Did it require following a moral code? Emma had explained the commission used "ethical" to mean operating in good faith and with transparency. Daphne had also asked whether the commission uncovered crimes like corruption in government contracts. Emma assumed the question was related to the class Daphne was taking, and the answer was yes, particularly when there was big money involved.

The disturbing moment had come when Daphne asked several questions about Frances Hill, chief of staff to the commission and Emma's boss. She'd wanted to know whether Fran worked on-site at commission headquarters most days or was more often out attending capitol events, whether she typically worked long hours into the evening, and most troublesome, what Fran's relationship had been like with her son, Johnny, when he was a child.

Fran Hill was a frequently discussed future candidate for congressperson, so media interest in her was always high. But after Johnny's tragic drowning, several less-than-reputable freelancers had presented themselves under false pretenses to try to obtain inside information regarding Fran, undoubtedly hoping for a high price from the tabloids.

When Emma asked Daphne why she wanted to know those things, she'd responded that she was "just curious." She'd looked away as she spoke, and Emma had been fairly certain the young woman was lying.

The exchange still bothered her.

There was a knock on Emma's door. Perhaps Daphne had forgotten something. "Yes?" Emma said.

Sidney Lane poked his head in, frowning, apparently loath to enter.

Emma and Sidney shared the same job title, but they had little else in common.

At age thirty-three, she was the youngest lead ethics investigator California's Hayden Commission had ever had, while sixty-year-old Sidney had been a gun-carrying agent for the Internal Revenue Service, investigating high-level financial crimes, before joining the commission ten years ago. And while Emma preferred simply styled clothing that varied little year to year and vintage furnishings, Sid was all about the latest thing. His exquisitely tailored suits were straight from the pages of upscale men's magazines like *Esquire* and *GQ*. His office was tech heavy and furnished with more metal and glass than wood.

"Are you planning to attend the governor's dinner celebrating the opening of the upgraded train station next Tuesday?" Sidney asked. "If you're busy, I could shift things in my schedule to cover for you."

As he spoke, he squinted at Emma's scribbled project notes on the wall behind her. He seemed especially interested in the timeline she'd created with a list of "next steps" marked in red. If they'd been secret, she wouldn't have left them up for anyone to see. Still, what Sid was doing was rude, and she wanted to get rid of him as quickly as possible. "I'm not planning on going. If you're available, that would be helpful."

Emma abhorred what she privately termed "wasteful busy-ness," the necessity in California's capital of spending time at events or meetings where the sole purpose was to be seen with important people to show that she and, by extension, the work of the Hayden Commission were important too. Fortunately, Sid relished rubbing elbows with Sacramento's power elite, so Emma routinely passed along many of those invitations to him.

She'd hoped a side effect of those transfers might be some goodwill from Sidney toward her, but nothing seemed to accomplish that.

Having gotten what he wanted, he gave a gruff wave. But as Sid turned to go, he nearly collided with Emma's analysts, Nick Lillard and Malia Ivanov.

"What is it?" Emma asked them. Through the curtness of her response, she hoped to signal that she was busy. She liked Malia and Nick but didn't want to encourage them to drop by without it having been prearranged.

Normally, her assistant, Hailey, would have waylaid anyone trying to get in, found out their purpose, and given Emma warning, but Hailey was out of the office at the dentist's this morning.

Malia was short and stoutly built, with frizzy black hair. A former congressional staffer, she was obsessively thorough. She'd just flagged a concern regarding the Community Fund for the tunnel that Emma was sure she would have missed had she still been in an analyst's role. Nick had sun-bleached blond hair and tanned skin that gave him the appearance of a laid-back, ocean-loving surfer. But he was a wizard at information technology and had quickly developed a reputation for working as hard as anyone in the building—he was often the last one there. Emma had high hopes that Nick would turn out to be as valuable to her investigative team as Malia.

He stepped toward Emma, extending a hand in which he held a small black velvet box tied with a red ribbon. "We brought you this," he said.

It looked like it might contain jewelry. Emma decided to hold off on any questions until she could see what was inside the box.

It turned out to be a vintage brass key ring bearing the image of a 1960s Ford Mustang convertible just like hers.

"We didn't know when your birthday was, but Malia saw this at a booth at Cesar Chavez Plaza, and we couldn't pass up the opportunity," Nick said. "That way we won't have to figure out a present later. When is your birthday?"

He looked at Emma so intently that it occurred to her—especially in light of the gift—that Nick might have a bit of a crush on her. It happened often in offices, lower-level staff idealizing and even romanticizing their supervisors.

Until now, she hadn't thought of that with respect to Nick's attitude toward her. In fact, she'd seen him hanging around Hailey's desk enough times to think there might be something extracurricular going on there. Regardless, this was an opportunity to remind him of the professional environment in which they worked. She began by ignoring Nick's personal question about her birthday.

"This is kind of you both. Completely unnecessary, but kind," Emma said. "I'm sure it's buried somewhere in the employee handbook, but there is a form for you to file in HR about this gift and its value. Even though we're not bound by government ethics rules, we have instituted similar policies because of what we do here."

"I took care of it," Malia said, not defensively but as though checking a box.

Nick said nothing, and Emma again felt the uncomfortable strength of his gaze. But after he and Malia had left, she considered the young man's longer-than-typical eye contact might be a sign of ambition rather than infatuation. She was his boss, and perhaps it had been an awkward attempt on his part to connect. Her thoughts were interrupted when her phone pinged. It was a text from Kate.

Fancy meeting for tea
at Second Chance?

7

Daphne's appointment with Emma Lawson had served its purpose. Not that it hadn't been interesting, but she'd needed a way to get through security downstairs up to the executive floor of the Hayden Commission headquarters.

Now she just had to locate Fran Hill's office.

She walked past the stairway she'd used to come up. It was the centerpiece of the short hall, with its curved oak banisters and plushly carpeted stairs. On her right was a closed door with a brass plate that read EXECUTIVE CONFERENCE ROOM. Across from that was the office of SYDNEY LANE, INVESTIGATOR. The hall reached a dead end at an elevator.

Daphne turned back, wondering what she'd missed, and saw that past an alcove with an unmanned desk and the closed door of Emma's office on her right was a hallway to her left. There was no other place to try. She guessed it meant Fran Hill merited a separate wing of her own.

She straightened up and smoothed the hem of her T-shirt. There was little else Daphne could do to smarten her appearance.

She reviewed her plan.

She would share with Johnny's mother the information he'd given her right before he died. She'd ask her what to do about the money. And having heard about the fire, she hoped Johnny's mother had already been to his storage space. She'd also check with her about that.

An elegant older woman seated at an impressive reception desk looked up at Daphne's approach. Her smile was professional, though it was something short of welcoming.

"May I help you?"

"I'm here to see Mrs. Hill," Daphne said.

"Do you have an appointment?"

Daphne shook her head, suddenly not trusting her English.

"Ms. Hill is not in. Would you like to leave her a message?"

The woman waited. Though not patient exactly, she seemed in no hurry.

Daphne felt tongue-tied.

"I'm a friend of Johnny's," she finally said.

A warmth laden with sadness surfaced in the woman's eyes. "Of course, I'll let Ms. Hill know. I can't make any promises, but would you be able to see her later today if she is available?"

Daphne couldn't stop a smile of gratitude from lighting up her face. The transatlantic travel, switching schools, the anxiety and uncertainty—maybe all of it would prove to have been worth it.

Daphne had provided her name and phone number to Fran Hill's receptionist, and with a sense of accomplishment she walked back the way she'd come, turning into the main hall.

As she approached the midpoint where the staircase was, she saw a group of people just beyond it waiting for the elevator.

She instantly recognized him. In the video chats they'd had, he'd looked a little different. But not much.

It can't be.

How? Has he followed me here?

Has he been searching the building for me?

Or is he at the commission on some kind of business?

Daphne's stomach seized up. She couldn't move.

She fought the crippling paralysis she felt and desperately scanned for cover.

A few steps away, a young woman in the previously empty alcove took off her sweater and hung it on the back of her desk chair.

Daphne walked hurriedly into the alcove until she was no longer visible to those out in the hallway.

Her heart thudded in her chest. She couldn't speak.

What could she possibly say?

The woman behind the desk appeared to be in her twenties. She had long, straight, black hair. She looked at Daphne curiously. "I'm Hailey Cha, Ms. Lawson's assistant. May I help you?"

Daphne wanted nothing more than to be helped.

But she didn't know what to ask for.

She couldn't confide in her. The whole point in coming all the way from Amsterdam had been to speak with Fran Hill in person—she'd wanted no emails or voice messages. No conversations with intermediaries that would leave a trail.

She turned to go, then abruptly stopped. She hadn't heard a bell or the elevator door open. Shouldn't it have arrived and left by now?

Suppose he saw me and has stayed behind?

Daphne peered around the edge of the alcove wall. He was gone. They all were.

"Is there something wrong?"

Daphne jumped at the sound of Hailey's voice. Then she had an idea. If she weren't alone, he couldn't approach her—he wouldn't dare. "Would it be possible for you to come downstairs with me? Walk with me to the front door?" She tried to think of a plausible explanation. "I just saw my ex-boyfriend here. He's angry about our breakup. I would like to avoid a scene."

If Hailey wondered who Daphne's boyfriend was and why he might be on the private third floor of the Hayden Commission, she didn't ask. She picked up her purse, whisked past Daphne, and checked the hallway in both directions.

Having confirmed it was clear, she said, "Come this way. There are back stairs."

She led Daphne to a narrow, unmarked door that Daphne hadn't noticed before.

But when Hailey stepped into the stairwell, Daphne didn't follow.

Hailey turned around and opened her palm to reveal a small, bright-pink plastic item. "It's a panic button. A rape alarm. If I press it, they'll hear it all over the building."

Daphne stayed close behind Hailey as she led the way down the three flights. She was relieved to find the lobby empty except for a security guy behind his desk.

As they passed him, he said, "You need to sign out."

"I'll take care of that for her, Richard, no problem," Hailey said.

She put her hand on Daphne's arm and stayed with her until they both were out the front door. She watched as Daphne looked all around. "Is he gone? Do you want me to call you a ride service?"

"No. Thank you. I'm fine now," Daphne said. Though she felt anything but fine.

He knows I'm here.

I'm running out of time.

9

IN THREE DAYS, the man who had killed Johnny Hill would receive his final payment. That would make a cool million in all.

He smiled at the thought of it.

It wasn't so much money. He'd seen fraud cases where people got away with a lot more.

The important thing was that this money would be his to control. No one pulling the strings, telling him what he could and couldn't do with it.

A million dollars.

It was enough to start over.

He wouldn't permit anyone to spoil it for him.

He'd not expected to have to kill again.

Yet here she was, unannounced and intent on ruining everything.

A fly in the ointment, which meant he'd have to be the spider in the web.

* * *

New City Hall

Alibi didn't like being tethered to his office, waiting for the mayor's call. He looked out his window. The olive oil stand only had a few customers in line.

Alibi's mother had said that safflower and canola oil were the fruits of the devil. She was of Italian descent and believed it must be "olio d'oliva" for pasta, salads, even to scramble eggs—and he was down to the last half inch in his bottle at home.

Alibi picked up his keys and phone, making sure the ringer was on, and closed his office door behind him. If the mayor wanted to see him in her chambers, getting there from the plaza would add only ten minutes.

He breathed in the scent of freshly baked rye bread and hot Polish sausages from the food stalls as he walked beneath old heritage cedars to the center of the square, where market booths ringed the William Coleman Memorial Fountain, installed in 1927. It featured three women symbolizing the Sacramento, American, and Feather Rivers, which flowed through and around the city. Criticisms had been levied at sculptor Ralph Stackpole's presentation of the stone women as stronger in build than many men, their arms uplifted to support the top bowl of the fountain.

It was one of Alibi's favorite pieces of local functional art.

As he joined the short queue for Bondolio's, he carefully scanned the area around him, a habit developed from years as a beat cop. A strikingly beautiful young woman approached the market by way of the diagonal walkway from J Street.

Her slight frame, pale features, and white-blonde hair stood in sharp contrast to the three women of the fountain, solid in their grace and strength. But it wasn't her ethereal appearance that had caught Alibi's attention. It was the fear that creased her delicate forehead, forced the corners of her mouth down, and caused her to turn her head left, right, then left again, her eyes wide.

Her gaze passed over him without pause, and Alibi concluded it was not just any man she feared—her boogeyman was specific.

When she reached the relative safety of the crowd of shoppers in the center of the plaza, she seemed uncertain of what to do next. He was wondering how far she'd walked under such stress when in a weary motion, she sat on the edge of the circular pool that formed the base of the fountain, into which sparkling streams of water arced and fell.

Alibi felt a stab of fear of his own, a conviction that she wasn't safe there. It was as though the shimmering water possessed the power to pull her under into unseen depths, so deep and icy cold that she would be lost forever. A pressure on top of his head spread to his chest, where it became a heavy burden that made his breathing labored. His eyes blurred.

It didn't make rational sense. If she inexplicably toppled over backward, she'd stand up in the shallow pool unaided, or worse case, he could wade in and pull her out. The cop in him fought for control, asserting that his real concern should be that she was exposed, that anyone with a weapon could strike her down with ease.

Deciding he didn't need to know which threat was real—mythical water demons or a bad guy with a long-range high-powered rifle—Alibi moved quickly and with authority to close the gap between them. When he reached her, he produced his identification and asked if anything was wrong.

She responded in an accent he didn't recognize—*Dutch? Swedish?*—that she was fine. She said she just felt a bit dizzy and needed to sit down. But as the ribbons of water continued to strike the surface of the pool below, Alibi's skin crawled, and beads of sweat formed on the back of his neck, despite the coolness of the day.

He couldn't have been more than seven or eight years old when he'd first had these experiences, and his mother had told him to heed the warnings. She'd said it didn't matter whether it was the gift of second sight from God, which she believed, or simply that he had a sensitivity to things in the here and now that others missed.

And if there was one thing Alibi knew for certain, it was that whether she was living or dead, he did not intend to cross his mother.

"Let's talk over here," he said, stepping far enough back so the young woman would have to stand and leave the edge of the pool. Once she'd done that, Alibi's breathing and heart rate slowed. "Is there someone bothering you? Are they following you?"

He thought she might say yes. Instead, her eyes slid away from him. He was pretty sure she was deciding which way to turn to fade into the crowd to make *him* leave her alone because he'd identified himself as a police officer.

He was about to reassure her, to tell her he would walk with her wherever she needed to go, no questions asked, when his phone pinged. It was Breno. The mayor could see him now.

Alibi hesitated, but he had nothing concrete to go on. The young woman had asserted she was fine, and his senses had settled once she'd left the vicinity of the water. Still, he kept an eye on her until she was out of sight, then hastily made his way back to New City Hall.

10

Second Chance Café

WHEN EMMA ARRIVED, there was a long line outside the door of the Second Chance Café. She was concerned that she wouldn't make it back to the office in time for her meeting with Fran when a motion from a row of tables set up European-style under the cafe's bright-blue awning caught her eye. It was Kate, raising a hand in greeting.

Emma hurried over to the small wrought-iron table, inhaling the welcoming aroma of mint tea. A plate was heaped with a selection of the cafe's fresh-baked scones and muffins. If the crumbs on a napkin in front of Kate were any indication, she had already finished one.

Emma opened her mouth to say thank-you but Kate, never one for small talk, spoke first. "Thank goodness they got that fire under control before it reached the upper floors. Though I suppose some of my things might be smoke damaged. But all that matters is Luke and you were gone before the inferno started. We've had enough adventures in this family for a lifetime."

Emma would have liked to leave it there—to let Kate persist in misunderstanding what had happened that morning. But they'd been through too much to keep secrets from each other. At any rate, she could see it wasn't going to be her choice, since Kate was looking at her with a familiar laser focus in her eyes.

"You were well away before the fire started? Or is that lad doing my head in again?"

"Luke is telling the truth," Emma said firmly. "He wasn't there." She reached for a raspberry muffin. "But I hadn't left. I was in the parking lot getting into my car."

Kate frowned. "You were still there? Outside the building? When the fire broke out?"

"I was outside," Emma began. "But I went inside to check on an employee."

Kate shot off another staccato stream of questions, her voice rising with each one.

"Inside? After the fire started? Briefly? To check?"

Emma was pretty sure that if sparks could have flown from her friend's gray-green eyes, they'd be doing so now.

Kate and Emma both had eyes others described as green, but while Emma's were bright, almost emerald, with gold flecks, Kate's and Luke's were a subtle gray green, as intense looking in their own way for their absence of color.

"Well, all right. It's not like you pulled a bloke from a burning building and carried him to safety."

Emma studied her muffin, hoping the pattern of berries might offer a hint in code as to what to say next. "I didn't carry him out," she said softly. "I had a cart."

She braced herself for a classic Kate Doyle lecture on her foolishness—on how she should have immediately called for help. Instead, Kate shook her head. "Fair enough. You had a cart. But you're okay? You're not one of the two the news is saying was injured?" Her gaze moved carefully over Emma's hands, then her face, as though checking for bruises or burns. Apparently satisfied, she asked, "Do they know what caused the fire? I saw online that bloke, what's his name, said it was radical far-left environmentalists who wanted to make a point about climate change."

"I hadn't heard that," Emma said. "If you mean the guy with the chain of bathroom supply shops who has his own radio show, he's a kook." Emma was accustomed to tuning out conspiracy theories that got ahead of the facts. They surfaced with every investigation the Hayden Commission undertook. "I think they'll find it was old wiring that caused the fire. The building seemed preserved in its original 1970s state. I was surprised to see that, since the facility is owned by Clad Corp. You'd think a billion-dollar chemical company could afford a simple remodel. My team reviewed a cleanup Clad Corp just completed of a toxic site they own near the old railway terminal in Sacramento. I give Clad Corp credit, they exceeded the legal requirements. But it does seem like they have money to burn." Emma realized what she'd just said. "No pun intended."

She was ready to leave the topic of the morning's trauma when something occurred to her.

"Daniel, the Clad Corp employee I met, said unpaid units have their items seized by the company and moved down to the warehouse, where they're assessed for value."

"Sure. That's the basis for those reality shows where people bid on storage units sight unseen and uncover a lost Van Gogh or a truckload of unmatched socks," Kate said. "It's a gamble."

"Right," Emma said, reaching for the thread that would make her random thought into a credible idea. "But suppose there was something in your storage unit you didn't want anyone to see, but you lost possession of it because you couldn't pay the fee. A fire in the warehouse would be one way—maybe the only way—to stop anyone from viewing it."

Kate looked thoughtful. "Maybe. It would have to be an item that held a secret so important that you were willing to commit arson to protect it, yet at the same time be something you could bear to destroy and never see again."

"Yes," Emma said. "I guess so." She realized she was leading Kate down an investigative rabbit hole, an exercise better suited for her work than for two friends celebrating a special day. She'd consider motives for the fire later. "Are you all set for the party tonight? I still can't believe you're getting married."

Kate shifted gears and beamed. "It's true. Though Breno's hopes that matrimony will make a respectable woman of me are doomed—it's far too late for that."

Kate had been fifteen when she'd discovered she was pregnant. She'd raised Luke on her own in Galway on the coast of Ireland until six years ago, when she'd moved to the States and by chance had rented a duplex across the street from Emma's house.

Emma thought of Breno, in his conservative suits and silk ties, and Kate, who favored all black clothing, preferably in leather or denim. Fashion choices aside, he and Kate did seem well matched.

Still, Emma couldn't help but wonder how much her own life was about to change. Guiltily, she took some comfort in the fact that no wedding date had been set.

Turning to the practical, she said, "I'd like to come early tonight, but after I meet with Fran, I have to—"

Kate waved her hand dismissively. "You're nearly all work and no play, but there might be hope for you yet. You're here now." She grinned. "Though perhaps I should make sure it's really you and not a clone or a hologram."

"It's me. The only magic is in this watch," Emma said, tapping its face. "I can't ignore your requests when I have it on. Your wish is my command."

Emma had once told Kate that she'd been seriously envious of two girls in middle school who had BFF—best friends forever—necklaces, each one half a heart that with the other made a whole.

It had come up in a conversation where Emma had revealed that she hadn't had a best friend in her entire life until Kate.

New Year's Day, Kate had surprised Emma with the purchase of two watches, each one engraved with BFF on the back. The make was the same, both from Throne timepieces in New York, but in deference to the difference in their tastes, Emma's was professional looking, a stainless-steel case with a white face, while Kate's was all black—band, numerals, face, everything. Emma didn't see how Kate could use it to tell the time, but Kate wore it as religiously as Emma did hers.

It was in view now on Kate's wrist as her hand hovered over a poppy seed muffin. At the last moment, she selected a sinful-looking iced cinnamon twist instead.

"Luke's chuffed about his internship with you at the commission," Kate said, placing the pastry on her napkin. "It's the first thing I've seen him look forward to in a while. How did he seem this morning?"

Emma pictured Luke lifting the heavy lamp, his muscles tense, his first thought at hearing the approach of an unidentified person having been to find a weapon. She decided to share only what was most important, what she sincerely believed.

"He'll be fine, Kate. He has you."

11

The Hayden Commission

EMMA MADE IT back to headquarters just in time. She was slightly out of breath when Fran's assistant told her to go on in.

Fran stood on the far side of her five-hundred-square-foot office next to a white oak conference table that could accommodate twelve, her head bent over a large book held open in both hands. Her stylish, blunt-cut hair—silver, with a single thick, black streak—shone in the light streaming through a floor-to-ceiling window at her back.

Emma paused on the threshold to take in the dramatic view of California's capitol building. A copper ball, gold plated with coins from the 1800s, a symbol of the state's historic gold rush, sat atop the white dome. Framed by a cloudless, robin's-egg-blue sky, it gleamed in the late-morning sun.

As the seconds passed, Emma felt awkward observing her boss without her apparent knowledge. She softly cleared her throat and regretted it—it was still raw from the fire.

When Fran looked up, Emma was taken aback, her own discomfort forgotten.

Fran Hill's name was known to political insiders nationwide. She'd spent a decade as a state senator, then two terms as mayor of nearby San Francisco, before becoming chief of staff for California's highly respected Hayden Government Ethics Commission, and she wasn't done yet. She was rumored to be planning a run for Congress when the current representative from Sacramento retired.

Though her career choices had not been conducive to self-care, Fran typically appeared untouched or at least unburdened by her outsize responsibilities. Emma considered her a role model for thriving in the life she'd mapped out for herself. But today, deep shadows were like bruises under Fran's eyes, and the fine lines around her mouth and on her forehead were pronounced, aging her well beyond her fifty-some years.

Fran seemed to sense what Emma was thinking. "I know, I look like hell," she said, offering a small smile. "I had a long night. I went through the last of Johnny's things. These are his books. Quite a variety." She gestured to an open box on the table. "Some on architecture and design, of course, but also a few on technology, and several cookbooks. I thought it would be nice to have them here with me." She placed the one she'd been holding into the box on top of the others. "Now I'm not so sure."

"I'm sorry," Emma said. Her eyes moved to a framed photo on Fran's desk of Johnny, a handsome young man with curly dark hair. He was smiling broadly in an image captured at his study-abroad program in Denmark only days before he'd come home for a visit to Sacramento and drowned in nearby Folsom Lake before he ever got to see Fran.

Mother and son were known to be estranged. Reportedly, this would have been the first time they'd been together in years. Perhaps to prepare himself for a potentially difficult reunion, he'd decided to go camping first.

Emma thought again of the odd interaction she'd had with Daphne VerStrate, the young woman who'd said she was a graduate student. As a public figure, Fran had taken her share of hits from the media and internet trolls over the years. But this was different, and Emma felt protective of her. No parent should have their child's death twisted and bandied about for money or sport.

Fran crossed to a pair of unusual chairs with painted dark-red frames and distressed brown leather seats. They looked like they might have been recycled from a stagecoach from the same era as the capitol dome. The entire room, except the high-tech equipment, reflected a streamlined and modernized Old West theme. Emma recalled Fran telling her Johnny had been responsible for the unusual furniture designs, doing the sketches himself. They were prototypes for a line he'd hoped to have mass-produced when he finished design school.

Fran sat down and motioned to Emma to do the same, a signal she was ready to begin their meeting. She appeared to gain focus when she moved into work mode. "So tell me, what's new on the train project?"

"There's this," Emma said, opening the folder she'd brought with her, withdrawing an advance copy of a press release from Governor Paul Lange's office.

As Fran gave the document her full attention, Emma appreciated the freedom her promotion to investigator provided her. Her first three years at the Hayden Commission, she'd been an analyst, subject to daily, even hourly, supervision. Now she led her own team. Fran had made that possible. Observing her today, Emma wished there was something she could do to help the older woman with her grief, but theirs wasn't that kind of relationship.

Fran interrupted Emma's thoughts. "Anthony Torgetti will be alongside the governor at the ribbon-cutting for the capital train station?" She frowned slightly. "*The Torgetti Tunnel* might have a nice ring to it, but if there were improprieties in the awarding of the naming rights, Paul may come to regret aligning himself closely with the young billionaire. Torgetti may soon be big news. As a Clad Corp board member, he's a person of interest in the company's lack of compliance with international climate change standards in the developing world. There's been some talk that the authorities may freeze his newfound fortune as a result."

Emma had not heard that about Anthony, but Fran often knew of powerful people's woes before others did. Still, having completed interviews and a far-reaching document review, Emma and her team hadn't found any ethical problems with the train tunnel contract. She reminded Fran of that fact.

"We haven't uncovered a single red flag, let alone any evidence to indicate that Anthony—Mr. Torgetti—did anything other than offer the most money for the rights to the tunnel's name. It appears to have been a fair and open bidding process." Emma removed a second paper from the folder. "But I wanted to draw your attention to an appendix to my report from last week. You may not have noticed it." She extended the one-page document to Fran. "Malia found gaps in oversight of the Community Fund specific to local train station upgrades. It looks like consultants rather than state or city employees were in charge of overseeing other consultants. Never a good practice. Not much on it yet, but I'm planning to request—"

Fran cut her off, though she took the offered sheet and gave it a careful look. "The state auditor's office will handle this. They routinely review all contracts."

"The issues may not be obvious," Emma countered. "Malia only found them because—"

Fran stopped her again. "Three hundred million dollars will change hands on Torgetti's tunnel-naming award. Ten times the money in the entire fund that Malia mentions here."

Fran's tone, though never sharp, had come close. *Probably to do with exhaustion—with her mind being on Johnny,* Emma thought.

Though Emma did wonder whether Fran might have given the green light to examine it further if Nick had raised the Community Fund concern instead of Malia. While not close friends, Nick and Johnny had gone to college together and had done a joint project on art and technology that won a campus-wide prize. Fran had been touched when Nick showed up at Johnny's funeral, and when he'd applied shortly afterward to do IT work for the commission, she'd expedited his hiring and assigned him to Emma's team.

Fran's eyes moved to the box of Johnny's books on the table.

Emma thought of something she should let her boss know now if their meeting was drifting to a close. "I told Sid he could take my place at the governor's VIP dinner at the station opening. I assume that was okay."

Fran smiled. "Sure, those things keep him happy, and we need him here. No one comes close to Sid's understanding of where the big money is likely to be hidden in corrupt government contracts."

12

EMMA DECIDED TO leave early so she could surprise Kate by arriving on time for the party. She could always work afterward—it was an open house, not a rave. It should be over by nine.

As she was considering what work to bring home, she recalled how Sid had studied her scribbled ideas on the poster-sized sheets on the wall.

Sid had never hidden his belief that Fran had played favorites when she gave Emma, the more junior investigator, the $30 billion train project, the biggest investigation the commission had ever undertaken.

He'd had no legitimate reason to feel that way.

Emma's investment and personal financial interest in the private preschool Kate had opened six months ago, Rainbow Alley, meant she'd been conflicted out of the only other commission project this year—examining pesticide regulations that would apply to all schools and day cares. So that had been assigned to Sid, and she'd been given the train project.

But Sid had gone so far as to suggest to Fran that he lead both the train and pesticide investigations, with Emma taking a back seat until something came along that "suited her."

Fortunately, Fran had declined his suggestion.

At the Hayden Commission, Emma and Sid did not oversee the production of tangible items whose quality could be objectively measured, like a chair whose legs might fall off or not. They trafficked in the marketplace of ideas, recommendations, and reports, easily undermined by sowing doubt about another staff person's performance. Emma suspected Sid was engaged in just such an effort with respect to her work on the tunnel.

The least she could do was not give him tinder to start the fire.

Another unfortunate choice of words.

She was beginning to think she had fire on the brain, though her brush with a real-life inferno had only been this morning. She supposed its dominance as a point of reference for everything in her life would soon wear off.

She carefully peeled the tape from the edges of her notes and pulled them down from the wall. Then she folded and attempted to fit the oversized papers into the large khaki satchel, fraying at the edges, that had served as her backpack and briefcase since college.

She tried several angles, but the papers with their bright-red-and-yellow lettering still stuck out at the top. She couldn't close the bag. It was a bit sloppy looking, but she decided they wouldn't fall out, which was all that really mattered.

There was a soft knock on the door from Hailey's alcove.

Emma called to her to come in, which Hailey did, closing the door behind her.

"How was the dentist?" Emma asked.

"Mr. Torgetti is here," Hailey said, looking over her shoulder as though the man were standing there, which Emma was pretty sure was not the case.

It wasn't like Hailey to get flustered.

"I have him waiting in the executive lounge. He said he's sorry to drop by without an appointment but wondered if you might have a minute."

Emma told Hailey to send him in. She ran her fingers through her hair and stayed standing to greet him. Then she thought of how Hailey had seemed and realized billionaires likely had this effect on everyone, especially if they were young and relatively handsome.

A moment later, Hailey showed Anthony Torgetti in, and Emma offered him a seat on the sofa. She sat on a chair across from him.

Anthony Torgetti was unassuming in appearance for one of the richest men in the world. In his late twenties, he was of average height, with medium-brown hair cut short. Fit though not buff, he wore a modest brown suit that looked like it had been bought off the rack. The sleeves were a tad too short. He was good-looking in an unthreatening way. He'd made his fortune by designing a new self-driving system for buses and delivery vans that was already in use by governments in Singapore and Vietnam.

"Thank you for seeing me, Emma," he said, giving her a slight smile, just enough to warm his features.

They'd spent several hours together in her office when she'd interviewed him on the tunnel project. It occurred to her now that his expression and movements were always understated. She wondered whether it was intentional—his way of not further intimidating those around him who, without any effort on his part, felt the power that came with his billions.

"I thought these files might be helpful to you and your team," he said, withdrawing a small black flash drive from the inner pocket of his jacket.

Emma hadn't seen one of those in a while. Nearly everything was shared virtually through cloud servers these days.

He saw her looking at it. "The information contained here is not something I'd want to have vulnerable to hacks. You might be aware that my finances are being looked at closely right now because of issues Clad Corp is experiencing internationally. In addition to being on the board, I'm a significant investor. Contrary to what's being said about me, I've let Clad Corp know if they do not aggressively institute policies to combat climate change in their international chemical division, I will move to withdraw my funds." His color rose. "I thought, given your position as an ethics investigator and the fact that you are already looking at the tunnel-naming award, providing you relevant background might put you in a position to help dispel some of these malicious rumors about me."

He extended the flash drive to her. Emma kept her hands firmly in her lap. As curious as she was about what was on the drive, they had rules at the commission about how information could be received from persons of interest in their investigations.

"I appreciate how forthcoming you are being," Emma said. "But I can't accept information from you in this way. It must be transmitted electronically from a verified email account to an encrypted and secure application on our end. We have to show that we've done everything possible to prevent leaks, to protect your information, and to be sure it's not altered or tampered with after we receive it."

Anthony's gaze dropped and his shoulders slumped. He briefly reminded her of Luke. No, of someone even younger, of a kid who'd been told it was raining so baseball practice with his buddies had been canceled. Emma was moved to come up with something that might work. "Just a minute," she said. "I have an idea." She went to Hailey's door and opened it, speaking in a low voice. "Would you see if Nick is available to come up?"

In the short time Nick had been with the commission, he'd done wonders to improve their cloud storage and upgrade their website. If anyone could protect Anthony's information and lock it down so it was safe from hacking but still met the commission's rules for transparency and ethical review, it was Nick.

A minute later, Hailey returned. "Nick went home. He wasn't feeling well."

Emma turned to Anthony. "Can we come back to this? If you hold on to that, I'll see how I might be able to receive and review it."

She wasn't sure he was listening. He seemed distracted by the papers overflowing from her bag. Then he suddenly smiled broadly. "That sounds like a great idea. You have enough on your plate if you're taking that much work home. I appreciate your looking into it. You know how to reach me."

Emma returned his smile and thought what an odd day it had been.

She was ready for a party.

13

The Alleyway

M INUTES LATER, AS Emma walked through the lobby, absorbed in work messages on her phone that had come in while she was meeting with Anthony Torgetti, she collided with Luke, his bike at his side.

She couldn't believe she'd again forgotten about Luke's first day at the commission. Then her concern shifted. Why was he only arriving now? It was nearly four PM. Being hours late wasn't a good way to start his first day.

"Sorry, security said I could leave this behind their station," he said. "Malia told me there are a lot of bike thefts downtown. I was glad to see it was still where I parked it when I arrived at two. This was the first chance I had to move it inside."

Emma was relieved. She smiled at Luke.

"The Kryptonite double dead bolt lock I gave you for Christmas is guaranteed to prevent that," Emma said.

"That lock would stop an amateur, but with the right tools, someone experienced might figure it out," Luke said.

Emma didn't argue, though she doubted his old Schwinn with the peeling paint would be top of the list for any thief. But she understood this wasn't about a rational weighing of the odds. With Luke's hypervigilance toward what might well be his prized possession, she thought it likely he'd be handing that bike down to his grandchildren.

She checked her watch. "Come on," she said, pointing toward the door. "We can surprise your mom and help her set up for the party. We'll put your bike in the back of the Mustang."

"What about Nick and Malia? I told them I was coming back—"

"It's okay," Emma said. Her phone was still in her hand, and she typed a quick message and hit send. "Hailey will let them know."

Outside, Emma said, "I have a reserved spot in the garage two blocks away—the commission doesn't have its own parking."

Luke walked his bike alongside her.

"How was your first day?" she asked.

"Good. Malia was great."

She noticed Luke didn't mention Nick. She'd wondered how they would get along. Nick seemed interested in learning new things one minute, then closed and easily annoyed the next. But he was young, twenty-six, and she put some of it down to the adjustment anyone had in a new job.

As they approached the intersection, Emma had a view directly into the alley across the street. She was shocked to see Daphne VerStrate standing there, her heavy camera on the strap around her neck.

Is she hoping to get photos of Fran as she arrives and exits the building?

"I need to take care of something," she said to Luke as they crossed the street.

She intended to find out exactly what was going on. But as she got closer to Daphne, she saw that the young woman had been injured. Possibly badly.

Daphne had her left arm cradled tightly against her body and was keeping it steady with her right hand. Blood soaked through her T-shirt below her wrist and flowed freely from her knee where her jeans had been torn.

When Emma reached her, she asked, "What happened?"

"I'm fine." Daphne winced as she said it.

Emma realized Daphne was looking past her shoulder at Luke.

"This is Luke. My nephew."

Although he didn't often call her Aunt Emma anymore, they'd both learned that the easiest way to convey the nature of their relationship was to employ the terms *nephew* and *aunt* in introductions.

"He works with you at the commission?" Daphne asked.

"Yes," Emma said, though she wondered how Daphne knew that. Then she realized that from this vantage point, Daphne had likely seen them leave the commission building together.

"How did this happen?" Emma asked.

"A car," Daphne said. "I jumped out of the way to avoid it and fell." Her voice was shaky.

"Did the driver stop to help you?" Emma asked.

Daphne shook her head no.

A near-miss hit-and-run had to be reported. There was the question of responsibility, of course, but Emma was also concerned there could be a drunk or otherwise altered driver who might run over a child walking home from school if they weren't found immediately.

"Where did this happen?"

"Not here," Daphne said.

"Where?" Emma asked.

"I'm not sure. I don't have a good sense of direction. By the river."

There were several rivers, and they were miles long. "When? Did you walk here like that?" Emma asked.

"Yes. Maybe forty-five minutes ago? I sat and rested before I started to walk home. I got turned around and ended up here instead."

"What kind of car was it?" Emma asked.

"Small. White. I don't know."

Emma knew from one of her investigations related to traffic safety that 30 to 40 percent of cars sold in the United States were white. Too bad the vehicle hadn't been a hot-pink convertible.

"It looked like that one," Daphne said, gesturing with her chin to a Toyota Corolla stopped at the light up ahead. "Or that one." Her eyes moved to a white Subaru Forester turning onto the street in front of them.

To Emma, those were two very different vehicles. The Corolla was an old compact sedan and the Forester a new SUV. "And the driver?" Emma asked. "What can you tell me about them?"

Daphne's eyes drifted up the front of the commission head-quarters. She shrank back against the wall of the brick building bordering the alleyway where she stood. "I don't know. The glare was great," she said.

Emma followed her gaze. There were windows on the second and third floors across from them, though they were obscured by the branches of a large oak tree that bordered P Street. "Did some-one up there have something to do with this?" Emma asked. "Someone from the commission offices? Are they in the commis-sion building now?"

"No," Daphne said, a little too quickly.

Just as she had earlier, Emma had the feeling Daphne was lying. But she couldn't piece it together. And if Daphne persisted in hiding things, there wasn't much she could do to help.

Emma became aware of Luke standing behind her. When she turned to face him, he was gripping the handles of his bike hard, pain in his eyes. Or maybe not pain.

Anger? At what? At the driver who caused this?

Emma resolved to model for him how to support someone who was in trouble without taking on too much.

To once again be the adult in the room.

Make that the adult in the alley.

She made eye contact with Luke and said softly, her back to Daphne, "It's okay. We'll make certain she's okay."

When she turned to Daphne, the young woman was trem-bling. Emma guessed she was in shock, in unbearable pain, or both. She regretted having pushed her so hard about the facts of the incident so soon. She wasn't an investigator on a case, she was a bystander who had to help. "Let's not worry for now about who did it," she said. "That will get sorted out. Someone will have witnessed it. Let's get you to a doctor. Sutter emergency room is the closest."

Emma flashed back to her own trip to the Sutter ER that morning in an ambulance after the fire.

"No." Daphne spoke sharply, then softened as she seemed to realize her tone. "Thank you. I don't need a doctor. I just need to lie down. I'm renting a room on Eighteenth Street. I don't think I can walk that far."

Eighteenth Street was closer to Matchbook Lane, where Emma lived, than it was to the Hayden Commission offices. Daphne must have really gotten turned around. In any case, Emma doubted that lying down would be an effective remedy for what ailed Daphne, not the way she was cradling her wrist and not with the visible shaking that had just stopped. She needed medical attention. "You should have that arm professionally evaluated."

"I'm fine," Daphne said again, though she neither sounded nor looked it.

Emma was losing patience. It wasn't helping matters to stand in the alley and have a debate. She raised her voice. "I understand this is difficult. It must have been terrifying. But you need to have that looked at. It probably requires an X-ray. It might need to be set."

Tears formed in Daphne's eyes.

Emma didn't feel the sympathy and compassion she wanted to feel. She was tired. She'd had enough.

She turned on her heel and said to Luke, "Stay here with her. I'll get the Mustang from the garage. I'll be right back."

14

"You are Lucas?" Daphne asked.

He thought about telling her his name was Luke. *Never Lucas.* But it had sounded nice the way she said it, with her accent, and he didn't want the first thing out of his mouth to be a correction. Anyway, fewer words were better when he felt like this. He and his counselor had agreed on that. So he nodded.

The sight of her injured and terrified, having barely escaped with her life after some idiot almost ran her over with a car, had thrown Luke back into the netherworld that had haunted him since last summer. The world of fear and violence and death that until then had only existed in comic books and video games, a parallel universe that had crossed time and space into his reality. The world in which he had killed a man.

"You work at the commission?" Daphne asked.

He looked beyond her down the alley so as not to stare and nodded again.

Her round blue eyes were pale, the lashes almost invisible, and her hair a silver blond that gleamed in the sun. She belonged on a stained-glass window on the wall of a church or on the big screen in a Jason Bourne film.

"Do you also work on the trains?" she asked.

His thoughts about how beautiful she was embarrassed him, even though he knew she couldn't have heard them. He shifted from foot to foot. One of his high-top black Converse shoes caught on the edge of the asphalt, and he nearly tripped.

Smooth, he thought.

He couldn't keep nodding as his only response.

"Yes. I'm on my aunt's team. She's responsible for the tunnel investigation."

Daphne stepped away from the wall where she'd been leaning and, while still cradling her arm, moved closer to him. At first it made him uncomfortable, but when she spoke, her voice was so low that he guessed she'd done it to enable him to hear her.

She looked no older than some students at his school.

"How many people work at the commission? Is it big?"

"Oh no," Luke said. "It's pretty small. Not like a big company or anything. There are the two investigators and their analysts. And people like accounting and personnel on the first floor. I'm not sure how many altogether. Maybe fifteen or twenty."

He was talking too much. He had to slow down.

"Do you know—" Daphne began.

She halted midsentence, and he turned to see Emma at the end of the block in the Mustang. She was stopped at the light, easy enough to spot since the convertible top was down.

"Could I talk to you?" Daphne asked.

Luke was confused. Wasn't that what they were doing?

"Tomorrow? Can I come talk to you tomorrow?"

"Okay," Luke said, buying time.

He didn't want to admit to her he was still in high school, that he was only an intern at the commission. Though he'd thought she might be his age, he was beginning to suspect she was older, the way she held herself and asked questions even while in pain.

He had second period at school free, and his mom was never home at that time. She'd be at work at Rainbow Alley.

"Could you meet early in the morning, say nine AM?" he asked. "I don't live far from where you're staying."

The light turned green. Emma was moving up the block.

"Great," she said, and for the first time she smiled. "Let me give you my number, and you can message me your address. I can't get my phone out." She looked down at her pocket, her hand still holding her other wrist.

He was entering Daphne's number into his phone as Emma pulled up to the curb alongside them.

"Luke, do you mind riding your bike instead of putting it in the car? I don't know how long this will take, and I don't want us both to be late for your mother's party."

15

New City Hall

IT HAD BEEN several hours, and Alibi couldn't shake what had happened with the young woman in the plaza. Or rather what hadn't happened. She'd done nothing wrong, and she'd said she wasn't afraid of anything. Alibi was certain that last had been a lie.

The thin arced streams of water splashing into the fountain's pool echoed in his mind. He was frustrated that he couldn't issue an all-points bulletin to locate her and ensure she was okay. But a problem with Alibi's intuition, or sixth sense, or whatever it was, was that since others couldn't see or feel what he did, getting them to act on it was often impossible. His only option was to be patient and to stay open to the next sign.

On top of it all, he still hadn't seen the mayor. Barely a step inside the building, he'd had a message from Breno saying the meeting had been delayed again and might have to wait until tomorrow. Evidently, whatever it was Mayor Melissa Ruiz wanted to share with him regarding Johnny Hill's month-old drowning had fallen in priority as her busy day had worn on.

With difficulty, Alibi set aside his thoughts about the woman from the fountain and the mayor's as-yet-unknown demands. He sat down at his computer and resolved to make progress on administrative tasks, the bane of his existence.

He managed to stick with it for more than an hour, responding to emails and reading boring memos, at which point he felt he deserved a reward. Engaging in real "crime-fighting" work qualified. He opened a window on his screen to view the incoming incident reports online.

The latest one caught his attention. Not so much on its own, but when he put it together with everything else that had happened over the last twenty-four hours, it didn't sit right.

He decided to review the known facts about the three cases that were bothering him.

First, there was the incident at the gallery last night. Red wine splashed across a valuable painting, the artist throwing a punch in retaliation. After which both parties had fled, no word from them since. According to the gallery owner, because the painting hadn't yet been sold, the insurance payout would go to the artist, not to her. She'd tried repeatedly to reach him, but his phone had been off. Nothing shocking in any of that, but in Alibi's experience, fights most often happened in and outside of bars, not in small art galleries. And people who suffered a significant financial loss, as that artist evidently had, were interested in restitution.

Then this morning there was the fire at the storage facility. Given that it had been ignited using a rag soaked in gasoline stuffed in a beer bottle and no organization or individual had come forward to claim credit for it as an act of domestic terrorism against Clad Corp, it was Clive Carter's opinion over in arson that it had been simple, stupid vandalism, albeit with unintended tragic results—the serious injury of an employee and one thus-far-unidentified fatality. Alibi couldn't say why he thought there was more to it than that, but he'd not been able to shake the feeling.

Finally, just in, there'd been a hit-and-run in the industrial area by the river, not far from the storage facility where the fire had occurred. A compact car had nearly plowed into a woman. Good Samaritans a half mile away had called 911. They'd said that from that distance it looked as though the woman had been injured, possibly seriously, from how slowly she'd gotten up. Though they hadn't gotten a good look at her, they thought perhaps she was a high school student. The victim had not come forward, and there'd been nothing from the emergency rooms, at least not yet. All they had was the 911 call.

Three separate crimes in twenty-four hours, each of which struck Alibi as having something not quite right about it.

Two with victims who haven't come forward, the gallery incident and the hit-and-run, and one with victims who should never have been there, the fire.

The incidents unsettled Alibi, like three small earthquakes barely registering on the Richter scale, but together quietly signaling that a tsunami was about to hit.

16

Midtown Condo

DAPHNE LIVED IN an upscale condominium complex in Mid-town, not at all what Emma had envisioned when the young woman said she "rented a room." It certainly didn't look like a student's place, reinforcing Emma's suspicions that Daphne might not be what she claimed to be.

Emma hadn't been allowed to leave the Mustang out front at the curb, not even for the brief time it would have taken her to help Daphne out of the car, then escort her inside and up to her apartment. So she'd turned her car key over to the young valet attendant. He'd paused only long enough to admire the vintage brass key ring before he leapt into the driver's side of the classic convertible and drove away with barely contained delight.

They were cleared by a polite concierge/security guard seated in front of a screen that provided live camera images of interior hallways and exterior doors to the building.

Inside Daphne's top-floor flat, Emma helped her get settled on an oversized red velvet sofa in the living room with a pillow under her head. At Daphne's request, she opened the curtains to reveal a stunning late-afternoon view all the way to the river. Then she went to get Daphne a glass of water. The kitchen was through a swinging door like the one Emma had in her home, but the similarity ended there.

In contrast to Emma's quirky and cozy midcentury space, the condo kitchen was modern and functional, with flawless sateen ivory walls and stainless-steel appliances.

Emma looked in the refrigerator for bottled water. There was hardly any food, not enough for more than a day or two—a few yogurts, two green teas, one prepackaged salad, and several hard-boiled eggs. Nothing to cook and nothing over an individual serving size.

When Emma returned to the living room, Daphne had already fallen asleep. Her eyes were closed, her narrow frame curled up on the sofa, one hand still cradling her injured wrist.

After setting both bottles of tea quietly on a table next to her, Emma went down a short hall and found two bedrooms, each with the doors open. One looked unoccupied. In the other, the bed was rumpled, as though it had been slept in. When Emma went to pull the comforter from it so she could cover Daphne, she glimpsed a carry-on suitcase open on the closet floor. It contained a single pair of jeans, a skirt, two T-shirts, and a bright-pink sweater, each compactly rolled. Kate would have been pleased—this was someone who knew how to pack.

There was nothing hanging in the closet. Out of curiosity, Emma checked the bureau—it was empty. Similar to the food supply, it appeared that Daphne only had enough clothing for a couple of days.

Then Emma noticed a small black backpack tucked behind the rolling bag. She took the blanket out to Daphne and gently covered her from her feet to her waist, not wanting to bump her injured arm and cause her pain or wake her. Satisfied that she was out, she went back to the bedroom and knelt in front of the backpack.

When she began to unzip the large outer pocket, she cringed at the sound of the zipper moving and stopped, worried she might be caught. But then Emma thought of Fran's tired and grieving face. This was her best chance to determine whether Daphne was here in some capacity that might cause Fran embarrassment or harm.

She wasn't sure what she hoped she might find. She assumed Daphne had her passport and phone with her, since she'd been out and about, but perhaps there'd be other identification in the backpack. Maybe a student ID card, something to see if Daphne Ver-Strate was her real name.

When all remained quiet, Emma unzipped the outer compartment the rest of the way. It was nearly empty, only two items.

There was a key ring at the bottom of the pocket. She pulled it out. There was only one thing on it, a Clad Corp Ideal Storage key card. Other than the small hole in it that enabled it to slide onto the metal ring, it was just like Kate's. Or Emma thought it was until she turned it over and saw *Johnny's Unit #316* handwritten in blue ink.

The other item was a leather folio. It contained a single photo, the same image Fran had of Johnny on her desk, but from the clarity and brightness of the colors, this one looked like an original printed from 35-millimeter film. It had something written on it too, on the back in pencil: *One year and one day.*

"Emma, are you still here?"

It was Daphne's voice from the living room.

Emma returned the items to the backpack pocket. She zipped it shut as quietly as she could, answering loudly to cover the sound. "Yes, I'm coming. I was just looking for painkillers for you."

She slipped out of the bedroom and into the bathroom. There was a first-aid kit on an open shelf above the sink. Emma didn't think Daphne would have brought that with her—the landlord had apparently thought of everything.

When Emma returned, Daphne was sitting up.

"Thank you for bringing me these," Daphne said, accepting the pills, then looking at the bottled tea. "Could you open that?"

"Of course, I'm sorry. Your wrist," Emma said, keeping her voice steady with an effort. She turned her back as she unscrewed the top, not wanting her eyes to give her away.

17

Matchbook Lane

THE MAN HAD a clear view of Kate Doyle's duplex from where he stood, hidden beneath a drooping willow tree in the side yard of a vacant house two doors down.

He could also see Emma Lawson's bungalow from there. Her Mustang wasn't in the drive. She must not be home yet.

The man didn't feel bad that he hadn't been invited to Kate's party. If he wanted to attend, he could wait until it was in full flow and walk in. One person would think another had asked him to come. He decided he'd keep that as an option as he observed the first two guests arrive.

He glanced at the time.

Didn't they know it was rude to be early, that their hosts might not be ready? Yet, as he examined his feelings, he found he empathized with them. When he'd seen the VerStrate girl earlier that day, and she'd seen him, he hadn't exercised the virtue of patience. He'd made a hasty decision. That had been unfortunate—not his usual well-thought-out plan of action.

But to err is human, and the man knew that acceptance of that fact would help him fit in when he started fresh.

Three more days. Really only two, since evening was drawing near.

What interested him now was that when he had been impatient—"the first to arrive," like the couple on Kate Doyle's doorstep— the girl had not gone to the authorities.

Not to the relevant agencies for fraud or money laundering, and not to the local police after the failed hit-and-run. He hadn't made himself hard to find, and yet no one had shown up at his door. The man thought about why that might be.

What is she waiting for?

Daphne VerStrate had been at the commission offices.

That had to be because suspicions were all she had, and she'd gone to Fran Hill for help in securing something that would stand up as evidence.

The man loved it when he figured something out that would have escaped everyone else. He felt a rush of pleasure run through him. And fortunately, Fran hadn't been there.

He wondered what Daphne's next move would be.

As more people arrived in fancy dress clothes to Kate's party, the man mulled over how to turn the million he would soon have into many millions more.

And at the thought of the money—his money—he knew he couldn't let this chance slip away. And he had the gun.

But he didn't like to picture it.

The light dimming in her blue eyes, pain racking her slender frame, and blood splattered in her gold-white hair.

He didn't deserve to be burdened with those images. But he'd demonstrated his dedication to his goals and his strength of character with Johnny Hill.

He was an experienced killer now—he'd earned that title through hard work and careful planning.

It didn't mean what people thought it did, some haphazard explosion of rage.

Dark clouds, heavy with rain, gathered above. The man wondered if he might have to cut short his surveillance.

He decided that if he did, it would be okay.

Soon he'd have all he needed.

18

Traffic slowed on Eighth Street, where construction had narrowed it from three lanes to one. Emma was concerned she might be late to Kate's party, but since there was nothing she could do about that, she decided to use the time to organize her thoughts about what she'd found in Daphne's apartment.

The most likely reason Daphne kept a photo of Johnny with her when she traveled was that they'd been involved romantically. The "one year and one day" might mean they'd been a couple for that long. Or it could be a reference to the future—maybe they'd planned something special in a year and a day. Graduation? Or even getting married. Although the photo could also support Emma's original theory that Daphne was researching a story on Fran and Johnny's relationship for the tabloids. Daphne and Johnny might just be friends. She could be showing that original photo as evidence of that—to make people comfortable giving her inside information.

Emma flashed back on the photos Daphne had taken of her in her office. Were those really for a presentation at school? Or would Daphne carry around a photo of her to use as a prop, just as she might be doing with Johnny's?

Then she thought about Daphne's limited supply of food and her few items of clothing. Was Daphne planning to be in Sacramento only a few days? That would make the whole "here for a quarter studying" thing a lie. Or did she intend to move into a dorm soon, buying clothes once she knew what local students wore?

Emma wished she'd been able to search the body of Daphne's backpack. Maybe there were answers in there.

Her phone pinged. It was Kate.

Breno is delayed.
Can you come early?
I could use a co-host!

Emma resolved to put Daphne out of her mind for the rest of the night—Kate deserved her full attention and support.

When she pulled into her driveway, there were a number of unfamiliar cars parked along both sides of the cul-de-sac. *So much for arriving early*, Emma thought. She'd intended to go inside her house and change, but given that she was already late, the rose suit she had on would have to do.

She'd barely put one foot onto the front porch of the duplex when Kate threw open the door.

She was wearing satin black capri pants and an off-the-shoulder black knit top that showed off her slim, fit figure. The flawless black polish of a pedicure that matched her manicure was visible through the open toes of her black kitten heels.

"You look gorgeous," Emma said.

Kate twirled and noticed Emma admiring her new bracelet. The cuff was hammered silver with a single stone in the center, a rich dark brown with slivers of turquoise and gold.

"Breno gave it to me as an engagement gift," Kate said, her eyes softening. "It's a boulder opal from Queensland, Australia. They're ethically mined, without toxic chemicals."

"And it's Luke's birthstone," Emma added, taking a step inside.

Kate smiled broadly. But her smile disappeared as her eyes fixed on Emma's suit jacket. "What happened to you?"

Emma looked down to see a trail of bloodstains from under her left breast to her hip, easily visible in the light. It must have happened when she was helping Daphne out of the car and upstairs.

"It's not my blood," she said quickly to Kate.

Kate's brows went up. "And who did you stab?"

Emma didn't think now was the time to explain that she thought the woman whose blood graced her jacket might have assumed a false identity to get a story for the tabloids, or that the same woman might have almost been run down by a crazed driver.

And to top it off, Luke appeared from the kitchen. When his concerned eyes met Emma's, she remembered what had looked like Daphne giving Luke her phone number in the alleyway.

If anything would ruin this night for Kate, it would be thinking her sixteen-year old son was on the road to trouble with a mysterious older woman.

"It's complicated," Emma said. "I'll explain later."

19

TRINA, A TEACHER'S aide Emma had met at Rainbow Alley, smiled warmly and came over to say hello. But when she got closer, her smile disappeared, and in a reenactment of Kate's reaction to Emma's jacket, she said, "What happened to you?"

Since Emma's response of *It's not my blood* had not gone over well, she said to Trina, "It's nothing, really," then turned to Kate. "I'm going home to change. I'll—"

"No, you're not. I need you here," Kate said firmly. Then she leaned in and whispered, "I don't know why Breno's late. It must be important. There's no telling when he'll show up. You know how thorough he is about everything. You can't leave me with this lot. Luke and his friends are helping, but I want you to get folks settled, to check on their drinks. The teens can't do that in this backward country, not even the older ones."

Emma knew Kate had made that last statement purely for effect. Though it was true that adults could legally buy drinks for those sixteen and up in Ireland, Kate would have been happy if Luke never drank alcohol—one less thing to monitor and worry about.

Kate took Emma by the arm and turned her around, away from the front door and toward the back of the house. "Borrow something of mine that will allow you to greet people without looking like you survived a zombie attack."

Emma closed Kate's bedroom door, opened her closet, and smiled.

Of course, everything is black.

But the problem with finding something appropriate turned out not to be the nonexistent color selection. Scanning the choices, Emma concluded it was unlikely anything of Kate's would fit her. There was the height difference of six inches, plus the curves she had that Kate lacked.

Kate returned to check Emma's progress and fixed her with a withering look when she saw there had been none.

"I can wash this off," Emma said, eyeing the bloodstains that looked ominously permanent in the rose linen fabric.

"No," Kate said, stepping into the closet, pushing hangers aside, looking for something.

"My skirt will work," Emma said. "All I need is a different top." She'd noticed a few spots of blood on the skirt but not enough to mention. She moved toward Kate's chest of drawers.

"Don't be daft," Kate said. "The whole point is to do this quickly so you can get out there and help me. Here," she said, pulling out a black dress that still had the tags on. "I ordered this online. It's too big for me."

Emma was skeptical.

The dress was beautiful—it wasn't that. A little black cocktail dress in a fine satin fabric, it had a Givenchy *Breakfast at Tiffany's* vibe, with thin straps and a low square neckline. But Emma had dressed professionally every day for so long, keeping any part of her body that might be deemed "unprofessional" under wraps, that she actually took a step back as though it might tempt her away from work and into a life of sin.

She caught herself. That attitude wouldn't get her out of Kate's room anytime soon. She took off her suit and the camisole beneath it, unzipped the dress, and had pulled it over her head when Kate produced a pair of scissors. She looked at Emma thoughtfully, then pulled up the zipper and cut off the tags.

"Wait," Emma said. "We don't know if it works yet. This must be an expensive dress."

"It is, and it does. Work, I mean," Kate said, grinning. "Look." She pulled the closet door open wide to reveal a full-length mirror.

While Emma didn't feel like Cinderella at the ball, she had to admit it wasn't bad.

As Kate was returning to her guests, she paused to say, "Those ballet flats will have to do. My shoes won't fit you."

Emma opened her purse and took out her lipstick. She owned only one shade, a deep red. After applying it, she looked in the mirror again. The neckline on Kate's dress was much lower than she was used to. The expanse of skin it revealed, though not tasteless, seemed overly bare. She considered asking Kate if she had a necklace she might borrow.

Then she thought of the red velvet box on the nightstand by her bed. In it lay a delicate gold chain on which hung a small gold pendant encircled with tiny rose garnets. It would look lovely with the dress's square neckline.

Her father had given it to her mother on their tenth wedding anniversary. *The year before she died. The year before he disappeared.* The necklace lay in that velvet box for over two decades. Yet for some reason, in a dress she would never have bought, at a celebration of the pending marriage of her best friend, whom she dearly loved, Emma felt it might be time to accept the past and embrace the present. At least where that necklace was concerned.

Maybe if there was a break later when Kate didn't need her help, *maybe* she'd go across the street and get it.

The doorbell rang. Emma took a last look in the mirror, smoothed her hair, and went out to make herself useful.

When she opened the front door, Alibi stood on the top step.

CHAPTER

20

Emma and Alibi had not yet said hello to each other when Kate, passing by with a plate of appetizers, caught sight of him. She swiveled on her kitten heels. Emma deftly stepped aside. It never paid to block Kate's outrage, feigned or real.

"Come in, though I don't know that I should be welcoming you," Kate said. She gave Alibi a brisk kiss on the cheek. "Where is Breno? He said he was delayed at work. How could you?"

Alibi put his hands up in mock surrender. "It wasn't me. It must be the mayor who had something important."

Kate's attention was caught by someone calling her from across the room. She handed Alibi the plate of mini corned beef and cabbage sliders and included Emma in her directive. "Check on the buffet and drinks, see what needs refreshing."

The backyard had been transformed. Brazilian and Irish flags hung along the fences beneath hundreds of twinkling fairy lights. The tables Emma and Luke had picked up that morning were covered with crisp white tablecloths and heaped high with plates of finger foods. Each item bore a small hand-lettered card indicating its country of origin and the main ingredients. Alibi made room for the sliders next to pastries filled with chopped chicken and reqeijão, a Brazilian-style cream cheese.

A rattan bar was positioned steps from the kitchen door to make restocking easy. On the central stone patio, Luke was setting up with two of his bandmates. He tested the reed on his saxophone while Terrance adjusted the stool for the keyboard and Linea did some last-minute tuning on her guitar.

There were protective canopies on tall poles over everything— the food, the instruments, and the bar. The forecast had called for rain, and heavy clouds darkened the early evening sky. Emma hoped the weather would hold until the party was over, but she wasn't surprised that Kate was prepared in case it didn't.

Alibi made a beeline to the self-service bar and returned with two open bottles of Guinness. "Do you think this counts as checking the drinks supply?" he asked.

"Yes," Emma said, gratefully accepting the beer. It was warm, the way Guinness should be served.

Alibi was wearing the same style outfit he always did—khakis, a dress shirt, and a dark sport coat. Tonight's jacket was hunter green.

No special party clothes, but he looked nice.

He hadn't said anything to her about the dress she was wearing.

She felt a little silly in it now.

"How are things?" he asked, his eyes roving the party, checking out the people who were laughing and talking.

Emma didn't take his lack of eye contact with her personally. He was conducting a threat assessment: *Who's here, what are they doing, what are they capable of doing next?* In her experience, homicide investigators rarely turned that function off. Although when she and Alibi had been in their "will we/won't we" dating phase, his attention, when he did settle it on her, had been complete. In those moments, she'd not felt second in his mind to anyone or anything.

As she watched him make short work of his Guinness—he wasn't a big drinker, but he liked the occasional beer—she wanted nothing more than to sit down with Alibi and talk like they used to. Really talk, like there was a future in what they said and the next conversation and the one after that were inevitable. But this wasn't the time or place for her to lose herself in conversation with Alibi. It was Kate's night, and Emma wanted to keep one eye out for whether and how she might be needed. So she asked a straightforward, work-related question of him instead. Besides, she was curious.

"Do you know what caused the storage facility fire?"

That got his attention. Alibi looked directly at her, his brown eyes warm and wide, a smile tugging at his lips. "So you heard about the fire?"

He was playing with her—clearly, he knew she'd been there.

"Do others know?" she asked.

"Yes."

She thought about that for a minute. "How? I threatened everyone I came into contact with that I would sue for violation of my medical privacy rights if they disclosed I'd been anywhere near that blaze."

She worried that if some enterprising journalist placed her at the Clad Corp building fire, they might reach back to the events of last summer when she and Luke had rescued the governor's granddaughter. In the violent resolution to that kidnapping, Luke, fifteen at the time, had needed to kill a man. That had been the big story, and the press would like nothing more than an excuse to revisit it.

Luke couldn't handle that, she knew it.

"Breno told me," Alibi said.

"Ah, that makes sense," Emma said. She was relieved that her involvement that morning wasn't common knowledge, at least not yet, though she wasn't thrilled with the Kate-to-Breno porous connection. She still lived in a world where what she told Kate remained between them. She returned to her original question.

"And the cause of the fire?"

"Suspicious," Alibi said.

"Really? Do you know who set it yet?"

"No. Excuse me a minute."

He crossed to the food table and returned with two small plates—one with vegetarian items for her, the other meat heavy for him. He popped a mini hot dog wrapped in bacon into his mouth. Emma made a funny face as he swallowed it. It didn't bother her when others ate meat, but she'd been a vegetarian for so long that it no longer looked like food to her.

"I've been thinking about the cause of the fire. Given that I was there," she said, smiling. "What's in a storage facility? People's stuff. Lots of stuff. So what you're likely to accomplish if you set a fire there is to destroy property, not to hurt people."

An odd look crossed Alibi's face.

"What?" Emma said. "Daniel Baptiste is okay, isn't he? That was just bad luck. And no one else was hurt."

Alibi shook his head. "There are things I can't talk about yet. It's an ongoing investigation."

Emma saw pain reflected in his eyes. Someone else had been hurt or worse. She didn't ask for more information—he would have told her if he could have. Instead, she focused her thoughts on what Daniel Baptiste had said about the facility's process for emptying units for nonpayment.

"At Clad Corp, when someone fails to pay, the company takes legal possession of their stuff and moves it to the basement, where it sits until management or experts can go through it and decide what to sell and what to junk. If someone who couldn't pay knew of that system and they'd stored things they didn't want other people going through—say, evidence of something illegal that they'd done— they might set a fire in the warehouse to destroy their own things."

Alibi reached inside his jacket pocket. Emma thought he was getting his phone. But he pulled out his blue notebook and a pencil and wrote something down.

When he'd put the notebook away, he said, "Well done, Sherlock. I think I'll have to advise arson to check that out."

"Am I Sherlock or Watson?" she asked, smiling. She was beginning to feel the beer.

"A very pretty Sherlock," he said, looking at her like he used to. She didn't mind.

"That's Kate's dress, isn't it?" he asked.

Emma was surprised. "How do you know? It fits me."

"It does fit you." He looked away as he said it.

Emma knew he didn't want her to feel that he'd checked too closely to see exactly how the dress fit. That behavior had been confusing when they were "almost dating," his not giving signs that he found her attractive. Since then she'd grown to appreciate it. She'd never seen Alibi ogle a woman, not even close, though she knew enough of his history to be certain it wasn't due to low libido or lack of interest.

"It would be good for us to talk," Alibi said neutrally, this time not giving anything away in his eyes. "Do you have time for coffee tomorrow?"

Before Emma could answer or even consider what his invitation might mean, he'd taken his phone from his pocket and stepped a few paces away. When he returned, he said, "It's the mayor. I have to go."

Just then Breno and Kate stepped out in the yard together, and people burst into applause. But Breno looked horribly uncomfortable and Kate didn't look much better. They came straight to Emma when they saw her.

Alibi raised a hand in farewell. "Congratulations, Breno, Kate. Sorry, I've got to run."

Neither of them so much as looked in Alibi's direction. Kate said quietly to Emma, "Breno needs to speak with you. Let's go to my room."

Her expression shut down any questions Emma might have.

Whatever this was, it was serious.

When they got there, Kate closed the bedroom door.

"What's going on?" Emma said, looking from Breno to Kate and back again.

"Sit down," Breno said.

Emma scowled at him. She didn't like being told what to do. But then Kate took her by the hand and led her to the end of the bed. Emma relented.

She kept her eyes on Breno.

It made no sense that he would be the one to tell her, but from the look on his face, she had to ask. "Is it my sister, Jasmine? Her children? Has something happened to them?"

Breno looked at Kate. She nodded encouragement.

"Emma," he said. "It's about your dad."

21

B RENO'S HAND MOVED toward his glasses but stopped halfway there. He seemed suddenly self-conscious, as though his discomfort with the news he was about to share was so great that he didn't know what to do with himself.

"Is he dead?" Emma asked.

"No," Breno said. "He's been arrested."

Emma's eyes opened wide.

She felt like someone in an old cartoon, staring at a piano plummeting from above about to fall on her head, frozen in a moment of awe at the horror and absurdity of the circumstance she found herself in.

Atticus dead, Emma could have understood.

She'd half expected it all these years.

But arrested?

For what?

She couldn't think of anything.

Then, slowly, she considered what might have changed in the two decades since she'd last seen or heard from her father. Perhaps, never having recovered from her mother's death, he'd gotten into drugs and been discovered in an alleyway, black tar heroin in his hand. Or maybe Atticus had taken a humdrum, corporate advertising job to survive—his wife had been the wage earner, after all—and despairing at having "sold out" his art, had committed a white collar crime, a scheme of fraud or money laundering.

Emma became aware of Breno and Kate looking at her, waiting for her to come out of what must appear to them like a trance.

She found her voice. "Why? What did he do?"

"At a reception hosted by a gallery showing your father's work, someone threw red wine on his featured painting, ruining it. Your father reportedly assaulted the person who did that."

Emma shook her head. There'd been a mistake.

Atticus's circumstances might have changed, but to his core her father was not a violent man. When he'd been angry—which had been rare—his voice had deepened and he'd folded his lips as though to stop himself from saying something he might regret. But he'd never, ever raised a hurtful hand to her, her sister, her mother, or anyone else. Even when her mother had seemed beyond reason, her father's only goal had been to protect her from herself and them from her.

Emma spoke firmly. "That's not possible."

She hadn't shouted, but her statement had sounded horribly loud to her in what until then had been a quiet exchange. In the stillness that followed, she fixed, belatedly, on the most important question, though she was afraid to ask. *Where is Atticus now?*

She'd lived for so long with the idea that if he was still alive, her father must be far away. Not in New York, Hong Kong, or even Antarctica. Those weren't far enough. At age twelve, she'd learned the meaning of *antidone*—the point the greatest distance geographically from where one was—and for her grandmother's apartment in San Francisco where she and Jasmine then lived, it was La Réunion, an island in the Indian Ocean east of Madagascar. Fittingly from Emma's perspective, it was the site of one of the world's most active volcanoes. She'd vowed to go there one day, where after twenty-four hours of flight time, she'd find her father waiting for her.

Even as an adult, she'd gone on believing that if he was alive, Atticus could not possibly be nearby. It had made sense to the part of Emma still trapped in childhood that only thousands of miles could prevent him from showing up at her door.

But now she knew the reality had to be different.

The incident at the gallery must have occurred in Sacramento. Why else would it have come to Breno's attention as the public safety liaison to Sacramento's mayor?

Bracing herself, she voiced her question out loud.

"Where is he?"

Breno didn't answer. He looked at Kate.

Emma didn't like that. What could be so difficult about that question?

"The alleged assault occurred at the Blue Heron Gallery in Old Sacramento," Breno said. "Your father had a rental car, and within minutes of that altercation, he left town—"

Gone? He's gone again?

Emma shouted, "No, that can't be." It came out almost as a scream.

As Kate tried to calm her and Breno looked stricken, without warning the door to the bedroom flew open, and Luke barged in. Flushed, he took in the scene: Breno looking guiltily at Emma, who, white and shaken, had just cried out in desperation and pain.

Eyes blazing with rage, Luke pulled his arm back, his hand clenched in a fist as he took a step toward Breno. Breno's hands flew up defensively in front of his face.

In what seemed like no more than a heartbeat, Kate had placed herself between them.

"Look at me," she said to Luke. She said it again, barking out each word, brooking no backtalk, playing the mom card for all it was worth. "Look. At. Me."

He turned slowly toward her, not relaxing his arm, still bent in a fighter's pose. She reached up and gently lowered it. "Breno had some difficult news for Emma, Luke, that's all." She slipped her arm through his and led him toward the still-open door.

An apologetic look in her eyes, she glanced back at Emma, who felt embarrassed and foolish.

Of course Atticus had gotten in his car and driven off at the first sign of trouble.

Wasn't that what her father did? Run and run again?

She moved to follow Kate and Luke. She would see what she could do to help them.

She would not chase after the shadow of a man who couldn't be bothered.

Then Breno said, "Your father is in San Francisco."

And that changed everything.

22

Eward, not wanting to miss a word.

"This afternoon your father was driving a rented SUV in downtown San Francisco when he made a wrong turn onto a one-way street and plowed head on into a Honda Fit, totaling that vehicle," Breno began. "The man at the wheel of the Fit got out and shouted at your father. Whether Atticus took that as a sign that the other driver was unhurt, we don't know. But we do know Atticus didn't stay to exchange insurance information despite the severity of the crash." Breno adjusted his glasses. "At that point, it legally became a hit-and-run. Atticus didn't get far. A witness wrote down the SUV's license plate number. Your father was taken into custody and is at the San Francisco jail."

Emma brought both her hands up to cover her mouth. It was a moment before she lowered them and spoke.

"How did you find all this out?" she asked.

"I knew from Kate your dad was an artist, and I remembered his first name, since *To Kill a Mockingbird* is one of my favorite books. I didn't think it was him at the gallery, though, because the last name was different from yours." Breno seemed to consider carefully, as he often did, what he wanted to say next. "I still thought it was an interesting incident to share with Kate—about the wine being thrown and the fight involving an artist. I mentioned to her the artist's name was Atticus Smit. She was the one who figured it out. You'd told her once that you and Jasmine have different last names because Jasmine took your mother's maiden name, Smit." He looked at Kate, as though for reassurance that he was getting this part of the story right. "The officer who was called to the gallery included an image of the ruined painting in his report. I recognized it as being similar in style to the one I'd seen in your office."

Breno pulled his phone from his pocket, quickly found what he was looking for, and extended it to Emma. She accepted the phone with both hands to hold it steady.

There could be no doubt.

The damaged artwork had the same flowing lines, the same shades of black and gray, and like the rest of Atticus's work, it wasn't a painting at all. It was a sketch in charcoal.

Moments later, Kate returned to find Emma rifling through her closet.

Emma pulled a long black leather jacket from its hanger. "Can I borrow this?"

"Of course," Kate said. "Where are you going?"

"To San Francisco. To see my father."

Kate's brows went up. She looked to Breno, who spoke tentatively, since Emma was already slipping her arms into the too-short sleeves of Kate's jacket.

"With the out-of-county hold in the system for the alleged assault," Breno began, "I don't think San Francisco will release Atticus, even if you make bail. You'll have to wait—"

Emma turned sharply toward him, her eyes wild. "Have the hold removed. Tell the mayor to make it happen." But she softened as she felt her anger fade, replaced by the almost unbearable memory of the loss she'd suffered decades ago, when one after the other, her parents had left her. Her boldness wavered. "Please. Tell her I haven't seen my father in over twenty years."

23

New City Hall

WHEN ALIBI ARRIVED at the mayor's chambers, she offered him coffee, freshly brewed and steaming hot, which he accepted. He'd pay for it later when he needed to sleep, but for now it was all he wanted.

She told him to sit, but that was as far as they'd gotten when her phone rang, and she was soon absorbed in a heated conversation. Seven twenty in the evening, and it felt to Alibi as though the mayor's day was just starting.

He used the opportunity to take a good look around. He'd been in her office many times, but typically Melissa Ruiz accomplished her business so quickly and efficiently that he had scant opportunity to do anything other than try to keep up.

He'd read the piece about the mayor's interior design choices in the Sunday Style section of the *Sacramento Bee*, so he knew the large-scale furnishings—the desk, credenza, hutch, and bookcases—were all of reclaimed Texas mesquite with accents of hammered iron. On the walls, in addition to photos of Ruiz with dignitaries from world leaders on down, there were colorful pieces of art, including a painting by Mexican artist Lourdes Villagomez that Alibi assumed must be a print—acquiring an original would surely have been out of the mayor's price range.

When Ruiz hung up, she joined Alibi in one of two plushly upholstered gold velvet armchairs positioned in a corner of the large space to create a feeling of privacy.

Mayor Melissa Ruiz was a tall woman, strong and fit with hair similar to Alibi's own—thick, black, and glossy and cut just above her suit collar. She'd served in the Air Force as an officer and a pilot, and her senior military background showed in her posture and bearing. She spoke curtly but not without warmth.

"We have an unusual situation regarding Johnny Hill's death. It was ruled accidental so wouldn't have come to you. I don't know how much, if anything, you know about it." She took a long drink of her coffee. Clearly, she could stand it hotter than he could.

"A fair amount," Alibi said. "As you know, the public reporting was in-depth and prolonged. And after Breno stopped by this morning, I took a look at the internal files." He didn't have to elaborate on the reason Johnny's death had gotten so much media attention. Anything Fran Hill did made the news, and the tragedy had been treated as a major story. "Cause of death was drowning, though sleeping pills and alcohol were found in Johnny's system, so there was the question of suicide. The press made much of that, some saying Fran's high-powered political lifestyle and lack of interest in parenting were contributing factors. But when all was said and done, it was ruled an accidental death."

"Correct," Ruiz said. "Johnny was believed to have been camping alone that night, at which time he consumed sleeping pills and alcohol, perhaps in an ill-advised attempt to deal with jet lag since he'd just arrived in Sacramento that day from Denmark." She shook her head. "So it is inconvenient, to say the least, that someone has waited until now to come forward to state that they witnessed two men by the lake that night, one who matches the description of Johnny in the news reports. And most troubling, it appeared to them that Johnny, if that's who it was, had difficulty walking and was being supported, almost half carried toward the water by the second man."

Alibi risked a sip from his mug. The coffee was now the perfect temperature, and it was delicious. If he could have purred, he would have.

Ruiz rose and crossed to a shiny Wolf brand gourmet coffee-maker on the credenza behind her desk. It had about as much in common with the ancient Mr. Coffee Alibi had as a thoroughbred did with a farmhand's lame mule.

Pot in hand, Ruiz looked inquiringly at Alibi. He shook his head no. The mayor refilled her own mug and remained standing.

"You might wonder why I am personally involved in this," she said. "The individual who says they have valuable firsthand information about what happened to Johnny Hill is only willing to convey it to the person 'at the top.' His words, not mine. And he wants to know if he can be put in a witness protection program if he has to testify in court as to what he saw. Obviously, he's way out in front of his skis. That's not how we do things. Fortunately, Breno, as the public safety representative for my office, has convinced him that when it comes to a possible homicide, you are the person at the top, not me."

Alibi took a moment. If there was something to what this potential witness had to say that even hinted at foul play, and if it could not be kept under wraps, he would have the media on him 24-7 for any scrap of detail they could get. If it reached the point where Fran Hill had to be informed, Alibi would also have a grieving mother on his hands, a politically powerful one, who would have to grasp that what had seemed a tragic accident might have been something so much worse than that.

"I'll talk to Breno and set up a time with the potential witness," he said. "This individual could be mistaken about the date or about what he thinks he saw. Even if someone else was there, that doesn't mean they bear any responsibility for Johnny's death. They may have left before the events that led to his drowning took place."

The fact that the mayor had refilled her coffee mug again and was drinking the contents at an alarming pace led Alibi to believe she'd jumped ahead to the worst-case scenario. Which was that Johnny Hill's death was not an accident. And it was not suicide.

In the worst case, Johnny Hill had been murdered.

Alibi had worked with Ruiz for several years and believed she was in elected office to do good for others, not to enrich herself. But in order to be reelected, she had to pay attention to how she was portrayed by the press. If her administration was thought to have overlooked the killing of the only son of a prominent

Sacramento political leader, Ruiz would pay dearly in the court of public opinion.

He couldn't fault her for wanting this handled with extreme care.

The mayor had to take another call. As she did so, she gave Alibi a wave indicating their meeting was over. He was down the hall, almost to the elevator, when his phone vibrated. It was a message from Breno.

Emma's father has been arrested and is being held in San Francisco.
Kate thought you should know.

24

On the Road

EMMA HAD BORROWED a jacket from Kate with the intention of leaving for San Francisco without delay. But as she approached her Mustang, it was obvious Fox and Crash had other ideas. The ninety-pound Rottweiler–German shepherd and twenty-pound puppy, a mini Bernese mountain dog, had four front paws between them up on her living room windowsill. They were barking an urgent request that she attend to them first.

As she got out of the car, she noticed her khaki bag on the floor of the back seat. No sense in having that along when she went to the jail. While San Francisco's violent crime rates were no more than Sacramento's, vehicle break-ins in the city by the bay were a real problem, and her handwritten wall notes on the train investigation were even more valuable than her computer tablet. It would be next to impossible to recreate them if they were stolen.

Having slung the bag over her shoulder, she climbed the few stairs and retrieved her key from beneath the planter to the right of her front door.

On a typical day, she walked from her office to the capitol building and from there to one or more agencies for investigative interviews or meetings. Lacking Kate's organizational skills, she'd more than once had to backtrack through a succession of locations to figure out where she'd left her keys. She'd decided that in her neighborhood, where break-ins were unheard of, she'd risk keeping a house key lightly hidden so that it was easily accessible whenever she got home.

Once she was inside, Fox jumped up and down as though bouncing on a mini trampoline, while Crash looked on, satisfied to let his small partner in crime do all the work.

The dogs trailed her through the kitchen, out the back door, and into the yard. She paced as they did their business, feeling bad that she was about to leave them alone again—maybe Kate would remember to send Luke to get the dogs after her guests had left.

Despite Kate's jacket, Emma felt a chill. The temperature had dropped, and the air seemed close and thick. Her thoughts turned to Alibi. She wondered whether she should ask him to intervene to get Atticus released, in case the mayor was unwilling or unavailable. But it might cause confusion to have two powerful people working behind the scenes on her behalf. Besides, she wasn't sure she wanted to tell Alibi that Atticus was back. She hadn't gotten used to the idea herself yet.

Once she had the dogs settled inside with fresh water and food, she decided to take five minutes to change so she'd be more comfortable for what could be a long night.

After hanging up Kate's cocktail dress with the jacket over it next to her suits, where she wouldn't forget to return them in the morning, she opted for a professional look: a pair of dark-gray tailored wool pants, a light-gray turtleneck, and stylish black ankle boots with a chunky heel. She figured it couldn't hurt when dealing with whatever bureaucratic snags might await her at the jail. On her way out, she grabbed a heavy wool pea coat from the front hall closet—she planned to drive with the Mustang's top down as long as the weather held.

She let the classic car's engine warm up while she checked the GPS program on her phone. It indicated she would arrive in San Francisco in under two hours, though traffic was unpredictable heading into the Oakland–San Francisco Bay Area at any time of day. She put on the knit SF Giants cap that she kept in the glove compartment. The dogs reappeared at the front window, paws up, though not barking this time, their eyes watchful, having monitored her preparation and aware she was leaving rather than coming home.

As she backed down the driveway, her mind strayed to work. The train project was not some obscure academic exercise. The near-constant congestion on the roads was the primary reason the new trans-bay tunnel was so hotly anticipated. Once it was open, a train from Sacramento to San Francisco would take the same two hours as a car if conditions were good, but the underwater tunnel wouldn't be subject to the hours of delays that could occur if the freeway or a bridge was narrowed or even shut down due to an accident —a situation that concerned Emma now.

Fortunately, as she approached the Tower Bridge, it was clear. With the road open ahead of her, she tried to prepare herself for what she might find at the end of it. She called up an early memory of Atticus, his arm around Margaret, Emma's mother, who held her baby sister, Jasmine, swaddled in a blanket. Emma, "the big girl" at five years old, had her hand in her father's on his other side.

All were smiling except Jasmine, whose face was hidden from view. Emma hadn't forgotten her sister—she'd been in the back of her mind ever since Breno uttered the words *It's about your dad.*

Jasmine was in England completing a master's program. Her four-month-old son, her two-year-old daughter, and her supportive husband, Reggie, had all relocated there for two years.

Emma had decided to wait to disrupt her sister's life until she had some idea of what this meant, including whether their father planned to stay for any length of time. Regardless, Emma doubted Jasmine would jump on a plane at the news Atticus was here. Even if he did have a reasonable explanation for his sudden disappearance within days of their mother's death (and how could he?), Emma was pretty sure it would be twenty years too late for Jasmine.

When Emma came off the bridge and merged onto Interstate 80, increasing her speed and causing the Mustang's powerful V-8 engine to roar, she allowed herself to consider why Atticus had come to Sacramento.

With her position at the Hayden Commission, she was a public figure—a quick Google search would have revealed to him her employment and its capital location. She experienced a glimmer of hope at the thought that he might have been planning to see her and then the fight and the arrest had gotten in the way. Suddenly, she had no shortage of memories of her father. They seemed to crowd into one another, each one demanding to be seen.

Once, she and Jasmine had made "soda pop cupcakes," their own recipe, which had failed to become solid when cooked. They'd sloshed the results across the living room carpet when carrying the delicious, sickly sweet concoction to eat in front of the television. When Atticus had come upon his daughters, smiling up at him, their faces shiny and sticky, dotted with soda pop cake, he'd not said a word about the mess but had returned from the kitchen with a bowl and spoon of his own and joined them.

Then there'd been the far more serious time when their mother had slipped on the concrete stairs to their apartment building. Emma thought it might have been a March day like this one, with an early rain. She'd been eight years old, and upon hearing that Margaret had "damaged several disks," she'd pictured tiny Frisbee-like objects, bright yellow, jutting out of her mother's upright spine.

Throughout the rest of Emma's childhood, Margaret's back had given her trouble. When the pain was at its worst, she was easily angered. When that happened, Atticus made her endless cups of tea, propped up her pillows, and entertained her with stories that made her laugh and sometimes cry.

Emma recalled how she and especially Jasmine had resented how often their father put their mother ahead of them. They didn't blame her. Their mother was hurt, what could she do? Instead, they found Atticus at fault for not fixing it. Why couldn't he make their family whole again?

There had been their walks to the Fourth Street Amtrak station, Atticus carrying a thermos of hot cocoa, appropriate even in summer in foggy San Francisco. Those happened during Margaret's good periods, when he felt she didn't need him right by her side. Emma remembered those treks to the station as some of the happiest times of her childhood.

It seemed ironic to her that Atticus had reappeared when she was in charge of a project that, among many things, would upgrade the very station she'd visited with him as a child. The one she'd imagined he'd fled to when he decided to leave her behind.

A soft drop of rain fell on Emma's face, then another, just the hint of a shower. She hoped she'd pass through it quickly rather than be forced to pull over and put up the top of the car.

She'd risk it.

She didn't want anything to slow her down.

25

Matchbook Lane

After his mom stepped in to prevent him from breaking Breno's nose, Luke had retreated into his room.

In the Marvel comic book world, scientist Bruce Banner transformed into the Incredible Hulk when angered, a giant green superhero/monster who grunted and crushed his way to victory over the bad guys. Last summer, Luke had had no choice but to use violence to rescue a child, and since then he'd sometimes felt as though the Hulk lurked within him. Luke's counselor had said that emotional volatility was normal under the circumstances. Still, when he'd asked her when he might feel like himself again, when the "episodes" would stop, she'd said reassuring things but had made no promises.

The party was winding down, though Luke could hear occasional bursts of laughter through his closed bedroom door. The forty or so people who had been packed into their modest backyard had come running inside when the rain started. They might have stayed—there'd been no lack of enthusiasm—but there wasn't the space to go on celebrating. The living room was just big enough for a sofa and the table where Luke and his mom ate, and then there was the kitchen. He didn't think anybody would want to hang out in the two small bedrooms.

He checked his phone again—he didn't want to think how many times he'd looked to see whether Daphne had messaged him.

There was no reason to think she would have. They'd already confirmed the time for tomorrow, and he'd sent her his address. But he recalled how she'd smiled when he'd said they could talk, and how the fear she'd seemed consumed by had lessened when she'd known he would meet with her—he hoped he could live up to whatever it was she needed from him.

He heard the doorbell ring, followed by cries of welcome and surprise. He wondered who could be arriving now.

A moment later his mom opened his door, her face flushed with excitement. "Come out and—"

"Can't you knock?" Luke didn't think before he said it. It was a habit, a well-worn line. He was actually curious why she looked so excited.

"Anthony Torgetti is here. You can tell him you're interested in the field of artificial intelligence—maybe he'll give you a job."

"Mom. I'm in high school. I'm working at Rainbow Alley and at Aunt Emma's commission. I don't need a job."

"Come on," she said, still smiling, undeterred, as she turned to go.

Luke followed grudgingly.

There were only a few people left, scattered in groups of twos and threes around the room, and he heard someone in the kitchen.

Mrs. Cleveland, who owned their duplex and lived in the other half, was seated at the table by the front window with Trina, a teaching assistant Luke knew from Rainbow Alley. He wished he could join them. He walked up to stand next to his mom instead, as he knew that was what she wanted.

Kate put an arm around him. "Torg, this is my son, Luke. He's sixteen."

It seemed weird to Luke that his mom had called him Torg. Though he'd seen the nickname online, it didn't seem like something you would do with a person unless you knew him well. And this guy was really famous, mostly for being so rich.

Still, Luke thought he looked pretty normal, like someone you would see anywhere and not really notice. He guessed he must seem good-looking to people his own age, clean-cut with nothing weird about him. Though to Luke, Breno looked more like a celebrity. His suit definitely fit better, his dark hair was thicker, and his teeth were whiter.

In fact, Torgetti looked kind of like a wannabe Breno.

The thought made Luke smile, which was good timing, because he hadn't been listening and realized everyone was looking at him happily, as though something was expected of him.

Fortunately, Torgetti seemed aware that Luke might have missed a step, since he recapped what must have been the most recent exchange. "So your mom tells me you're interested in artificial intelligence. Any particular aspect of AI you're researching?"

Luke blushed. *Researching* was definitely a stretch for the reading he was doing for an independent study project at school.

"Luke is also working at the Hayden Commission as an intern," his mom interjected.

He was embarrassed that she seemed determined to broadcast his résumé just because this guy was someone famous, although he guessed that was what moms did.

"They do good work," Torgetti said. "I was just there today. I've had a couple of interviews with Emma Lawson, one of their lead investigators."

"Emma's a dear friend," said Kate.

Torgetti's eyes moved toward the sounds in the kitchen. "Is Emma here?"

"No," Kate said. "She was, but she had to leave early."

Torgetti nodded. "It's been a long day for a lot of us. I just wanted to stop in and congratulate you."

There was a soft roll of thunder, and they all turned toward the front window. It looked like the rain had stopped, though the night sky was gloomy, and the moon was barely visible behind the clouds.

Trina assisted Mrs. Cleveland in getting to her feet. She was ninety and still lived alone. Luke saw his chance. "I have to help Mrs. Cleveland home. It was nice to meet you."

Torgetti pulled at his shirt collar. He suddenly seemed unable to figure out what to do next. The smooth manner he'd maintained for a few minutes seemed to have left him like a borrowed coat that had slipped to the floor. It made Luke find him more likable.

Anthony Torgetti didn't throw his weight around as Luke had imagined a powerful guy who had ten thousand times, maybe a million times, the money of anyone else in the room would. Luke had seen some posts about Torgetti being headed toward legal trouble. But it seemed to Luke like it was the usual hating on someone successful by random people online who had nothing better to occupy their time.

He headed to his room to get his coat to go next door. It could start pouring rain again. But as Luke stepped away, Torgetti pulled an envelope from his inner suit pocket.

"I almost forgot, this is for you," he said, looking first at Breno and then pushing it somewhat awkwardly toward Kate. "Luke, you too," he said, catching his eye.

Luke almost reversed course.

A gift from a billionaire?

He really wanted to see what was inside.

26

West Sacramento

ALIBI SET THE takeout bag from Delicious Island Fare on the kitchen counter and removed his coat. There'd been plenty of food at Kate and Breno's party, but he'd left too early to sample much of it.

At least he'd had a chance to spend time with Emma.

He poured himself a glass of Tempranillo red from Berryessa Gap winery up the road and filled a bowl with the spicy, deep-fried Chicken Katsu that was a specialty of the nearby Hawaiian restaurant. As he sat down and dug in, he wondered whether being with Emma had triggered his craving for the dish, a favorite of Tommy Noonan, Alibi's longtime friend and his first partner in homicide over a decade ago.

Tommy had dated Emma—that was how Alibi met her.

Though Alibi couldn't say he'd never thought about Emma in lustful ways while she was seeing his good friend, turning those fantasies into reality was a line he never would have crossed. Not that Emma would have cheated on Tommy; he was quite certain she wouldn't have. But even after Tommy had tragically died last August, despite undeniable sparks between them, Alibi and Emma had never managed to move past the friend stage. And the longer Alibi knew her, the more he suspected that had nothing to do with

Tommy—or, for that matter, him. Emma was as driven and single-minded about her career as anyone he'd ever met, and with the exception of Kate and Kate's son, Luke, there seemed little space in her life for anything else to take root.

One of the things Alibi liked best about his apartment was the open-plan kitchen and living area. It meant the view of Sacramento's Tower Bridge was visible from wherever he sat, though tonight its golden span, usually beautiful against the night sky, was shrouded by fog and heavy low clouds.

He felt the gloom seep into his mood.

His recent attempts at dating others had ranged from awkward to disastrous, in part because he didn't seem able to put the possibility of romance with Emma entirely out of his mind. He even found himself thinking of ways to "run into her"—ridiculous for a grown man.

He tried to look at the positive. He'd made progress tonight by directly suggesting coffee. But the mayor had phoned before he'd closed the deal. In fact, all told, this evening the mayor had cost him a free meal at Kate and Breno's and a firm date with Emma. On top of that, she'd landed him with the possibility of reopening Johnny Hill's case, which would make no one happy, least of all the murderer.

And having an unhappy murderer was rarely a good thing.

As he finished the last of the chicken and rose to rinse out his dish, it occurred to Alibi something important had been missing when he'd gone over the internal files on Johnny's death.

There'd been nothing about Johnny's phone being logged into evidence. Had it been lost in the lake when he drowned? Or if there was a killer, had they taken it? And what about Johnny's computer? If he'd left that in Denmark, which seemed likely on a short trip, had anyone accessed Johnny's cloud accounts?

Alibi pulled his notebook from his jacket pocket and added those items to his to-do list. While he was at it, he jotted down a reminder to share Emma's thoughts about a motive for arson in the storage facility fire with Clive Carter, his counterpart in the fire department.

Clive should be able to get a warrant for the list of names of those who had failed to pay for their storage units in recent months. Once he had that, they could cross-check criminal histories to identify the individuals most likely to have stored something they felt was worth committing arson to destroy. If the guilty person had no prior criminal activity, they could be overlooked. But it was a place to start.

As he dried the bowl and fork and put them away, Alibi felt himself slipping into work mode. He didn't like it—he had to draw the line somewhere.

He retrieved the book he was reading from his bedroom, *Turpentine*, by Spring Warren, a mystery adventure story set in the Wild West in the 1870s, guaranteed to provide a brief escape. He brought it back to the table where he'd left his half-full glass of wine.

His phone lay next to it.

Without overthinking it, he sent Emma a text.

The mayor plied me with her super-caffeinated brew.
Not going to sleep anytime soon.
Call me if you want to talk.
Alibi

He'd decided not to say anything about her father. He thought Emma had said he'd died, but he must be remembering that wrong. Breno hadn't given him much to go on. He'd let Emma share that information with him in her own time, if she wanted to.

He'd just reached the point in *Turpentine* where a bomb explodes at a gun factory when from the corner of his eye, he caught sight of something outside his kitchen window.

A silvery wisp that from that angle had the shape of a man.

It was impossible for anyone to be out there.

Alibi was on the ninth floor, and there was no balcony.

But he gently set the book down and concentrated on the image outside. He felt his mother's presence, gone five years now, and the floating apparition became clearer, taking the form of an athletic young man. He had dark curly hair and was clean-shaven.

Alibi knew who it was.

He'd seen him that morning.

Well, not "seen him," exactly. He'd viewed images of Johnny Hill in the press clippings and in the autopsy photos in the confidential file from the coroner's report.

The figure became less solid as it floated up and away from the window. It was increasingly hard for Alibi to see. He didn't turn to get a better view—he knew he would gain no knowledge by facing Johnny's silver shadow head on.

Alibi quieted his thoughts, and as he sat still and open and stripped of even his own expectations, a bolt of lightning split the sky, and with it his shimmering vision of Johnny Hill was cleaved perfectly in two.

27

Best Bet Bail Bonds

IT WAS JUST past ten PM when Emma pulled her Mustang into a parking space across from the Hall of Justice on Jeff Adachi Way, a narrow side street named for a longtime San Francisco chief public defender, considered by many to be a champion for criminal justice reform and police accountability. She hoped the fact that she'd found convenient parking on a street named for a defense attorney would prove to be a good omen in her quest to see Atticus released tonight.

She checked her phone. She had five new messages.

The first three were from Breno. He had "signed" each one, a requirement in city government, so that if the city was sued (which it often was), it was possible to know which employee had said what, even in the briefest texts.

> Your father is at Intake & Release
> 425 7th Street.
> Breno Silva

> Successfully removed out-of-county hold. Go to any bail bonds service across from Hall of Justice. They'll walk you through next steps.
> Breno Silva

Kate sends her love.
Breno Silva

The next one was from Kate.

Love you.

Emma smiled. Evidently, Kate hadn't been willing to rely on Breno to deliver her message.
The last one was a surprise.

The mayor plied me with her super-caffeinated brew.
Not going to sleep anytime soon.
Call me if you want to talk.
Alibi

As Emma latched the convertible top in place, she mused that it was unlikely Alibi's message had been a random "let's talk for no reason" text. Maybe Breno had gone to Alibi instead of the mayor to deal with the out-of-county hold.

The rain had stopped, which was fortunate, since she'd not thought to bring an umbrella. It was cold out, but not too bad. She kept the Giants cap on and buttoned up her pea coat.

When she reached Bryant Street, she was faced with a half dozen twenty-four-hour bail bond establishments. She chose one that proclaimed FAMILY OWNED AND OPERATED in red letters beneath the name BEST BET BAIL BONDS.

Inside, it was empty except for a young woman with dishwater-blond hair and small, dark eyes. She sat hunched over on a stool in front of a computer behind a thick Plexiglas partition.

She looked up but didn't smile when Emma came in. She slid a form the size of an index card toward Emma through an opening at the bottom of the partition, then turned her attention back to her screen.

There was a line on the card for the inmate's name. Emma couldn't remember the last time she'd written *Atticus Lawson* on anything. It felt very strange. When she was done, she slid the card back to the woman, who looked it over, entered something into her computer, and after a beat said, "No record. Not there."

Emma felt the tiny bubbles of optimism and hope she'd permitted to float to the surface on her drive over burst. Until she remembered Breno had said that her father had used the last name

Smit, her mother's maiden name. Emma offered that to the woman, who said, "Spell it."

Emma did, but rather than coming back with *Eureka, here he is*, the woman scowled and squinted and leaned forward to peer at her screen before saying, "Hold on." She rose stiffly and disappeared through a door behind her. When she reappeared, she was trailed by a second woman, this one with a perky brunette bob and a broad smile.

"Let's see what we can do," she said in an upbeat tone, navigating to a new screen. "Hmmm. Mr. Smit is on an out-of-county hold. He'll be transported to Sacramento for processing on a charge there. We're sorry, we can't help you." Her voice now had all the warmth of a prerecorded robocall, probably because she'd concluded they'd make no money, since it wouldn't be possible for Emma to post bail for Atticus.

Without another word, the brunette went back through the door from which she'd come. Fortunately, the first woman seemed energized by her coworker's lack of compassion. She asked Emma, not unkindly, "Were you aware of this hold? Do you have any paperwork related to it?"

"I have a text," Emma said, taking out her phone. "From the Sacramento mayor's office, indicating the hold has been removed." She was in the process of locating Breno's message when the woman announced proudly, her surliness gone, "I found him. I had to refresh and get to his new status. Atticus Smit. The hold has been removed. He can be processed for the San Francisco hit-and-run. Twenty thousand bail."

As Emma was hoping the credit available on the two cards in her wallet combined would be sufficient, the woman said, "You pay ten percent of the total bail for our services, and we process everything for you. Only if Mr. Smit does not show up for his court date is the full twenty thousand due and payable, and it is your responsibility."

Not show up? Run away? Atticus? *That's what he does.*

But it was a risk she'd have to take. No, not quite that. It was a risk she wanted to take.

She said to the woman, "Okay. If it comes to that and twenty thousand dollars is the price of admission to see my father again, I'll pay it." She pulled her bank card from her wallet. "For now, put the two thousand on this."

28

Inmate Intake

A LARGE DEPUTY WITH a buzz cut behind the counter in the Intake and Release Center for the San Francisco jails was in full uniform. He had a badge and everything, though no firearm, which Emma found comforting. Maybe that meant this was a safer space than outside. On her short walk from Best Bet Bail Bonds, she'd seen three police officers with holstered weapons.

There were two people in front of her in line. Following very brief conversations, the officer directed each of them to take a seat in the waiting area. But after scanning Emma's driver's license, he stepped away to confer with a woman at a desk behind him, who consulted her computer screen. Then he moved to the far end of the counter. "Over here," he called to Emma.

She felt a knot forming in her stomach. She walked quickly—better to get whatever it was over with.

"Follow me."

He led her down a hall to where another officer, an older man with dull eyes and a glum manner, sat next to a metal detector. He searched her purse carefully and then wordlessly returned it to her.

No one here seemed interested in small talk.

Emma supposed the steady flow of people with problems coming in and out of the jail—some having reached the lowest points of their lives—likely wore down even the most compassionate among the officers and other employees. The expedited treatment she was receiving must be because the mayor or maybe Alibi had called ahead.

"Will he be able to leave with me now?" she asked the officer with the buzz cut, speaking to his back as they walked briskly past a series of unmarked dark-wood doors.

He didn't answer but stopped abruptly in front of a closed door, just like the others they'd passed. He knocked once, then opened it without waiting for a response.

His broad form blocked Emma's view.

She'd thought he would stay with her or at least give her some instructions about what would happen next, but all he said was, "You can go in," before he quickly turned and left.

Emma concentrated on breathing, which had suddenly become difficult.

Air in. Air out.

The small room had gray walls and was minimally furnished with a scuffed wooden table and three chairs. The sole occupant stood with his back to her, apparently oblivious to her existence, as he surveyed items on the table before him. She could feel the pounding of blood in her ears. Her knees felt weak.

She took one step inside.

She had only his back to go on, but the man standing a few feet from her was far too short to be her father. Although she was much taller now than she'd been at age eleven.

Would that make Atticus seem shorter?

There was something in his bearing that was familiar. But she couldn't be sure.

It's been so long.

He was dressed in a gray tweed jacket with suede patches at the elbows and dark slacks. The most striking thing about him was his salt-and-pepper hair, which was thick and wavy and neatly trimmed above the nape of his neck. It caught the light from the ceiling fixture above him.

She took another cautious step forward. The chunky heel of one of her boots dragged on the linoleum. The man turned at the sound.

It was unmistakably Atticus Lawson.

Unmistakably Emma's father.

As he seemed to fully appreciate her presence, his skin blanched white, and his green eyes, rimmed with red from exhaustion or stress, blinked several times, as though he was checking whether he was seeing things.

Not the welcome she might have hoped for.

Then Emma understood. She was the same age now that her mother, Margaret, had been when she died.

As a child, she hadn't thought she looked anything like her mother—she had her father's eyes, which was what most people commented on. Besides, to an eleven-year-old, she and that glamorous thirty-three-year-old woman with the dark-auburn hair, high cheekbones, and deep red lips might as well have been from different species or even different planets. But now that she was grown, having looked at old photos of Margaret, Emma could see the remarkable resemblance between them.

The moment seemed to drag on. As they maintained eye contact, neither saying a word, Emma carefully considered the new reality she was in.

Her father was alive. Standing before her. And other than the transitory effects he'd shown during that first moment of shock, he looked the picture of good health. His skin, the color having returned quickly, was warm and only lightly lined around his eyes and mouth. His thick hair shone. His weight was right in proportion to his height. His arms and legs appeared slim and strong in clothes that, while modest, were nicely tailored.

All of which, when taken as a whole, made Emma want to kill him.

CHAPTER

29

On the Road

I T WASN'T THAT Emma had pictured a Hollywood-type reunion, she and Atticus rushing into one another's arms, Atticus sobbing with joy at having found her at last. In fact, in all the thinking she'd done since she'd heard the news about him—dredging up old memories and indulging her curiosity over what he looked like—she'd not pictured the moment they would see each other for the first time after so many years.

In retrospect, shock was an understandable reaction on his part, even absent the strong resemblance to her mother—the changes in her from age eleven to age thirty-three had to be even greater than those she'd observed in him.

But since then, things seemed to have gone from bad to worse.

Once he'd grasped that she was his daughter, not the spirit of his deceased wife, Atticus had seemed distracted and if anything displeased by Emma's arrival. He'd turned back to the table and continued collecting and organizing his things, which had evidently been returned in a jumble in a plastic bin that now stood empty.

He'd tucked a brown leather wallet into the inner pocket of his tweed jacket and scooped up several small items she couldn't see, putting those in his front pants pockets. Finally, he'd lifted a black cell phone as though about to make a call, but Emma could see the darkened screen. She might have realized the battery was dead before he did. She pushed herself off the wall where she'd remained for support and, after testing the stability of her knees, took one step and then another toward him, removing her phone from her purse as she did so.

When she reached him, she silently offered Atticus her phone. He looked at her as though she were a stranger or worse yet, a nuisance, scowling deeply in a manner she didn't recall him ever having adopted before, at least not when looking at her.

"We have to go," he said abruptly, striding past her out of the room without so much as a glance back.

Emma had to hurry to keep up through the lobby and out the front door onto Seventh Street, which was well lit. Despite the late hour, there were people coming and going to bail bonds offices, the jail, the intake center, and the police department up the block.

Atticus looked to each side and then over his shoulder, not fearful exactly, but as though he expected someone might emerge out of the shadows at any moment. It definitely wasn't a look of pleasant anticipation.

Emma thought for the first time since she'd arrived about how many missing pieces there were in the story Breno had told her about the gallery.

Who was the man who'd thrown the wine at Atticus's painting? Why had he done that? And why on earth had Atticus assaulted him afterward?

She decided to try to take whatever was happening right now less personally, since her father must have a lot on his mind that had nothing to do with her.

She focused on the immediate issue, which was getting them home. "My car's this way," she said, moving toward the intersection, where she pressed the button for the walk signal.

Then she noticed Atticus's arms hanging loose at his sides. He wasn't carrying anything. Everything he had with him fit in his pockets.

"Do you have luggage? Where are your things? Your clothes, your art supplies?"

She smiled at the last question. She'd never known Atticus to be without at least a sketch pad and some drawing charcoal.

He didn't answer.

She realized she didn't know when he'd first gotten into town, where he was staying, or how long he planned to be here.

Had he come with only the clothes on his back to the gallery reception, intending to return to wherever he lived right away, and ended up here in San Francisco instead?

The number of questions she had seemed to be increasing, and they had begun to make her feel dizzy.

"My things are at my hotel," Atticus said, still looking around.

"Here? In the city?" Emma asked. "We should go get them now."

He grabbed her hand and, after looking briefly both ways, pulled her with him across the street without waiting for the light to change.

She experienced déjà vu, a vivid flashback to when she'd been little, really little, at the beach. Atticus had taken her hand, his enthusiasm clear, smiling and laughing, pulling her toward the ocean. It had been a calm day, low waves rolling gently to the shore, but she'd been frightened as they approached the expanse of gray-blue water stretching to the horizon, endless and unknown. Then she'd felt her small palm pressed against his larger one and her own fingers entwined safely in his. He'd held on tightly to her when their toes touched the cold water, and she'd shrieked, but not with fear—with astonishment. She'd felt safe and as though anything might be possible.

This wasn't the beach, and Atticus 2.0 was unpredictable at best, but he had again taken her hand in his.

He increased his pace. She had to hurry to keep up. He was beginning to remind her of Kate in that regard. When she pointed out the Mustang, Atticus approached the driver's side. "Keys," he said firmly, dropping her hand and extending his, palm up.

She spoke calmly but felt the need to suppress laughter at the ridiculousness of his request. "You can't drive. You were just arrested for a hit-and-run."

There was that scowl again as he jogged around to the passenger side. She unlocked his door—nothing automatic on the 1967 Mustang—then went back around to unlock and open her door. She started the engine to let it warm up and rolled down her window.

She needed the air.

"Can you put the top down?'" Atticus asked.

Maybe he needed even more air than she did.

She looked outside. The clouds were still heavy and dark, but perhaps the rain was done for now. "It will be cold," she told him. "And it's a two-hour drive." She appraised his tweed jacket and open-collar shirt doubtfully, then recalled she had a knit throw in the back seat and reached for it, handing it to him.

"Which way to your hotel?" she asked.

"I'll get my things tomorrow," he said, his gaze fixed straight ahead through the windshield.

"It's a four-hour drive round trip from Sacramento to San Francisco," Emma said. "I know it's late, but it would be easier if we—"

"In the morning, I'll take the train," he said flatly, even coldly, leaving no room for discussion.

It felt to Emma as though he couldn't leave San Francisco behind fast enough. Which was odd; he'd loved it when they'd lived there. He'd said it was the best place in the world.

They drove through the city streets without exchanging another word.

Emma felt exhausted, one drama after another catching up to her—the storage facility fire with its twenty-foot wall of flames and her desperate attempt to revive Daniel Baptiste, Daphne Ver-Strate's suspicious probing questions about Fran, Daphne's presence outside the commission headquarters, her story about being run down by a car, and Emma's discovery that Daphne and Johnny Hill had been together in Denmark. Not just together, but most likely in love and remembering or anticipating something "one year and one day" from about a month ago. And now this.

Now Atticus.

It was all too much. Then Emma thought about Alibi 's text to call her "anytime" and Kate's message, *Love you.*

She wrapped herself in what was known to her, in what was good.

When they reached the Bay Bridge, she chanced a glance and saw that Atticus had fallen asleep. His chin rested on his chest and his eyes were closed. The throw blanket had slipped off his legs onto the floor. She wanted to reach over and pick it up, to cover him and make him warm, but she wouldn't risk taking her eyes off the road, not at the speed they were traveling.

There was a distant roll of thunder as they exited the bridge. When Emma eased into the left lane for Interstate 80 to take them home, a streak of lightning split the sky and the rain poured down. She yelped, and Atticus sat bolt upright.

The torrent of drops was cold and heavy. It stung her face and hands, distorted the view through the windshield, and with the top down was getting them soaking wet.

She had to cross four lanes to take the first exit, which deposited them in Emeryville, the gateway to San Francisco from the East Bay, with shopping malls and lots of new townhouses and apartments. She pulled over, put the top up, and sat back, catching her breath, looking around for something on which to dry her face.

Atticus handed her the blanket and said, "Are you hungry?"

Emma hadn't eaten much at Kate's, not even the plate of snacks Alibi had brought her.

And they still had an hour's drive to go.

"Yes," she said.

"Good. Because I'm hungry," he said, and his eyes warmed as his lips turned up in a genuine smile that Emma had all but forgotten.

30

Berkeley

EMMA RECALLED AN all-night diner from her university days in Berkeley, only a few miles up the road from where they were now. She hoped it was still there.

Ten minutes later, she could confirm that it was, although very few cars were in the lot at this hour. The rain was still coming down. It had slowed to more of a shower than a downpour.

Emma and Atticus walked together, their shoulders touching as they crossed to the diner's door. Emma was five foot six and, in her boots, nearly five eight, so Atticus had only two inches on her in height. It felt strange to her to no longer have to crane her neck to look up to see his face.

Inside, the diner was as she remembered it, a dozen tables in a narrow space better suited for half that many. The grill was visible behind the counter. A young woman transferred eggs and hash browns to one plate and a toasted bagel to another, then delivered them to an elderly couple at a corner table toward the back.

"Sit where you like," she called over her shoulder as she headed back to the grill.

They took the nearest table. The place mats were laminated menus. *Eggs All Day* stood out in a banner across the top. The rest of the fare consisted of burgers, grilled cheese, and other items that could easily be fried up on a grill.

More from habit than anything else, Emma reached for her phone to check her messages, then decided against it. She wasn't much for "being in the moment." She preferred anticipating, analyzing, looking ahead, and preparing for what would come next. But she wanted to be present now.

Atticus removed a pair of gold-rimmed glasses from his jacket pocket and put them on to read the menu. They reminded her of Breno's.

She wondered if Breno and Kate had managed to enjoy the evening at least a little bit. She worried that the news of Atticus had blown a hole straight through it. At a minimum, she hoped they'd had great engagement celebration sex after everyone left, and then she realized she didn't know how that could happen comfortably in the tiny duplex with Luke one door away.

Kate had not discussed with Emma where she, Luke, and Breno planned to live after the wedding, and since there was no date set, Emma hadn't felt the need to press. But as much as she didn't want them to move away, not even one block or one street, she didn't see how the duplex could work for the three of them. They would have two incomes to afford something bigger.

Emma already knew what she wanted to eat—the eggs and hash browns looked good—but Atticus seemed to be having trouble making up his mind.

That's when she noticed that the hand lying next to the place mat, his left hand, bore a plain gold band on his ring finger.

A wedding ring.

It was old and tarnished and looked to Emma like it was the ring he'd worn when he was married to her mother.

Has he never taken it off after all these years?

The waitress approached with a pot of coffee. She filled Atticus's mug. Emma didn't decline as she normally would and ask for tea. Detached, she observed the dark liquid flow into her cup while her mind stayed on Atticus's ring.

Atticus ordered a burger and fries. She ordered her eggs, scrambled.

She couldn't stay silent any longer.

"Are you married?" she asked.

He reached for the ring with the fingers of his other hand and rotated it back and forth slowly in a practiced motion that she remembered.

"Yes," he said.

Emma waited.

He sipped his coffee, looked around, and said nothing more.

Emma puzzled through it.

Does Yes *mean someone new? It must. You don't say* Yes, I'm married *if your wife is dead, do you?*

She didn't feel able to push him on it, not on something that big, not yet. But the idea of small talk seemed blasphemy to her now. Whatever words passed between her and her dad, in their reunion after so long, had to be important.

She wanted him to go first. But he said nothing. He just kept turning that ring around and around.

She blurted out, "What happened?" It was all she could think of to say when what was racing through her mind was wound up into a tight ball inside that one little phrase. *What happened? Why did you leave? Where did you go? What have you been doing? Why didn't you contact me? Don't you love me? Why don't you love me?*

Atticus didn't respond.

Emma gulped for air. It was audible.

He looked up.

She realized she might hyperventilate if he didn't say something soon. She tried to slow her breathing.

His ring was like a flashing neon light. She couldn't look away.

"Do I have . . ." She paused, thinking how to word it. "More siblings?"

Atticus smiled, that soft smile again, and shook his head no.

If he hasn't been following what happened to us, if he doesn't know anything current about Jasmine, now is the time for him to ask.

Or was it going to be down to her to tell him he had two grandchildren?

Atticus reached for his coffee and took another sip. He'd never been much of a talker, other than his storytelling. Still, Emma felt something inside her competing with the wonder and joy of being seated across from him. It was the jolt of anger she'd experienced in the jail when she'd first processed that he was happy and whole, a feeling that threatened to build into a truly stark and powerful rage unless her father gave her something more than a nonspecific one-word marital status. And he'd better give it soon.

Emma's brow wrinkled. She scowled at him. She was breathing hard, the picture of someone fuming, ready to blow their stack, when Atticus laughed. He laughed out loud. He leaned back in his chair, tipped his head up, and laughed until tears flowed down his cheeks.

Emma screwed up her face even harder and bit her lip to keep from screaming at him.

Has he lost his mind?

His mood seemed to shift without warning.

Finally, Atticus shook his head and said, "You look just like you did when Jasmine beat you at chess for the first time. Four years younger than you, and she whooped you. That was the face you made before you upended the board, rooks and knights and bishops flying all over the place."

He wiped his tears away and smiled broadly at her.

"My stubborn, competitive, beautiful girl, determined to have things your way or not at all. You haven't changed."

His memory of her, *some evidence he remembered her at all*, was part of what she'd been seeking. She gave in. She even smiled a little.

But she still had so many questions.

"Will you stay with me?" she asked him.

She heard her own voice, childlike and plaintive. She didn't care.

When he said nothing, she nudged him. She clarified. "While you wait for your court hearing?"

"My understanding is that might not happen for some time, maybe a month or more," Atticus said. "If so, I'll have to go home and come back."

"Where is home?" she asked.

The waitress chose that inopportune moment to deliver their meals. Atticus turned his attention to her, said thank-you, and asked for catsup. He took a bite of his burger and afterward said, "It's good." Then he said to Emma, "I'll be here a few days, at least." He took another bite and after finishing that said, "We can talk about everything you want to later. But for now, let's eat."

31

Midtown Condo

D APHNE WASN'T HUNGRY, but then she never really was. Some people assumed she starved herself to achieve her model-thin weight, but she'd never been very interested in food. Her mother's theory was that growing up watching her three brothers eat would have put anyone off their appetite—they weren't known for their table manners.

Daphne smiled at the thought of Finn, Ruben, and Lars. Especially Finn, her younger sibling, the only one still living at home. Though he could be annoying at times—judging by his friends, most fourteen-year-olds were—she missed him.

Daphne had slept straight through after Emma Lawson dropped her off, but now it was midnight, and she was wide awake. She'd not called a physician. Her father was a physiotherapist at a primary care clinic in Utrecht, where they lived. He'd provided the medical care when Daphne or one of her brothers climbed too high up a tree or raced too fast on their bicycles, spraining an ankle or a wrist or coming home with more cuts and scrapes than he'd been able to count.

Daphne had witnessed his assessment and treatment of their injuries for years, so when she'd located a first-aid kit in the condo's bathroom, she'd been able to clean and bandage her various wounds herself.

She appreciated that the flat had come so well equipped, an advantage of the short-term furnished rental over a hotel room, though it had been expensive. She'd had to dip into the $10,000 Johnny had been paid for the designs he'd submitted as part of an unsuccessful application to California's new train tunnel Community Fund.

She'd wanted to wait to get Fran's advice before spending any of it, but she was pretty sure that money was Johnny's free and clear.

She still couldn't believe the chain of events that had led to Johnny's death. *To his murder.* It had all seemed so innocent at the time.

Now she knew it had been anything but innocent for the killer.

She hoped Johnny's mother had gotten to his storage unit before the fire.

Daphne hadn't, and she thought there might be evidence in there that could help get a conviction. Johnny had kept journals since he was a teen, and once he'd started designing, they'd been filled with his notes and sketches. If he'd gone to the storage unit on this visit, before he met with the killer, perhaps he'd added his most recent journal. That would have the notes and designs that would prove the killer's motive for murder.

One of her worst moments had been after Johnny's death, when she'd gone into his email. Anything Johnny had ever written or created had become precious to her. She'd been stunned to find his account in the cloud had been cleaned out. Not only the inbox but also all the old archived emails and even the "trash" had been permanently deleted.

That was when she'd been certain it was murder.

As she thought about it, she realized that given the destruction of so much of the evidence—what had been in the cloud, possibly the storage unit contents—her testimony might be the only thing that could convict Johnny's killer. Would she have to come back to the States for that? Did they let foreign nationals testify?

She decided to worry about that if it came to it. If she survived that long.

She'd thought Fran would have contacted her by now, but there'd been no calls or messages on the pay-as-you-go phone she'd gotten for short-term use on this trip. Had Fran's receptionist forgotten to tell her? That seemed impossible. She'd been the picture of efficiency.

The purple-black bruises on Daphne's left hip and thigh were more painful than her wrist and knee injuries. She shifted to find a better position on the couch.

Emma Lawson hadn't believed what Daphne had told her about the car trying to run her down. But it was true, every bit of it. Except for the part about her not knowing who had been driving. She wasn't ready to expose Johnny's killer yet. Not until she had solid evidence of his crimes.

And she realized now just how careful the killer had been.

Fran was her only remaining hope.

Daphne lay back and closed her eyes. Her mind drifted to the man she'd met in the alleyway. *Lucas.* She was certain he was from Ireland, probably the west coast. He had a slight accent that was easy enough for her to recognize, though he'd obviously been here a long time. He was American in more ways than he was not.

The kindness in his unusual gray-green eyes had been important, but she recalled most the fear she'd seen there too. Not for himself, but for her. As though he knew exactly what it was like to want to help someone so much that you were willing to die for them, if that's what it took.

She was very glad she would see him in the morning. Lucas worked at the commission. He could get to the third floor whenever he wanted. If she hadn't heard from Fran by the time she saw Lucas tomorrow, he would help her figure this out, which reminded her of something she wanted to ask him.

After she'd wrapped her wrist and arm and there'd been time for the analgesic pills in the first-aid kit to take effect, she'd finally been able to use her phone without too much pain. The first thing she'd done was to check the Hayden Commission site online.

A photo of Johnny's mother was there, as was one of Emma Lawson. Lucas's name was the last on a list of interns, though he was listed as *Luke*. But the man Daphne had seen waiting for the elevator and again behind the wheel of the white car, the man she was sure had killed Johnny, was not on the staff page for the commission.

The website appeared to be well maintained and up-to-date.

Lucas had said he'd only started today, and he was there. So while there might be another explanation, some glitch in the commission's IT process or system, Daphne thought it more likely that the absence of his photo meant the man who'd killed Johnny didn't work there, and that he'd followed her there today.

The condo building had good security, a guard in the lobby and cameras on all the doors. It was the primary reason she'd chosen it. But would it be enough to stop someone so desperate to silence her that he was willing to run her down in broad daylight?

Daphne felt a chill.

With difficulty, she stood and double-checked the dead bolt on the apartment's front door. Then she remembered the business card from the man who'd approached her in the public square and said he was a policeman.

That had been odd, though she supposed she must have looked very nervous. She took the card from her pocket and read his unusual name aloud.

Alibi Morning Sun.

The American police had been last on Daphne's list of anyone to go to for help. She'd seen too many movies depicting their "tough guy, guns first" approach. She'd feared they might not believe she was innocent in all of this and she could end up in jail or worse. But Lieutenant Morning Sun had not looked like the policeman in the movies, not with his long hair, and he hadn't worn any kind of uniform. Still, he'd shown her his identification with an official seal. And surprisingly, he'd had a caring, if intense, manner.

Daphne had to think to remember the day of the week.

She'd arrived on Monday; that meant today was Wednesday. Everything was taking too long, and time was not on her side with Johnny's killer looking for her.

By Friday, if Fran hadn't responded and she and Lucas hadn't figured out another plan, she would call Alibi Morning Sun. She put his card securely back in her front pocket.

THURSDAY, MARCH 11

32

I T WAS WELL past midnight. Fortunately, the man did not require much sleep. Like artist Leonardo Da Vinci and inventor Nikola Tesla, he'd found a few hours a night to be optimum.

He marveled at the masses who, like sheep, followed "the science" of the day that proclaimed eight hours of sleep the magic number for renewal of the senses. He was sharper and more attuned when he hadn't dulled his thought processes by putting them out of commission for extended periods in each twenty-four-hour cycle.

Only two days left. He had big decisions to make. *Life and death decisions.*

No better time to make them than the middle of the night.

Who will die first?

That question was not easily answerable.

Like the age-old riddle: Which came first, the chicken or the egg?

Should I butcher one or break the other?

He moved to the window and trusted the moonlight to guide his way.

33

Matchbook Lane

E MMA GLANCED AT the watch Kate had given her. It was two
thirty AM. She had no doubt that when she and Atticus pulled
into her driveway, Fox and Crash would rush to the window, barking at a volume that might wake the dead and would certainly
wake her next-door neighbors who had a new baby and needed all
the uninterrupted sleep they could get.

"We have two dogs," she said to Atticus, by way of preparation. The *we* would require an explanation at some point, since
Crash belonged jointly to Emma and Luke, and Fox was Jasmine's.
But now was not the time. "I'll need to run inside to stop them
from barking. As soon as I have them settled, I'll come back out
and get you."

"Sounds good," Atticus said. They hadn't had dogs when she
was growing up, but he'd always liked them, pausing to dole out a
scratch here and a "Good boy!" there to any that crossed their
path.

But to her surprise, when she coasted to a stop in front of the
cocoa-colored midcentury bungalow she'd called home for eight
years, it was dark and quiet. No barking. No dogs. "Luke must
have come to get them, knowing I might be late," Emma said, as
much to herself as to Atticus.

Her father raised an eyebrow.

He was probably waiting for her to say who Luke was. But as far as Emma was concerned, he could keep waiting.

She'd been doing it for years, and petty or not, it didn't bother her to even the score a bit by withholding some information of her own. Besides, something as important as who Kate and Luke were did not deserve to be discussed in the car at two in the morning in passing.

When they got out of the Mustang, Atticus started up the front steps, but Emma silently motioned for him to follow her around the attached garage to their left instead. They passed through a gate, then had to duck beneath magenta bougainvillea in need of a trim cascading over the fence separating her property from the neighbors.

They reached a bright-blue door on the side of the garage. Emma felt around beneath the welcome mat, retrieved the key, and opened it. She leaned in and flicked on the light switch by feel.

To address a shortage of affordable housing, the California legislature had enacted laws preventing local jurisdictions from limiting garage conversions. Emma had jumped at the chance to take advantage of the new rule last fall.

The large space was simply furnished. There was a vintage black leather sofa that opened into a comfortable double bed and a square table with four chairs in the center of the room. To the right was an enclosed bathroom and to the left a galley kitchen. There were musical instruments in a row against the back wall, including one of Luke's saxophones, an electric guitar, and a drum set.

The only window was over the kitchen sink. During the day, it provided a view of the backyard that was shared with the main house, with its colorful mix of native and drought-resistant plants, including Emma's favorite, Tango Hummingbird Mint, which true to its name attracted hummingbirds as well as butterflies.

Because Emma had designed the conversion with Luke's band practice needs in mind, it was insulated throughout like a recording studio. That was also the reason for the dearth of windows, since even double-pane glass permitted some sound to escape. To compensate, Emma had a large skylight installed in the center of the room, which meant sleeping on the converted couch could feel like camping, since it offered a broad view of the night sky, complete with stars.

Emma sometimes thought that in another life she would have liked be an interior designer. But Atticus appeared indifferent to his surroundings. He made no comment and seemed to be waiting for her to give him directions.

She obliged. "Please make yourself at home." It came out more formally than she'd intended. She crossed to the refrigerator. She did her best to keep it stocked with yogurt and other snacks for Luke and his bandmates, but the supplies had been depleted. "Not much here. We can shop tomorrow."

She handed Atticus the key to the studio.

"There's a separate key for the front door of the main house under a terra cotta planter at the top of the stairs that you started to go up. If you could put it back after you use it, that would be helpful."

"You're not much for security, are you?" Atticus asked.

She tried not to sound defensive. "It's a safe neighborhood, and this is a dead-end cul-de-sac. No through traffic."

His eyelids drooped. It occurred to her that perhaps he was being even less communicative than she remembered since it was closing in on three in the morning.

"I swim early. I leave here around five AM," she said. "Though I'm not sure I'll make it to the pool tomorrow, given the time now. I've a hearing in the early afternoon, but if you change your mind and would like me to drive you to the city to pick up your things rather than taking the train, I'm happy to do that any time after three PM."

She became aware that she was babbling when Atticus stepped forward, moving slowly and evenly, as though not to startle her. When he reached her, he opened his arms and wrapped them around her. He didn't pull her close, but his arms encircled her completely. His touch was steady and unwavering.

Emma kept her head down and her eyes closed.

She didn't know what to do, or even what to feel, whether to return the embrace of the person she'd once loved more than anyone in the world or to strike out, beating her fists against his chest, hurting him as he'd hurt her through his absence for more years than he'd been present in her life. Before she could decide, Atticus had dropped his arms and stepped back.

She looked up. His face was open and unguarded. She breathed more easily.

There would be time to welcome and return his hugs, if that was what she wanted.

34

I N THE MORNING, Emma dressed in jeans and a sweater, then carefully hung her lucky suit in a garment bag. It was a sea-green skirt and jacket with vintage ivory buttons that she'd purchased to celebrate her first day as a Hayden Commission investigator eighteen months ago. With Atticus sleeping in the garage studio, another first, she felt it was appropriate to wear it today.

She picked up her gym bag, prepacked for the pool, and took both that and the garment bag to the front of the house. In her sleep-deprived state, she wanted to make sure she didn't forget anything.

She returned to the kitchen and put the kettle on for tea, in compliance with Dr. Branco's instructions yesterday to drink plenty of fluids to counteract the effects of smoke inhalation.

She and Atticus hadn't made plans, unless you counted possibly going to San Francisco later to retrieve his luggage from the hotel. And this morning she realized they'd not even determined how best to get in touch with each other once she left the house. He didn't have a working phone, and she'd not yet provided him her cell number or email.

From a drawer next to the refrigerator, she withdrew a notepad and pen as well as some tape. She wrote down her contact information and Hailey's as a backup. Then she retrieved her personal laptop from the small second bedroom she used as a home office.

She placed the computer on the kitchen table and added to her message to Atticus that he could pick it up there for his use, so he'd have a way to communicate with others, including her, until his phone was working again. She also reiterated her offer to drive him to San Francisco to get his things from the hotel.

When she could think of nothing more to say, she hesitated over her signature. She was uncertain whether to write *Love, Emma*. She settled on just *Emma*.

The path back for them, or maybe it was forward, was uncertain in her mind, and she preferred not to get ahead of herself.

When she stepped outside, note and tape in hand, the air was cold, crisp, and beautifully clear, as often happened in Sacramento after a hard rain.

She passed through the side gate, folded the note in half, and taped the small square of paper firmly in place in the center of what she already thought of as "Atticus's door."

There was no sound from within. He was probably still sleeping, though given the studio's prodigious soundproofing, an absence of noise told her nothing about whether he was still there. She willfully tamped down her anxiety, reminding herself that worrying about Atticus's whereabouts, something she had worked hard to give up on long ago, could become her new full-time job if she let it.

When she reached the front yard, Luke was coming out of the duplex. He had Crash and Fox leashed and behaving reasonably well until they caught sight of Emma and employed their combined one hundred plus pounds to pull him across the street to get to her.

Luke had gotten quite a bit stronger over the last year, and she was certain he could have stopped them if he wanted to, but he seemed content to let them have their way, at least in this.

She checked her watch. It was not yet seven.

"Before-school band practice?" she asked him.

"No," Luke said. "The dogs set my schedule this morning."

As if to make his point about who was in charge, Fox pulled her leash from his grasp so she could greet Emma properly through nonstop consecutive jumps. She seemed to be reaching greater heights, which Emma guessed was a natural result of her legs having grown longer in the four months since Emma's sister, Jasmine, had left to study abroad.

Though beloved, Fox had drawn the short straw and been made to stay behind, since Jasmine and her husband, Reggie, had agreed the kids took priority, and it was enough to descend on Reggie's parents in their small home in the UK with a baby and a toddler without also bringing a puppy along.

It would be temporary, though two years felt like a long time, which was what was required for Jasmine to complete her master's program at the prestigious London School of Economics and Political Science, an opportunity that she and Reggie had agreed she couldn't pass up.

Emma would not have said yes to such an extended dog-sitting gig if Luke had not made the commitment with her. She and Luke had co-owned Crash for five years now, and it had worked well.

"I'm headed to the pool soon," Emma told Luke. "But I'll walk with you first, if that's okay."

She was curious how things had gone once she'd left the party, still concerned her drama with Atticus might have ruined the evening for Kate.

Or for Breno.

She'd have to get used to treating them as a unit as far as most activities went, although she hoped Kate, an avid follower of celebrity news, never mushed their names together in a Bennifer-like nickname, not even in jest.

Brate? Kreno?

The very thought of it made Emma shudder.

She and Luke had started up the hill of the cul-de-sac when Luke asked, "Where did you take off to last night?"

Emma didn't hear judgment in his question. It sounded more like curiosity and possibly concern. Not unreasonable; she doubted Luke had ever seen her as emotionally vulnerable and distressed as she'd been after she'd gotten the news about Atticus from Breno, not even when she and Luke had been fighting the bad guys together.

She gathered Kate had decided it was up to Emma to determine whether and how she wanted to tell Luke about her dad.

Luke's dad had been a thuggish type, and though Kate was vague on the details, Emma thought he might have been the reason Kate had abruptly pulled up stakes and moved Luke from Ireland to California.

Emma didn't think Luke even knew his dad's name, and it was highly unlikely he'd have the opportunity for a reunion with him in the future like Emma and Atticus were having now.

She opted for being brief and direct. "My father is in town unexpectedly. That was what Breno told me last night."

Luke's eyebrows shot up. "Hasn't he been gone, like, forever?"

"Yes, he has," she said. "But he's here now. I don't know for how long. And I'll be spending time with him."

Luke frowned. "Are you okay?"

Emma was touched that his first thought was of her. "I think so," she said.

Crash and Fox had treed a squirrel, and the subsequent barking made conversation difficult. Emma was grateful for the time Luke had to process the information while he got the dogs moving forward.

As it turned out, Luke had news of his own. "At work yesterday, Nick directed me to organize some electronic files about Anthony Torgetti's contract on the tunnel."

Emma asked, "Was it interesting? Did you find something?"

"No. But he was at our house last night. At Mom's party, after you left. He was asking about you."

Emma hadn't seen Nick there, and she didn't know how he might have ended up being invited.

An after-hours event wouldn't help her efforts to narrowly define their relationship as work focused.

"Does your mom know Nick? Does Breno?"

"Nick? No, why?" Luke stopped walking and looked at her like she'd radically changed the subject. Then he smiled as he realized what the misunderstanding had been. "Nick didn't come to the party last night. Mr. Torgetti did. Late, like after nine o'clock."

That makes much more sense, Emma thought. Working in the mayor's office, Breno knew just about everyone there was to know in the capital.

"He gave my mom and Breno a wedding gift," Luke said. "Or I guess it's an engagement gift. It's a honeymoon. Kind of. He included me. I didn't know he's part owner of that new airline, Cross World Flights. He gave us three round-trip tickets to wherever they fly, which I guess is just about anywhere."

Luke had become animated when telling her. He sounded both surprised and happy about it.

Emma had to admit it was pretty cool.

"You should go to La Réunion near Madagascar," she said. "It has one of the most active volcanoes in the world, and it's got to be close to the farthest point away from here."

Luke grinned. "How long would that take?"

"Twenty-four hours," Emma said.

They'd reached the duplex, and Luke opened the side gate. He unleashed the dogs, letting them into his backyard. As she watched him, his dark, curly hair still damp from his morning shower, his black T-shirt, jeans, and high-top black Converse echoing his mother's fashion choices (though she doubted Luke would see it that way), Emma felt a strong surge of love for him. He was not without his troubles, but he was an exceptionally thoughtful and kind young man. On impulse, she said, "I'd like you to meet Atticus. My dad. If you want to."

He smiled. "Yeah, okay."

Luke was almost to his front door when something else occurred to her. Since her yard was twice the size of Kate's, Luke often dropped the dogs off there when he went to school. She called after him, "Atticus is staying in the studio. It would probably be best if you keep the dogs with you until Crash has had a chance to meet him. I'm sure Fox will be okay, but you know how protective Crash can be if someone shows up at either of our houses without a security clearance from one of us."

35

Atticus awakened with a start when he heard the roar of an engine. It was so loud he thought it was a plane taxiing down a runway. Then he realized it was the sound of the V-8 in his daughter's Mustang as she backed down the driveway only a few feet from where he lay in the converted garage.

Had she said something about leaving at five AM?

It couldn't be that early. The sky was a soft blue through the skylight overhead. Dawn had passed.

He rolled over and buried himself under the covers. He hadn't slept well, and it wasn't the fault of the sofa bed, which had been comfortable enough. He'd had the dream again. The one where he struggled to lift Margaret off the kitchen floor in their old apartment in San Francisco. She'd not been heavy in real life, but try as he might, straining his arms, his legs, his back muscles, putting everything he could into it, he could barely get her a few inches off the ground. The worst part was he could hear the girls, Emma and Jasmine, crying and calling to him. But he couldn't leave Margaret to go to them. She wasn't safe, and they wouldn't be safe, unless he could lift her, carry her, and take her away.

He pulled the covers off and sat up. He felt clammy and hot. A shower might help. It sometimes did. Although he'd be putting back on the same clothes. Maybe there'd be something in the main house he could wear.

Nothing of Emma's would fit him, even if she did have sweatpants or jeans he wouldn't look ridiculous in. She'd mentioned someone named Luke. She hadn't used a tone that made him sound like a lover, but this Luke had access to the house and the dogs, whoever he was.

Maybe he'd left some clothes there.

When Atticus stepped outside, he was struck by the beauty of the day. He'd known it wasn't raining; the skylight in the studio was an early-warning system for that. But the purple-pink bougainvillea that covered the fence between Emma's yard and the neighbors were extraordinary, the sky was cloudless, and the sunlight gave everything a light golden glow at this early hour.

When he turned back to close the door, he saw a small square of paper taped in the center of it. He pulled it down.

Emma's note to him was clear, helpful, and even generous. But it was hard for him to connect its brief and dry style and structure with the Emma he'd known.

Obviously, an adult would write in a different way than a child. But his Emma had been creative and energetic and loving. He'd had hopes of her becoming an artist like he was or a writer or a dancer. It had been a complete surprise when he'd met this tightly buttoned-up young woman—analytical, professional, and clearly accomplished in her work. He'd Googled her, so he knew her job title and some of her accomplishments, but he still wasn't quite sure what she did for a living. Whatever it was, it was impressive, and that hadn't been surprising. But her joy for life, the spontaneity he remembered, if it was there at all anymore, was below the surface. That made him sad, not in small part because he suspected that his having left when he did, the way that he did, was at least part of the reason she seemed so different than he remembered.

He pocketed the note and went to the front of the house, removing the key from beneath the planter as directed.

As soon as he opened the door, he corrected a major error in his earlier impression. This was the home of a highly creative person, and a joyful one. The colors of turquoise and orange against white and blond wood made it energizing, even as there were areas of sanctuary within it—the corner writing table, a soft area rug with several books next to it. It looked like Emma might still lie on the floor and read as she'd done as a child.

At least some of what he remembered in Emma was there. She just hadn't been willing to show it to him. Not in the first twenty-four hours. He laughed at his hubris in thinking he might know anything yet about the young woman he'd left behind two decades ago.

One of the young women.

He and Emma hadn't talked about Jasmine. She'd been harder to find online. He wondered if he'd meet her again soon too, though he had things to settle first, and nothing was guaranteed, he knew that. He located the laptop in the kitchen and picked it up.

He would've liked to tour Emma's house, but he felt that would be intrusive. He would ask her to show him later, if she wanted to. On his way out, he did glance around to see if the sketch he'd given her before he left was up on the wall, or any of the others she might have kept. They were not.

For a moment he felt as forgotten as he imagined she must have felt for all those years.

He put the main house key back under the planter, but when he returned to the studio, he kept that key in his pocket. He didn't like the idea of anyone being able to let themselves in without his knowing, whether he was there or not.

He set up Emma's laptop on the table and logged in using an incognito window, which would keep him anonymous and not record his browser history, since he'd have to return the computer to Emma at some point.

He opened his email. No new messages.

He began to type.

I'm sorry I wasn't able to call you last night. My phone wasn't working. There's been more excitement here than I expected. But you shouldn't worry. Everything is fine. This might take a few more days than we'd planned. I'll keep in touch, although it may be hard for you to reach me, at least until I work out my phone situation. I want you to remember

everything we agreed upon and know that I will follow
through. I've already seen Emma.
Don't be frightened.
I love you.

Atticus read it over.
It was the best he could do. He hit send.

36

They had an open-campus policy at Thompson High School, so all Luke had to do was sign out in the office, indicating his reason for leaving. He was nervous but wrote neatly, *Forgot Assignment.*

When he arrived home, he went into the bathroom and looked in the mirror, running his fingers through his hair. The bike helmet had flattened it. He was wondering if he could pass for eighteen when there was a soft knock on the front door. He opened it, and Daphne stood on the stoop.

She wore a light-blue, flowing skirt that ended in the middle of her calves, a darker-blue tank top, and a bright-pink knit cardigan draped over her shoulders, her arms free, since the left was bandaged from elbow to wrist. Her nearly white short blond hair, blue eyes, translucent skin, and even her pale feet in thin leather sandals stood in stark contrast to the bright colors.

It was as though she were a black-and-white photograph and someone had photoshopped the outfit onto her.

She was even more beautiful than Luke had remembered her.

Daphne seemed to be studying him, and then he realized she was probably waiting for him to invite her inside or at the very least say something.

Anything.

He stepped aside so she could come in.

"Would you like a drink?" he asked her.

He blushed when her eyebrows went up.

It was the only thing he'd been able to think of to say. He hadn't meant alcohol. It was what his mom said when people came over.

Daphne looked around, taking everything in.

Luke hesitated before starting toward his room. He wondered if it would be obvious when she saw it that he was in high school. But he felt strangely exposed in the living room with the large window facing the street. Besides, he hadn't asked her her age, but she couldn't be much older than he was.

She smiled when she saw the acoustic guitar leaning against his desk, then looked at him questioningly, as though asking permission.

When he said, "Sure," more loudly than he meant to, she didn't seem to notice his nervousness.

She lifted the guitar, sat on the end of his bed, and picked out a few notes, humming softly to herself. It was a minute before she looked up. This time her gaze landed on his saxophone on the other side of the desk. His good sax, the one he used for performances, was at Emma's in the garage studio. But he kept the first one he'd ever owned, bought at a yard sale, as a backup.

"Do you play?"

"Yes," he said.

"Would you play?"

"Now?" he asked.

She nodded.

He thought she might be buying herself time before she got to the purpose of her visit. He recognized the strategy as one he employed in new situations.

"It's a tenor. It will be loud in this small space," he said, and then smiling, he added, "It's not like picking up and strumming a guitar."

"Will we bother someone?" she asked, looking toward the door.

"No," he said quickly.

Perhaps she thought he had roommates, though he doubted she'd be able to guess anything about them. His mother was so organized, no sweaters or shoes left around in shared spaces to show that a woman lived here. There were Irish knickknacks, miscellaneous books, and a water bowl and dish for the dogs.

Still, Daphne might have concluded he lived with a parent or two. He wondered whether young people in Europe stayed at home with their families after high school the way a lot of them did in the United States.

He retrieved a new reed from his desk drawer and moistened it between his lips. After inserting it in the slightly battered horn, he moved to the far corner of the room, as far as he could get from the bed where she sat.

He said again, "It will be loud."

She smiled. "It's okay."

He played a few bars of "My Funny Valentine," an old blues standard. It was the first thing he thought of. He followed that up with a fast and tricky improvisational run. It was what he was known for.

Then he worried she might have thought he was showing off.

"That was wonderful," she said.

Luke knew he was good at this one thing, and he'd heard in her voice that her brief compliment was genuine. He felt better.

He put the saxophone back. Though he didn't want to be, he was aware of the time. He had to be back for Honors History by ten, and it was a fifteen-minute bike ride to school.

He looked at her expectantly. She must have had a reason for coming. It couldn't have been just to see him.

It took her only a beat to get started once he'd shown he was ready to listen.

"Did you know Johnny?" she asked.

Luke frowned. "Johnny?" He mentally ran through the guys at his school, checking if there was anyone named Johnny, before remembering she couldn't possibly know any of them.

"Johnny Hill," she said. "His mother works at the commission where you work. Johnny was studying in Denmark when I was also studying there. We met, and . . ." She seemed to realize she was providing information he might not need. "You don't know Johnny?"

He shook his head and then watched helplessly as her face seemed to collapse in on itself. She squeezed her eyes shut tight and covered her face with her hands.

Suddenly, Luke realized who Johnny was, who Johnny's mother was.

Johnny Hill, who died last year. He drowned.

Luke had heard about it, of course, because Emma worked for Johnny's mother, Fran Hill.

Daphne hadn't looked up. She hadn't uncovered her face.

Luke said, "I know who Johnny is. I never met him, and I haven't met Fran yet. Yesterday was my first day at the commission."

She stood and put the guitar back gently, almost reverently, where she'd found it. Her voice was shaky. "Then I don't think you can help me."

"I might be able to," Luke said quietly. "If you tell me what it is that you want."

Everything about her was light—she was so pale and thin, almost fragile. He watched her closely, ready to say yes to whatever she might ask.

He didn't want to disappoint her.

Her eyes searched his. There wasn't hope in them, not exactly, but she sat back down. "I am eighteen now," she said.

Luke felt relieved. She was only two years older than he was. Maybe one and a half. But her next words made that unimportant.

"Johnny and I planned to be married. Soon." One tear, then another, overflowed onto her cheek. "But I was seventeen when he met me, and he was twenty-three, so he didn't want to tell his mother. They weren't close. It took him a while to decide he should still tell her, even if her reaction might not be to welcome me." She said it proudly, as though Johnny had been brave to want to declare his love for her to someone who might not approve.

Luke thought if he were Johnny's mom, he might not like it much either, what Johnny had done—twenty-three and seventeen. But Daphne looked at him with such openness, he felt her need for him to understand. So he fought to keep his disapproval from showing and gave a small nod.

It was enough for her to go on, though it seemed she might have sensed something in his manner that caused her to feel she had to explain.

"It wasn't anything wrong. In the Netherlands, when you are sixteen, it's okay. How do you say it here? It's the age of consent.

To be together. But not to marry. For that, you must be eighteen. That's why Johnny waited to tell his mother until after my birthday in January. He thought perhaps she would be happy if she could plan our wedding with us." More tears fell. Daphne didn't wipe them away. "I don't know whether Johnny had a chance to tell her. But he is her only child, and I want her to know that I loved him, and that she has me, that we might remember him together. I tried to accomplish this by speaking with her yesterday. I went into the commission offices. There was security to sign in."

Luke felt confused. He wanted to better understand what had happened, why it was so important to her to see Fran, to come all the way to the United States. Why not call her, write her a letter?

"It must have been so awful when you heard," he said. "How did you find out?"

"I went to meet Johnny at the train in Copenhagen. He was to have taken it from the airport. When he wasn't on it, I waited for the next one. I checked the airport information. His flight from California had been on time. There were no emails or messages from him. Then I checked his social media account. Someone had posted what had happened." Daphne stopped and shook her head. "That he had died."

Luke felt strange standing over her. He sat down on the edge of the bed, leaving space between them. She looked at him, her blue eyes red rimmed.

"I wanted to tell his mother about us. About the things I found. And about the money."

She opened her bag, removed a key ring, and set it next to her. Then she took out a thin notebook, perhaps a journal.

Luke had wondered what she'd meant by "the money," but he forgot about that when he saw that the only thing on the ring was a white plastic key card imprinted with the words IDEAL STORAGE. It was like the one his mom had, but with a hole in it so it could be slid onto a key ring as Daphne had done.

He pointed to it. "Is that yours? Or is it Johnny's?"

She wasn't listening. She'd opened the notebook and was looking for something.

She read out a name. "Shaylene Wilson. Do you know her? She also works at the commission. I found her on the staff page on the website."

Luke said, "No."

"Yesterday, Shaylene, who works for Fran Hill, said she would give Fran my email and phone number. I've heard nothing. I wonder if she forgot, though she didn't seem the type to forget."

"That's possible," Luke said. "But if she forgot or Fran wasn't in, I'm sure she will tell her tomorrow. Or perhaps Fran received the message but hasn't had time to respond yet. Did you let Shaylene know it was urgent?"

Daphne frowned, as though she was trying to remember, and then said, "I don't think so. Should I have? I thought all messages were passed along promptly in a place like the commission."

"That explains it then," Luke said. "You just need to be patient." Her face fell, and he could tell that had been the wrong thing to say. "I'm sure that's hard, but—"

"No." Daphne spoke harshly. "No, there is not time."

She looked away from him, but before she did he thought he saw fear in her eyes again, like he'd seen yesterday in the alleyway. When she looked back, her openness had returned. She spoke quickly, with obvious excitement. "Will you tell Fran Hill for me? If I give you the message? Will you go there now and tell her the things I wanted to say?"

Luke had to be back in school very soon.

"I can't right now, but I can do it at two o'clock. That's when my shift begins at the commission."

Daphne smiled. She leaned across and put her arms around his neck to give him a brief hug. When she sat back again, she was still smiling.

He could see the joy and relief in her face.

Luke went to his desk and tore a blank piece of paper from a notebook and picked up a pen, but when she saw what he was doing, she said, "No. I don't want to write it down. I will tell you about it, and then you can tell her."

That didn't sound like such a good plan to Luke.

"Suppose Fran isn't there when I go to find her? Wouldn't it be better if I have a note to give her? That way it will also be certain to be correct and clear."

Daphne spoke sharply. "No. Oh no. I can't have something that can be lost and might be read by someone else. I can't. There is danger, and—"

Before Daphne could finish her sentence, Luke heard the dead bolt on the front door to the duplex turn.

They both jumped, startled.

His mom shouldn't be home yet, but Breno had a key.

Luke put his fingers to his lips, indicating to Daphne that she should stay quiet. He didn't want Breno to know he was alone with Daphne in his room when he should be at school. His mom would totally freak out if Breno told her.

Luke slipped out of the bedroom and closed the door behind him just as the front door was opening. A strange man stood on the front stoop, looking as shocked to see Luke as Luke was to see him.

Luke was scanning the room for a weapon when the man said, "You must be Luke. I'm Atticus, Emma's dad. This key was in her kitchen drawer, labeled with your name and your mom's. Emma told me the dogs were here. I thought I'd take them for a walk."

Luke willed the tension in his muscles to relax. He could do nothing about his palms and the back of his neck, where beads of sweat had begun to form.

He walked toward Emma's father and managed to say, "Great. Let's go around the back and see the dogs." He stepped out on the porch and quickly pulled the door closed behind him.

He didn't want Emma's father going inside and finding Daphne. He didn't want to have to explain Daphne being there to Emma either.

They'd just gotten down the front stairs, and Luke was about to take Atticus around to introduce him to Crash and Fox, sparing a moment's thought as to how badly that might have gone had he not been home and Atticus had tried to meet Crash on his own, when out of the corner of his eye, he saw Daphne emerge from the side gate and without looking back hurry down the cul-de-sac toward the main street.

"Look, I think that's Emma," Luke said, putting a hand firmly on the man's arm to turn him so he was facing up the cul-de-sac and away from Daphne. "I guess not. It must have been my neighbor. Emma looks a lot like her."

If Emma knew he'd described ninety-year-old Mrs. Cleveland as her doppelgänger, she wouldn't be happy, but Luke had bigger concerns at the moment.

"It's faster if we go through the house into the backyard."

Luke stepped aside so that Emma's father could go up the stairs first, then used his body to block any view of Daphne, though she should be approaching the main street soon.

Once they were settled and Luke had turned his attention to getting Atticus and Crash acquainted—Fox was already on board, since Atticus apparently gave excellent puppy tummy rubs—he decided Atticus must not have seen Daphne. He hadn't reacted, and she'd slipped away so quickly.

37

Second Chance Café

ALIBI HAD ARRIVED early, confirmed with Marie the arrangements Breno had made over the phone, and ordered a large black coffee. He stood in front of the café sipping it slowly, wanting to make it last. He typically came to Second Chance midmorning, but the same long line he was used to seeing snaked out the front door now. He guessed they must be busy all the time.

Marie Jones had started the business after her early release from prison twelve years into a life sentence for dealing crack with her then boyfriend. She was one of three thousand inmates given a second chance at life on the outside by the First Step Act, which remedied gross disparities in sentencing for crack-versus-cocaine-related crimes. With help from community organizations, Marie had raised the money to open the café last year, where true to its name, she trained and employed others who had been previously incarcerated and at-risk youth.

Marie's son, Jeff, was seven when she began her sentence. Now nineteen, he helped her manage the place. Its popularity was due not only to the support of local legislators and businesses but also to the excellent coffee and freshly baked pastries she served.

Marie occasionally let Alibi hold meetings in "her office," the picnic table out back that had RESERVED painted in bold letters on the top. She didn't hold a grudge against the side of the system that had put her inside, including the police. When asked, Marie asserted that poor policies were at fault—if she blamed anyone or anything, it was the old-school "war on drugs" and the politicians who had built their careers on it.

Jackie O rolled up in front of Alibi on her bicycle. It was sleek and silver blue. She'd once told him it was "a gravel bike," which she said meant it was good for city riding and on the dirt—he wasn't sure where gravel came into it. He preferred his transportation to have four wheels, though he could see the appeal of a bike ride on a beautiful day like this one.

"Morning," he said. "If you want something to eat or drink, bypass the line. Ask for Marie's son, Jeff."

As Jackie O walked her bike to the back to lock it up, it was easy to see how she'd gotten her nickname. Tall, with dark eyes and dark hair in soft waves, she could double for a young Jackie Kennedy, the wife of U.S. president John F. Kennedy. Years after his assassination, the widow Kennedy wed billionaire Aristotle Onassis, which led to her forever being known as Jackie O.

Since the moment he'd arrived, Alibi had been scanning the sidewalk, checking out people as they approached to make sure he didn't miss the witness, though he didn't have a description of him. The man had refused to give his name or to come into the department, insisting instead on "a public place." They'd traced the number he'd called them on, but it had come up as a pay-as-you-go unregistered phone.

In the end, Breno had sent the man a photo of Alibi, leaving it up to their unknown informant to initiate contact. The whole thing was a little squirrely for Alibi's taste, but he figured it was in keeping with the last twenty-four hours in this town. Plus, the mayor wanted this meeting to happen. So happen it would.

Jackie O reappeared. "Should I get us a table?"

"No. Marie is letting us use her office."

Noting she was empty-handed, he asked her, "You're not hungry?"

She shook her head.

Just then a man in his thirties, pushing a stroller, started toward them. His eyes were fixed on Alibi. He had short blond hair and was of medium height and in good shape. There was a transparent vinyl hood with a blanket obscuring Alibi's view of whatever was in the stroller. *Maybe a baby, protected from the sun.* But Alibi didn't like unknowns.

When the man came within a few feet, he said to Alibi, "Are you Lieutenant Morning Sun?" His voice was clear and steady. He didn't appear nervous. He wasn't looking around, checking for anyone. Still, the stroller bothered Alibi.

He took his identification from his inner jacket pocket and showed it to the man, who studied it and nodded. He hadn't flinched when Alibi reached into his pocket, which Alibi took as a good sign. The man didn't seem accustomed to having a weapon drawn on him by those in authority.

The man turned to Jackie O. "Who are you?" He didn't sound angry, just as though he had a right to know.

"I'm Dr. Oliver. I work with Lieutenant Morning Sun."

"Right. You lot always come in pairs," the witness said, without hostility.

Alibi said, "We've arranged a table in the back so we can have some privacy. If there's anything you'd like to eat or drink, we can get that for you."

"I prefer to sit up here," the man said.

Since the witness had specifically asked for a public place, Alibi didn't find it unreasonable that he didn't want to go in the back. In fact, he liked consistency in a person's behavior.

Jackie O spotted a four-top where people were getting up to leave. She hustled over to claim the table for them. Alibi and the witness joined her there, where the three of them waited, standing, while Jeff, the owner's son, used a clean dishtowel to wipe down the table.

The witness kept hold of the handle of the stroller at all times.

Alibi decided if there was a baby inside, it must be dead asleep. It never made a sound, nor did the man check on it. He'd known people who were homeless who kept their possessions in a stroller. But this man looked recently showered and shaved, with clean clothes and a decent haircut. That didn't mean he couldn't be unhoused and have made a special effort, but Alibi didn't think so.

Jeff, who was a pleasant, affable young man, smiled as he shifted the table sideways to make room for the stroller. "Y'all want anything else?" he asked.

Alibi looked to Jackie O and the witness, but neither ordered anything. They all sat down, Alibi on the witness's left with the stroller between them, Jackie O to the witness's right.

"We appreciate your contacting us," Alibi said. "Is there a name you would like to use while we talk today?"

The man said, "You can call me Bee. Spelled B–E–E. And I noticed you wondering who I have in here." He pushed back the blanket from the hood of the stroller to reveal a very old, very large calico cat. Its long frame was thin, and its fur was patchy in places. But it was watching them, alert enough.

Bee said, "This is Charlie. I bring him everywhere." He looked again at the cat, this time with clear affection. "I wouldn't want him to die alone while I was out."

That made sense to Alibi. He had new respect for the guy.

"Would it be all right if I record our conversation today?" Jackie O took her phone and held it up for Bee to see. "I can take notes if you prefer, but I always worry I'll miss something important trying to write things down."

Well done, Alibi thought. Jackie O's reference to "something important" was a good way to make the witness feel valued, which he was.

Still, it surprised him when the witness said, "A recording is fine."

That was another good sign. The only way a recording would be a risk to the witness was if he didn't intend to tell the truth.

Having gotten Bee's approval, Jackie O set her phone on the table and pushed record. Alibi identified himself, as did Jackie O for the benefit of the recording, and Bee followed suit, giving his presumably assumed name.

"We understand you have information about Johnny Hill's drowning," Alibi said. "If you could tell us about that, we would appreciate it. Start wherever you like."

"Okay, sure." Bee said. "I like to go up to Folsom Lake and bird-watch. So does Charlie." He looked at the cat as though for confirmation, but he appeared to have fallen asleep. "It's not the only place we go, but it's one of our favorites. There are always sparrows and wrens, but sometimes you can see whole flocks of gulls fly in to roost on the lake. Anyway, on the second of February, we went up really early. It had been raining for like a week, and it was the first clear day. Charlie was itching to get out." Again he looked at the cat, who hadn't moved. "That's how I'm certain of the date," Bee said, leaning toward the phone and speaking a little louder, as though to be sure it captured that point. "We got there before the sun was up, it was that early. There was a full moon, so it wasn't too dark. We started out high on the eastern shore of the lake—that's where I parked—and we walked down through the trees. This stroller has good wheels."

Alibi noted that as the first piece of useful information—the fact that Bee said he had a car. They could check with the park service; they might keep a record of who went in and out via the access road.

"Charlie and I usually move closer to the water after the sun rises, since that's when the gulls might come. But early, we find a good spot in the trees to listen to the sparrows sing. That's Charlie's favorite thing."

Alibi nodded, wondering how well the old cat could still hear.

"I was laying back, listening to the birds—they were noisy, they call it the dawn chorus—when I saw these two guys coming from the direction of the campsites at Beal's Point. I didn't see exactly where they started out. But I'd be surprised if they stayed there. Like I said, it had been raining for weeks. It would have been pretty muddy. Not at all pleasant."

Alibi took a sip of his coffee and immediately regretted doing so, because it seemed to break the flow for Bee, who stopped talking. But then Bee appeared to notice Jackie O's pleasant, interested expression, which had not wavered. She was clearly listening intently, waiting for him to go on, which he did.

"I didn't know it then. But one of the guys was Johnny Hill. He didn't have a hat on. He was wearing a jacket, all dark clothes, but the biggest thing was he couldn't walk on his own power. The other guy was supporting him, an arm around his waist, with Johnny leaning against him. It looked like Johnny might be really drunk or sick. He was dragging his feet. I'd taken out my binoculars, so I could see them pretty well. These are the ones I use." Bee took a compact pair of binoculars from his pocket and set them on the table.

Jackie O said, "Do you mind if I take a photo?"

"Just a minute," Bee said, sliding the binoculars closer to her and leaning back away from them, pretty much guaranteeing he would not be in the shot.

Alibi didn't know if capturing his image had been her unstated objective, but she went ahead and picked up her phone, the red recording light still on, and snapped several shots of the binoculars. Alibi noticed she was careful to capture the brand name and magnification on the side.

"There's a big outcropping of rocks there," Bee continued, when Jackie O had set the phone back down. "I watched them walk around it. It's not really a path. There's not a swimming beach there, but it takes you down to the lake. I figured they were going to sit on the shore to watch the sunrise, or maybe it would make the guy who was sick feel better. Like I said, Charlie and I go down there sometimes to see the gulls up close."

Bee went quiet, as though he was thinking about something.

Alibi gave him a moment, during which he glanced at Charlie, who had slept through Bee's story. Of course, he'd been there, and Alibi expected the cat could have told it himself if he'd had the words.

"That's extremely helpful," Alibi said. "Can you tell me anything about the other person who was assisting Johnny?"

Bee didn't hesitate. "He looks like me."

The back of Alibi's neck prickled. "What do you mean?"

"Same build, same height, same weight, you know," Bee said calmly.

Looking at Bee, Alibi wondered for the first time whether that might be his actual nickname. His hair was a pale blond, not what he thought of as a honey color but maybe close enough to yield the nickname Bee.

"Did you see his hair color or eye color?" Alibi asked.

"No," Bee said. "He wore a hooded jacket and gloves. But he was white. I caught a clear glimpse of his face. Like I said, the moon was bright, and these are pretty good binoculars."

"Was there any other way that the man who was with Johnny Hill reminded you of yourself?" Alibi asked.

"No, it was more a feeling than anything else."

The prickling at the back of Alibi's neck increased.

He looked at Jackie O in a manner that he knew she would recognize as him offering her the floor. Sometimes it helped to mix up the voices the witness experienced, even if the questions might end up the same.

Jackie O asked, "Can you tell us, how did you know it was Johnny Hill that night?"

"I didn't know it then. But I've seen the pictures of him since. His hair is dark, kind of curly. Mainly it was his face. It wasn't hidden. It was him." Bee didn't sound defensive, but he was adamant. He had no doubt.

Jackie O asked, "Was there anything else about either of the men that stood out for you?"

Alibi liked that question, though he didn't know what else Bee might be able to add.

"Yes. Johnny had on white shoes, which I mainly noticed because of how muddy they were. But also, they had a bright-yellow stripe on the sides, neon almost. It showed up in the dark, even partly covered with mud. I remember thinking everything else both of them wore was dark, but here were these splashes of yellow. It made me think of the yellow-breasted chats. They whistle and chirp and make this chittering sound. Charlie and I used to see a lot of them around here, but not so often anymore."

Alibi caught his breath. He didn't trust himself to say anything. He'd seen in the reports the shoes Johnny Hill had been wearing when his body was pulled from the lake. That information had not been released to the press.

They were white trainers with distinctive bright-yellow stripes.

What Bee's reason was for coming forward now and whether he was telling the truth about another man being there were still open questions. In fact, the possibility that Bee had done Johnny harm couldn't be ruled out. But one thing was certain. Bee had been there that day, and he had seen Johnny Hill.

CHAPTER

38

Blue Heron Gallery

DESPITE HAVING FINALLY seen Atticus after twenty-two years, Emma found she had more questions than ever. She didn't know where he lived. She didn't know if the person he'd married was like her mother or completely different. Most of all, in the "old questions" category, she still didn't know why he'd abandoned her and Jasmine, his two little girls, all those years ago. And she had new questions. Why had Atticus come to Sacramento? How long had he originally planned to stay, and how long would he stay now? What had happened at the gallery? Who was the man who'd thrown the wine, and why had Atticus assaulted him?

Having finished her swim, Emma was almost at work, but she didn't see how she'd be able to concentrate. She made a snap decision, stepped on the gas, and drove past the commission parking garage. She turned left on Capitol Mall, then right on Front Street, where she pulled into the first available parking space.

After putting the top up on the Mustang, she took out her phone and easily located the address. The Blue Heron Gallery, the site of her father's alleged assault on a wine-throwing stranger, was only three blocks away. It was a gorgeous spring morning; the crisp air would do her some good.

She had to admit she wasn't exactly sure what she hoped to gain from this excursion. At nine AM, the gallery was unlikely to be open. For that matter, she didn't know if it would open at all today. She wasn't sure what damage, if any, had been done to the premises, or if there were insurance or crime scene requirements that might keep it closed for some time.

She passed a T-shirt shop whose window featured Sacramento Kings and River Cat shirts, then a jewelry store that displayed pendants of jasper stones and blue topaz by local designer Susan Rabinovitz.

A small sign indicated that Rabinovitz did jewelry repair from her gallery, Little Relics, near where Emma lived. It occurred to Emma to bring her mother's necklace there to have it cleaned and a safety clasp added so she could wear it without fear of it coming loose and being lost.

Emma already felt calmer. She liked being in Old Sacramento, walking in the early-morning light along the raised wooden sidewalks bordering the cobblestone streets. Of course, she'd heard the disparaging comments by other locals, that it catered to the tourist trade and was too commercial or even too tacky for anyone serious to find enjoyment there. But what they were missing, Emma thought, was right there in the name: *Old* Sacramento. In a few miles along the Sacramento River, there were nearly fifty historic buildings dating back to the 1800s.

As she approached the turn to the gallery, she decided her goal was a simple one, easily met. She wanted to make real and tangible some part of one of the many mysteries surrounding Atticus, and she could do that by seeing where the showing of his artwork had been held. She increased her walking speed in a manner that would have impressed Kate and soon found herself standing a few doors away from an elevated wooden sign bearing the painted image of a flying blue heron.

As though the timing had been orchestrated to coincide with Emma's arrival, a woman emerged from the door beneath the sign. Tall and elegantly full-figured, with heavy black hair past her shoulders, she appeared to be in her late forties, maybe early fifties. She wore a long red-and-white dress in a geometric pattern with a wide black belt and a handcrafted large silver necklace.

The woman leaned against the building and took a cigarette and lighter from her bag. Emma thought it likely she worked at the gallery, given the hour and her stylish dress, and the proprietary manner in which she stood suggested she might even be the owner. Then it occurred to Emma that maybe this woman was the reason her father had come to Sacramento.

Maybe she'd even been the cause of the fight. She was close enough to Atticus's age, and attractive—

Hold up. Emma froze stock-still where she stood, still several doorways away. *Could this be my father's new wife, here to pick up his work, to deal with the aftermath of the altercation, and now she's stepped outside for a moment to gather herself?*

Emma tried to appear casual, resisting her desire to break into a run, wanting to get to the woman before she finished her cigarette and went back inside or left.

She'd begun to consider what she might say to her, but when Emma reached the front of the gallery, she forgot the woman was even there. Visible through the large front windows was a roomful of charcoal drawings in flowing lines in black and gray and white. Some large, some small, but all unmistakably Atticus's work. Emma stared, spellbound.

The woman dropped her cigarette and ground it out with the two-inch heel of a stylish black shoe. She smiled at Emma. "Extraordinary, aren't they?"

Emma squinted at the bottom right corner of the closest drawing, trying to make out the scrawled signature.

The woman followed her gaze. "These are all by Atticus Smit. Are you familiar with him? He only works in charcoal."

Emma managed a slight nod but didn't turn away from the drawing. The woman evidently took Emma's transfixed, nearly dazed expression to be that of a true connoisseur of the arts, someone who could lose themselves in a piece if it spoke to them. "I'm Lanelle Rogers," she said. "This is my gallery."

That got Emma's attention.

"I'm the artist's daughter, Emma Lawson." Emma didn't explain why she and her father had different last names. There could be lots of reasons for that.

As it turned out, no explanation was necessary, since Lanelle said, "I see the resemblance. The emerald eyes."

Emma heard the faint echo of someone speaking to her long ago. *You have your father's eyes.*

She looked at Lanelle, whose high heels had a cross strap in a flamenco style. Emma could picture her raising one arm over her head, castanet in hand, and dancing away. She shook off the illusion.

"Would it be possible for me to go inside?" Emma asked her. "To look more closely at my father's work?"

"I guess so," Lanelle said, stooping to pick up the cigarette butt she'd crushed under her foot. "The insurance appraiser came yesterday, and the police have been here, so I don't see why not. Don't touch anything." She held open the door for Emma. "Not because of fingerprints or CSI or anything like that. There might be stray glass, you could hurt yourself, and then I'd have another insurance claim on my hands."

There was a long, thin table in the middle of the room with a half dozen wineglasses on it and a few bottles. Tiny glints of broken glass sparkled on the dark-wood floors. "I couldn't have the cleaners in yesterday," Lanelle explained, "They'll be here soon."

A smaller table at the back of the room had a laptop on it and a display of postcards, some of which Emma could see bore images of Atticus's artwork. There were chairs on either side. It must be where sales were conducted.

All the art on the walls was Atticus's. Emma circled the room slowly, pausing in front of each of her father's creations. The thumbnail image Breno had shared on his phone of the largest piece didn't do it justice. It must be eight feet wide by eight feet long. Though splattered with red wine that obscured some of it, the outlines of a locomotive engine barreled toward the viewer, the front out of proportion with the rails, which curved audaciously upward into a night sky as though reaching for a waning moon.

There were several other pieces featuring trains streaking past against various backgrounds, similar to the one Emma had in her office. It looked as though Atticus had done a series that stemmed from that original idea.

In the back of the room, a small five-by-seven drawing depicted two little girls, one taller than the other, holding hands, with nothing else in the frame. Emma recognized it as identical to one of her and Jasmine that he'd finished not long before he left. It might even be the same drawing. She felt tears prick her eyes and waited for the moment to pass.

Lanelle had seated herself at the smaller table and was looking at the computer. Emma decided the direct approach would be best. "Would it be all right if I ask you a few questions about what happened at my father's reception? I want to help him if there are charges or a court case. You mentioned the police have already been here?"

Lanelle took no time to make up her mind. "Please, sit," she said. She closed out the program on her computer and turned her full attention to Emma. "I had a brother who was an artist. That's what sparked my interest in having this gallery. He had some legal trouble. What is it you would like to know?"

It did not escape Emma's notice that Lanelle spoke of her brother in the past tense.

She had lots of very specific questions, but as an investigator, she knew it was best to let any witness start with what they saw as the beginning and follow that wherever it took them. "If you could just tell me what happened."

"Well, let's see," Lanelle said, leaning back in her chair and looking around the room as though recreating the scene in her mind. "We had a good turnout. People were having a nice time. I introduced your father, and he said a few words. He was kind of shy, but funny."

She smiled at Emma and waited, as though permitting her a moment to recall similar experiences. But Emma drew a blank when it came to what the nearly sixty-year-old man she'd bailed out of jail might look like speaking in front of a group of interested art patrons. So she said nothing but gave Lanelle a smile, which seemed sufficient to prompt the gallery owner to continue.

"We had a photographer who took pictures at the reception before things got crazy. She'd already left by then. If you'd like me to send those to you, I'm sure there are good ones of your dad and also of his art. If you write down your contact information, I'll message you the link."

Emma nodded and jotted it down for Lanelle, even though she didn't know how she'd feel when she saw the photos, a whole side to Atticus's life that she'd known nothing about.

"Your dad mentioned in his comments to the crowd that he had a daughter who lived in Sacramento. Not your name, but that must be you." Lanelle smiled. "Unless you have a sister."

Emma felt her heart contract.

Atticus definitely knew I was in Sacramento.

Before she could recover her composure and think what to say to Lanelle next, a shadow blocked the sunlight at the front door to the gallery, followed by a loud knock.

39

"CAN'T THEY SEE the closed sign? Just because we're sitting here—"

Emma interrupted her. "I know him. He's a police officer."

"I already gave a statement," Lanelle said. She sounded like she didn't want her time with Emma cut short.

"He's a friend," Emma said, getting up to let Alibi in.

When she opened the door, she and Alibi said the same thing at the same time. "What are you doing here?"

Alibi responded, "I'm here on a case."

Emma said, "I'm here because of my father."

She couldn't remember specifically what she'd said to Alibi about Atticus. She generally let people assume he was dead, which she'd thought was true until last night.

She walked Alibi over to Lanelle and made introductions.

Lanelle's attitude changed. It was Emma's impression that she liked what she saw. The gallery owner's eyes moved in a bold appraisal of Alibi's dark eyes, his rich olive skin, his long, thick black hair, and his body, which was tall, strong, and lean.

"I understand you're a friend of Emma's and a police officer?" Lanelle said, exuding charm she'd not displayed for Emma despite having been helpful. "We were just discussing Emma's father's show. There's nothing new from the statement I provided the officer who was here two nights ago, but—"

Emma felt time slipping away from her. Whatever Lanelle might have decided, she and Alibi were not contestants on a reboot of *The Dating Game.* "Alibi, sit," Emma said. "Lanelle, please go on. You said my father had just presented to the group?"

Alibi remained standing, his gaze roaming the room.

Emma thought she saw something close to wonder in his eyes.

"These are all your father's?" Alibi asked.

"Yes," Emma said.

With effort, Emma looked back at Lanelle. She was afraid she might lose it in a big way if she let herself consider what it meant to her that Alibi was so affected by her dad's drawings.

"Lanelle? What happened next?" Emma asked her.

She was grateful when at the sound of her question, Alibi's cop side reasserted itself as he sat down and turned his attention back to Lanelle. He took out his little blue notebook and pen, which gave Emma comfort. If anyone could help her dad out of the criminal implications of this mess, it would be Alibi.

"We made some sales," Lanelle said. "Then a young man, maybe in his thirties, a glass of wine in his hand, approached your father. His face was red, and he was scowling. I was pretty sure he was drunk. I couldn't hear what he was saying, but he started crowding Mr. Smit, your father. It is my responsibility to protect our artists from rude and angry people. I managed to make my way over to them. There were a lot of people, and—"

"Could you hear anything the young man and my father were saying to each other when you got close?" Emma asked.

Alibi frowned slightly. Maybe she shouldn't have interrupted a witness midsentence, but Emma didn't care.

"The man verbally accosting your father wasn't making sense." Lanelle hesitated. "He said something like, 'It's your fault,' and 'You blackmailed her,' and . . ."

Lanelle seemed unwilling to go on.

Emma kept her expression neutral to show she was ready to hear anything Lanelle wanted to say.

Lanelle almost whispered, "He said to your father, 'You killed her.'"

Emma's stomach dropped. "Killed who?"

"The guy said something about his mother, but I couldn't tell if that was the person he was saying your father had killed or if his mother had told him about it," Lanelle said. "It really seemed to be just a drunken rant. I'm not sure the guy even knew who he was talking to—"

"Did Atticus respond?" Emma interrupted.

"Yes," Lanelle said. "Mr. Smit—Atticus—said, 'That's crazy. She lied to you.'" Lanell's brow wrinkled briefly as she appeared to do her best to recall anything else. "I think that's everything your father said. Because then the young man threw the wine at the painting, and he pushed your father, who pushed him back, and the young man fell. He hit his head on the side of that table leg." Lanelle gestured to the table on which the bottles of wine and glasses sat. "The young guy's head was bleeding down onto his forehead. That's why I think people in the back thought your father had punched him or attacked him. But Mr. Smit was just defending himself, trying to get away from this man who shoved him first. As soon as the other man fell down, your father ran out. All he wanted was to get away. He wasn't interested in hurting the other guy."

Lanelle paused, her eyes searching Emma's to make sure she understood that her father hadn't been at fault. Then Lanelle looked earnestly at Alibi, and Emma appreciated that this, at least, wasn't flirting. She appeared to want to demonstrate she wasn't lying, that she wouldn't look away from a police officer when she said these things. For her part, Emma was certain Lanelle's story was true. *Of course Atticus ran away. That's what he does.* She almost wished he'd stood his ground and slugged the guy.

Lanelle seemed to interpret Emma's downcast expression as continued concern that Atticus might be in trouble. "If you're worried about your dad, don't be. The officer who came that night asked whether I wanted to press charges for property damage. The table leg is only scratched—it can be fixed. And the wine damage to the painting was done by the other guy. Besides, I only make a commission if it's sold. Your father is the one who suffered the financial loss. My insurance company should cover that for him, since it occurred in my gallery. In any case, I don't expect that other guy to reappear. He has a lot to answer for. That painting sells for twenty thousand dollars. Plus he seemed in a big hurry to leave when I said I was calling the police."

Twenty thousand? Emma thought that if Atticus was routinely making that on a single drawing, maybe he would like to fund his grandchildren's college education, since he hadn't helped with hers and Jasmine's.

Regardless, the good news was her father hadn't assaulted anyone, and it sounded like he shouldn't be in any trouble legally for what had happened that night.

But murder?

And blackmail?

What on earth has Atticus been doing for the last twenty years?

CHAPTER

40

Delta King

EMMA CALCULATED HOW many postcards she needed. One of each of Atticus's three available drawings for herself and Jasmine was six, plus Luke might like one, and one for Alibi, who clearly had been taken by Atticus's art. That was eight. While Emma was considering whether to get a postcard for Kate and one for Hailey, Alibi said to Lanelle, "We'll take a dozen, thank you." He handed Lanelle his credit card.

"Your phone number?" Lanelle asked, her voice dropping an octave to a huskier tone. Since there was no physical charge slip anymore and Alibi had inserted his card in a portable point-of-sale device, Emma doubted very much the phone number request was a routine step in the transaction. But if Alibi noticed the gallery owner's less-than-subtle hint that she'd like to see him again, he didn't act on it, reeling off what Emma knew was the public line for his office.

When they got outside, he said to Emma, "Coffee?"

She was about to say yes when she realized she was hungry. After her mile-long morning swim, she usually picked up something at the convenience market next to commission headquarters, but she hadn't made it in to work yet today.

"Could we go somewhere that serves breakfast?"

"Delta King okay?" he asked.

The Delta King was a majestic authentic paddle-wheel river-boat built in 1927 that had been converted to a hotel and restaurant. Its storied past included being partially submerged in the San Francisco Bay for years before being restored and settled in its current place of honor at the Riverfront Dock in Old Sacramento. Emma could see it three blocks straight ahead of them where the street met the waterfront, which must be why it had come to mind for Alibi.

Emma had always wanted to go there and for some reason never had. She followed Alibi down the gangplank and then up thickly carpeted stairs to the Pilot House restaurant, which was beautiful with dark wood, stained glass, and chandeliers. A mouthwatering buffet was set up against the far wall. There was outdoor seating on the deck with a 180-degree view of the river, downtown Sacramento, and the Tower Bridge beyond.

A young woman in a nautical-looking dress greeted them warmly. "Are you guests of the Delta King?"

When neither Alibi nor Emma answered in the affirmative, she said, "I'm sorry, but breakfast is only for those staying at the hotel. The Fly Swatter is open on Third Street and serving breakfast now."

The Fly Swatter? Emma guessed the name must be tongue-in-cheek, intended to attract tourists.

She'd resigned herself to finding out what the Fly Swatter's specialty could possibly be when Alibi produced his identification and said, "I'm here with Ms. Lawson on a case. If it would be possible for us to have a table somewhere quiet and have breakfast during the interview, I would appreciate it. Of course, I will pay full price for our meals."

The host's eyes grew wide as she looked at the laminated card nestled in a small leather folder next to his badge. It identified Alibi as head of major crimes for the city of Sacramento. She asked if they would wait a moment and returned quickly with another woman, who said they should follow her. They were escorted to a private outdoor table at the end of the deck.

Emma did not sit down. When the Delta King staff left, she said quietly to Alibi, "I'm not sure I can stay under these circumstances."

Alibi sat and unfolded the crisp white linen napkin onto his lap. "What circumstances?" he asked.

"You using your position paid for by the taxpayers for private gain."

Alibi smiled. "Sit."

Emma remained standing.

"Sit, and I'll explain," he said. "Then if you want to leave, we can."

Emma sat down and folded her arms. A waiter appeared with coffee, which Alibi accepted, and Emma declined. When he began to describe the buffet and à la carte options, Emma said politely, "Would you please give us a minute?" Then she turned her attention to Alibi, channeling Kate's laser-like interrogative gaze.

Alibi seemed unfazed. "The incident at the Blue Heron Gallery was referred to major crimes due to the value of your father's painting, as well as a question about the extent of the injury to the other man if an assault, in fact, had occurred."

Emma opened her mouth to say it had not. Alibi raised a hand to forestall her.

"You were speaking with the owner about the case before I arrived. I need to get a statement from you regarding why you were there and what if anything you learned that my team might want to follow up on."

Emma opened her mouth again, and this time he let her speak. "There's nothing to follow up on. You heard the gallery owner state clearly that she witnessed the altercation, there was no assault, and what did occur was not Atticus's fault."

Even as she said it, a small voice in Emma's head intoned *murder, blackmail.* Admittedly, those things might be of interest to Alibi's major crime team.

Alibi said, "As you can see, we are talking about the case. I could have taken you to headquarters to do that, but just this morning I interviewed another potential witness off-site. It's not uncommon, and it doesn't seem that you picked up on my telling the staff here that 'I will pay' for our breakfast. No taxpayer funds will be misused. Okay? Can we eat? I thought you were hungry."

Mollified by an ethical resolution to the question of payment, Emma led the way to the buffet, where they filled their plates. She chose a vegetarian frittata, fresh-fruit salad, and a mini iced cinnamon roll. Alibi selected scrambled eggs, bacon, and herb-roasted potatoes.

When they retook their seats, they ate in silence. Emma was surprised by how hungry she was.

When she'd sat back and begun sipping her tea and he was on his second cup of coffee, Alibi asked, "How are you?" It wasn't said in his professional tone.

She hesitated. "I don't know."

He said nothing, giving her time.

"When my mother died, my father—Atticus—disappeared without explanation. Last night was the first I've heard from him, let alone seen him, in more than two decades." She looked out at the river and then back at Alibi as she posed the question she'd been afraid to ask.

"Are you concerned about the accusations against my father of murder and blackmail? Given that the gallery owner didn't think there was anything to it?" She couldn't keep the hope out of her voice.

Alibi asked, "Where does your father live?" When she didn't answer, Alibi said gently, "It may be nothing at all. But even if it is something, there's a question of jurisdiction. Unless he's accused of crimes that happened here in Sacramento, it would be a matter of referring the information to the appropriate local authorities to see whether they think it's worth pursuing."

Emma said stiffly, "I don't know the answer to that question."

Her cheeks flushed. She felt embarrassed and angry, though not at Alibi. At Atticus.

She softened her tone as best she could.

"My father is staying with me. I don't know for how long. I don't know where he lives now or where he's lived since he disappeared from San Francisco twenty-two years ago. He's only been here one night. I just learned that he knew I was in Sacramento when he made this trip, but I don't know if I'm the reason he came."

It was Alibi's turn to gaze out over the water. He seemed to be thinking. "Based on what we know so far, a man has levied unspecified, possibly drunken accusations at your father, which your father flatly denies. Unless that man surfaces and wants to make his claims formal, this won't go anywhere. If we ran down every sloppy, angry interaction like this one, we'd have no time to solve real crime."

Emma felt her shoulders relax.

"Do you want to talk about your father?" Alibi asked. "About how you feel? About what happened before, not what is happening now?"

"No," Emma said. "Not yet."

"Well, then there's something I'd like to speak with you about," he said. "If you're ready for a total change of subject. Can I vent a little about what's been happening with me?" He smiled.

Emma nodded. Alibi wasn't one to vent. She wasn't sure he would even know how. He was undoubtedly just taking the focus off her troubles to lighten her mood. She appreciated it. She picked at the cinnamon roll as he spoke.

"I've had an odd twenty-four hours. I think you might be right about the arson relating to someone wanting to destroy something illegal. We're going to run that down."

Emma was pleased. She hadn't thought before of the potential application of her investigative experience to crimes like arson, outside of the scope of the commission.

"And now we've had a strange report of a near-miss hit-and-run. Yesterday afternoon a woman was almost run down in the industrial section near the river. We've not heard anything from the possible victim. Yet observers, admittedly from some distance, report she may have been seriously injured."

"It wasn't serious," Emma said.

Alibi studied her. "What do you mean? Were you there?"

"No," Emma said. "I wasn't there. It's not like I'm at every bad thing that happens in this town," she said, thinking of the fire. "I know the woman. I mean, I met her yesterday. I saw her shortly after she was injured. She may have a broken arm, but I think that would have been the worst of it. And she flatly refused to see a doctor."

Alibi pulled out his notebook and pencil. "Start with her name, and tell me how it is that you know her."

Emma didn't understand why this was so important to him. He must get a dozen reports of random small crimes per day in a city of five hundred thousand. But his look was intense, so she did her best to be helpful.

"Her name is Daphne. I don't recall her last name. I can get it for you. It's Dutch. She identified herself to me as a student at the University of California at Davis on a joint program of study with the University of Amsterdam. I gave her an informational interview on government and ethics for a paper she's doing."

Alibi printed rapidly in neat block letters.

"When I was leaving work yesterday, I saw her in an alleyway across the street from the commission headquarters. She'd been injured and told the story of a car that almost ran her down. I wasn't sure whether to believe her."

Alibi looked up from his notebook. "Why not?"

"I felt she might have lied to me earlier about being a student. Just a sense I had, that she might be nosing around the commission to get a story on Fran."

Emma didn't want to admit to Alibi that she'd gone through the woman's backpack. And she couldn't think what relevance the photo would have to a hit-and-run. It couldn't be Johnny who'd tried to run Daphne down. He was dead.

Alibi had an odd look on his face. "Did you say she's Dutch? Does she speak with an accent?"

"Yes. She's Dutch and she speaks with an accent," Emma confirmed. "She's lovely. Striking." It was hard to think of Daphne and not think of how she looked.

Alibi sat very still, as though listening for something far away. "Striking how? In what way?"

"Fragile," Emma said, though it felt odd that was the first thing that had come to mind. "Pale-blue eyes, very thin, short ash-blond hair, almost silver."

Alibi stood abruptly. He pulled out his wallet and dropped a fifty-dollar bill on the table. Emma was sure it was too much for what they'd ordered. This was Sacramento, not New York. And who carried cash these days?

He took her hand. "Let's go."

They walked to her car in silence.

When they reached the Mustang, Alibi leaned in and pressed his lips lightly on hers, lingering there—it wasn't what a friend would do. His lips were warm. When he stepped back, Emma wanted to feel that warmth again.

* * *

Matchbook Lane

The man had seen her arrive last night, right after the party started—his choice of the willow tree as his vantage point had been excellent.

She'd climbed the stairs with the bag over her shoulder, the colorful poster-size sheets sticking out. Then she'd reached under a planter next to the door and let herself inside.

A break-in, in this quiet neighborhood, would normally be risky. But knowing the location of the key, he could walk up the stairs like a relative or friend who had every right to enter the house, whether Emma Lawson was home or not.

He'd noticed that one error many people made was to define those who looked like them as "good" and those who didn't as "bad." The man pitied them—their world views were built on a flawed understanding of human nature.

Philosophy fascinated him. But now was not the time.

He focused and fleshed out his plan.

Emma's dogs weren't in the house. Several cars had gone by and they hadn't come to the front window to bark, as he'd seen them do yesterday. Still, the fact that they existed at all did add to his time pressure. He wouldn't want them returning in the middle of his little visit. He would quickly lift a few valuable items to make it look like a random burglary.

Would Emma Lawson keep cash in an easy-to-find place in her house? Did she wear expensive jewelry?

Ideally, he wanted things that would fit in his pocket, though he supposed he could grab a laptop or tablet and carry it out as though it were his.

The only thing he needed to take, what he'd come for, was her notes so he could see what next steps she had planned on the investigation. Then, if her most immediate questions would lead her to him, he would take action. Emma Lawson would move to the top spot on his list.

The man straightened his back and lifted his head. *I belong here. I belong here.* He repeated his mantra and exuded confidence as he climbed the stairs. He shifted the planter, and with satisfaction, his fingers closed around the key.

41

The Hayden Commission

Alibi had walked with Emma to her car from the Delta King, holding hands, not talking. When they'd gotten there, he'd leaned in and kissed her lightly on the lips.

Lightly, but not casually, Emma thought.

An hour later, when she tried to review the latest reports Nick and Malia had sent up on the tunnel project, she had to reread every other sentence. She touched her lips with the tips of the fingers of one hand.

It was no use trying to work.

She decided to walk to Rainbow Alley to ask Kate for an update on the end of the party, since Luke had shared only the news about Anthony Torgetti's gift of a trip anywhere in the world.

As she closed her office door behind her, it occurred to her that she hadn't traveled, other than for work, for as long as she could remember. She found herself wondering where she and Alibi might go together.

Somewhere tropical? Stretched out on the beach, then diving beneath the waves and surfacing in each other's arms. Or perhaps a cabin on a pine-covered ridge? Snowed in for days, where the only entertainment to be found is under the covers, on top of the covers, or on a rug on the floor in front of the heat of the fire . . .

Still daydreaming on her way to the elevator, she noticed Sid's door was ajar. That gave her an idea. She thought about it for less than a minute.

On the one hand, Emma was about to do something impulsive, which didn't usually end well for her. On the other, she felt empowered and protected in this odd mood she was in. And it was high time she confronted Sidney Lane instead of tiptoeing around his bad behavior where her work was concerned. No more trying to buy him off with invitations to VIP events.

Sid needed to understand she was on equal footing with him now and she'd appreciate it if he'd stop fuming and pouting about the train project. Maybe they could even help each other by collaborating. He had financial and IT skills she lacked, and she was analytical and could find investigative gems that eluded him.

She would propose an alliance.

Later, Emma would wonder if it had been lack of sleep or the high she'd been on as she considered lust-based travels with Alibi that had caused her to forget who Sid was and how poorly he would react to a proposal that they play nice and work together.

But in the moment, her bad idea seemed like a good one. She turned back and knocked on his door with confidence.

There was no answer.

Through the gap, she could see Sid wore a headset and was absorbed in something on his computer.

She took a step into the room and was about to speak to get his attention when she caught a glimpse of his screen. It was angled so she couldn't see the whole thing, but she caught enough of it to be certain the content was related to the tunnel project. She saw the words *Community Fund* at the top, which was the area Malia had flagged as problematic.

Sid was consumed by what he was reading, his back to her, so she took a silent step closer.

Interspersed with the text were several thumbnail images of an outdoor seating area, a café or restaurant. It was familiar to her, but she couldn't quite place it.

As though sensing something in the air, Sid looked up. The first thing he did was abruptly shift the monitor toward him to block her view. The second was to rapidly click the mouse several times. She was sure he was shutting the program down. Only then did he remove the headset and glare at her.

She expected him to say something like, *Didn't your mother teach you to knock?*

Instead, he seemed to want to draw her into a staring contest. It was unnerving.

Since he wouldn't avert his eyes, neither did she, until hers started to burn, and Emma decided there was no point to whatever this was. And while she didn't think being direct was necessarily the best approach with Sid, it was her go-to-move.

She began by dropping her *Let's form an alliance* plan.

Instead, she made clear that the train project belonged to her.

"That was the train tunnel project you were viewing. Is there anything I can help you with, based on my three months leading that investigation?"

"No," Sid said. "I was looking for something else. I navigated there by mistake."

Wow, you are a bad liar, she thought.

She wondered if he'd tried that when he worked at the Internal Revenue Service. She doubted it, although if he had, maybe that was the reason he'd had to find a new job.

"There were outdoor images there," she said, her tone even, ignoring his scowl and the tension in the room. "I don't have those in my Community Fund files. Where were they taken? Would you mind opening that program again so I can have another look?"

Sid's expression changed. His smile was more frightening than his glower. He focused it on her. "I don't have time. I'm late for a meeting." He stood and loomed over her.

It was clear to Emma that he was waiting for her to leave, after which she was certain, from the way he kept glancing sideways at his keys on his desk, that he planned to lock his door. She was insulted that he thought she might be capable of searching the browser history on his computer after he left, though it had crossed her mind.

As she walked to the elevator, she could hear him start down the stairs.

The sense of well-being that had surrounded Emma faded. A thudding pain started in her temples. Those images on Sid's monitor bothered her. She didn't know why. But some sort of connection had been made in the back of her mind.

42

Clad Corp Ideal Storage

A LIBI CLOSED HIS office door and locked it.
What had he been thinking when he kissed Emma?
Half-kissed her.

It didn't matter, whatever it was, there was no taking it back.

When he'd stepped away, she'd leaned toward him as though willing him to kiss her again, to show her he meant it. Had he read that right?

Alibi might never know. Because he'd fled.

For an intuitive guy with a sixth sense regarding danger and death, he was pitiable when it came to figuring out what women wanted.

He kicked off his shoes and lay down on the couch with one of the throw pillows under his head. He intended to take a moment to try to sort out what was happening with Emma, but his office was a poor place to do that.

Another woman's face came into view.

It was not that of a woman he wanted.

She was blond, fragile, and striking. And now she had a name. *Daphne.*

He was still waiting for Emma's assistant to forward her last name.

Daphne had asked Emma questions about Fran Hill. Those questions had bothered Emma, making her wonder whether the young woman might not be who she said she was. But suppose Daphne was exactly who she said she was. Suppose she was that and something more. Alibi thought of the image outside his ninth-floor window last night, of the silvery spirit of Johnny Hill cleaved in two by lightning.

Daphne had studied in Amsterdam and Johnny had studied in Denmark, both in the last year. Alibi didn't know the geography of Europe. Could the two young people have met?

He was reaching for connections, and he wanted to be patient, to let the pieces come together on their own. But he saw Daphne's haunted face in the plaza, large as life, and he knew that people who tried to kill and failed often tried again.

And succeeded.

His phone rang, and Alibi jumped, startled.

Carlos's name flashed across the caller ID.

"Hello, Carlos—" Alibi was interrupted by a knock on his office door. "Carlos, just a minute."

"It's locked." Jackie O's voice was muffled from the other side of the door.

Alibi opened it for her. He saw her take in his stocking feet and his shoes on the floor next to the throw pillow that had fallen when he'd jumped up. He said into the phone, "Carlos, Jackie O just came in. Can I call you back?"

A torrent of words burst forth from the other end of the line. Alibi took the phone away from his ear, though he could still hear every word. When Carlos finally took a breath, Alibi said, "That's great. Congratulations to you and Marc. No worries." He smiled at Jackie O. "We have everything under control here."

Jackie O picked up the pillow, put it back on the couch, and sat down. "I caught some of that," she said. "The babies are here?"

"Yep, the babies are here," Alibi said, retrieving his shoes and moving to his desk chair to put them on, hoping to find his way back from where he'd been—from thinking about Daphne on the edge of the fountain and Johnny Hill in the lake.

His brain seemed to be on a loop.

He needed to get out of his office. He turned to Jackie O. "Looks like Carlos's paternity leave starts today. He's the lead on that Clad Corp arson case from our end. Do you want to accompany me to the storage place? Since it was arson, we have to treat the fatality as a possible homicide."

It wasn't technically in Jackie O's job description to visit the scene, since the fire wasn't thought to be gang related. But Alibi had taken the view, which Jackie O had endorsed, that all cases could be gang related, thereby expanding her investigative reach and the experiences she was having during her department fellowship.

"Sure, let's go." She smiled and stood up.

"Did you ride your bike?" he asked. "We can put it in the back of my truck."

"I have a better idea. I'll race you there. Loser pays next time at Second Chance."

"I always pay at Second Chance," Alibi said.

Jackie O was already out the door. She called over her shoulder, "I know. So next time won't be any different."

Fifteen minutes later, after being held up by construction on I Street, Alibi reached the storage facility. He pulled onto the shoulder across from the main lot. At first, he thought he'd gotten there ahead of her.

Then he heard Jackie O's voice.

"Not bad. I saw the holdup on I Street when I came in this morning. I'm thinking about what I'll have at Second Chance. Maybe one of their famous wild blueberry scones?" She was standing next to her bike at the top of an overgrown pathway that came up from the river—a shortcut with no traffic lights.

"You knew about that construction?" Alibi said, smiling. "If you did, the game was rigged. No scones for you. Will your bike fit in the cab of my truck? I can lock it inside. It doesn't look like you'll be able to get to the bike racks."

The entire Clad Corp Ideal Storage property, which was several blocks long, was cordoned off by yellow crime scene tape. The parking lot was empty. Two beat cops, one at each end, were stationed to prevent unauthorized entry. A sign atop the building said STORAGE: 24/7 ACCESS, but people would be out of luck until the arson unit cleared the site for use.

Within minutes Jackie O had popped off the bike's front wheel and loaded it and the bike into the passenger side of the truck.

"Neat trick," Alibi said.

They crossed to the big lot. Alibi intended to walk the perimeter outside the caution tape, but as they got closer, he could see a lit-up reception area inside the building where an employee of the facility was going through paperwork.

Alibi approached one of the beat cops, who recognized him. "Is there a cleared entry route? We'd like to get inside."

"Yes, sir. Stay within those cones." The officer pointed to a marked-off path that would take them there.

As Alibi and Jackie O approached the glass front doors, the woman he'd noticed looked up and called out, "We're closed."

Alibi held up his ID.

She scurried over and pushed the door open, though she didn't move aside to let them in.

She was a small, gray-haired woman. IRENE was embroidered above IDEAL STORAGE on the pocket of her shirt, and a badge pinned below that said MANAGER. "I thought you all were done for the day," she said. She looked and sounded tired.

"I'm sorry to bother you. My colleague, Dr. Oliver, and I will remain outside in the designated areas. But could you show us from where we're standing what the access is to the place where the fire occurred? I understand it was in the basement."

"You don't want to go there? You just want me to tell you?" Irene asked, looking skeptical.

"Yes," Alibi said.

Irene pointed to a large freight elevator and then to a stairwell with a closed door. "Either of those will take you downstairs, though once you get there, there's a closed door that says 'No Public Access' before you can get to Building 2."

Alibi went to pull his notebook from his inside jacket pocket but then noticed Jackie O tapping away on her computer tablet, so he stopped.

"I've already explained about the sprinklers not going off down there," Irene said. "We had our inspections, all properly signed. They work just fine in the main building. Last week some kids smoking set them off. That's why we have all the no-smoking signs. It must be that the explosion blew out the sprinkler system in the warehouse. I already told your lot that."

"I'm sure the fire department made note of it," Alibi said reassuringly. "Is that door usually locked?" He pointed to the one she'd identified as providing access to the basement.

"No. Since our employees spend so much time going back and forth, it's left open. But anybody would be noticed who didn't belong down there, and we do lock the warehouse itself when we're not in there."

"I'm a little confused about the layout. There seems to be a basement and a warehouse, or are those the same thing?" Alibi asked mildly, as though he were just a country cop who didn't understand much. Which sometimes was true. "What do you mean by Building 2? I thought that door led to the basement of this building."

The woman's tense look left her. She appeared to be on comfortable ground answering these questions. "A wide hall on the bottom floor connects Building 1—that's where we are—to Building 2, which is the original building, a warehouse from a plumbing supply company. It was here before this building was built. That old one, Building 2, is just one big space, but it's double height. It goes up to our second story here. We call it the basement because you get to it by going down one floor below reception in Building 1."

"Got it. That's helpful," Alibi said. "We're going to quickly walk around both buildings outside." Then as though it were an afterthought, he asked, "Do you know who was working Tuesday night? I gather Daniel Baptiste was here from midnight to when the fire occurred. Was there anyone with him?"

"No one was with Daniel. It's a quiet time right now, no one moving in or out like the first or last of each month. That's when we put on extra staff. There was a customer, that lady who was here getting her stuff. That was a good thing, or Daniel wouldn't still be with us above ground."

"Do you have a business card, in case I have follow-up questions?"

Irene turned toward the reception area, evidently expecting Alibi to follow. He hesitated, but it was on the opposite side of the building from the access to the basement. The team from the arson unit must have cleared it or Irene wouldn't be working in there.

There was a long counter with the stack of papers on it that Irene had been going through when Alibi arrived. Behind it was a crowded display of packing boxes, padlocks, and other supplies.

As he watched while Irene searched for her card, Alibi thought of Daphne. On the off chance that the fire and whatever was happening to her were related, he decided to ask now and apologize later to Clive Carter in the fire department if he'd overstepped. "I understand when someone abandons their unit, the items can be sold, per your contract with the renters, and that's what ends up in that warehouse?"

"Not exactly," Irene said, as she rummaged in another drawer, trying to find her elusive business card. "Everything goes down there that people don't want, but only a fraction is sold. Most of it is junked."

"How often do you take things out of the warehouse to sell or junk? Is it daily?"

"Oh, no. We don't have the staff for that. My daughter and I do most of the review. Once in a while we have an expert look at something like art or coins, but we have to pay them, so it has to be really promising. Probably once a week or every two weeks. It's a big space. We have room for things to sit."

"Would it be possible for me to get a list of people whose units were abandoned over the last month?" Alibi consciously used the word *abandoned* to imply the owners no longer wanted their property. *Seized for nonpayment* would be a much more inflammatory way to characterize what went on here, though it was arguably more accurate.

Irene looked up at him, her voice weary rather than accusing. "Why? Do you plan to contact them?"

"No, just a quick review," Alibi said. "If there's someone we'd like to talk to, we'll come back to you with a warrant for your specific records on them. We won't contact anyone without you knowing about it first."

"I don't know," Irene said, considering. "I don't think I can give you that information."

Alibi didn't want to push it. "One more question. Do unit owners get only one key each?"

"We give them two keys, one that's meant to go on a key ring. They're next to impossible to copy, and they have to pay a pretty steep fee if they lose them."

She finally found her card and was extending it to him when a door at the end of the counter opened and a young woman came through, wearing the same style shirt as Irene's but bearing the name THERESA and no manager's pin. She had a large black purse slung over her shoulder, keys in hand.

"Mom, can I go? I've—" She stopped when she saw Alibi. She was short, like her mom, but slim, with heavily mascaraed lashes framing large, dark-blue eyes.

Alibi accepted the card from Irene.

He and Jackie O had just reached the bottom of the ramp outside the front doors when the young woman hurried after them.

"Are you here about the fire?" she asked, her eyes bright with interest.

43

THERESA MIGHT JUST have been bored or interested in what gossip she could get to tell her friends, but Alibi was never one to turn down a willing potential witness.

He didn't think she could be much over twenty years old.

"Yes, we're here about the fire," he told her. "We're going to walk around and get a sense of the layout. It would be great if you could join us. Point out anything you think might be important. That would be helpful."

She glanced over her shoulder. Her mother was no longer visible at the counter. "Sure, why not?" she said with a smile. As they started out, she dug into her shoulder bag and withdrew a small tin of mints. "Want one?"

"No thank you," Alibi said.

Jackie O smiled and shook her head.

They walked around the parking lot, staying on the outside of the caution tape. Alibi didn't see anything remarkable. They rounded the corner to the back of the building.

Alibi noticed a small panel next to the back door, identical to one at the front entrance. He turned to Theresa. "Do people usually park back here? Where does that door go? Is it open to the public?"

Her eyes slid away from him. "Nobody uses it. It's locked all the time."

"That looks like it's for key cards," Alibi said, pointing to the panel. "Do you know who might have a key card to this door?"

Theresa's smiling, interested expression of a moment ago was gone.

She seemed to want to look anywhere but at Alibi as she answered. "My mom and I do. But it's for emergencies only. Nobody uses that door."

He kept his tone mild. "Since it's an emergency exit, can it be opened from the inside without a key?"

"I guess so. I don't know," Theresa said. "I've got to go." She left, disappearing around the side of the building opposite from where they'd come.

Alibi wanted to know what she was hiding, but no point in chasing after her when she was clearly upset. They could follow up with a formal interview. Meanwhile, Jackie O was taking photos with her tablet of red graffiti on the back wall. It was illegible, but bright, and could have been put there recently.

"You think that's anything?" he asked her.

Jackie O didn't answer. She lowered her tablet and raised her head as though she'd heard something, then put up a hand to indicate Alibi should stay where he was as she jogged in the direction Theresa had gone. He waited for what felt like a very long few minutes and was starting to get concerned when Jackie O came back around the corner and waved for him to join her.

When he did, it was clear this was where everything had happened.

Caution tape restricted access to the building for at least thirty feet, maybe more. Where evenly spaced windows had once been, all across the wall at head height, only the frames were left, and those were charred and melted. The window glass had all been blown out by the force of the explosion, the fire, or both. The ground within the taped area was littered with it.

Jackie O had an arm around Theresa at the edge of the tape. Alibi approached them slowly, and when he got close, he could see the young woman had been crying.

Jackie O said to her gently. "Why don't you tell Lieutenant Morning Sun what you told me? You won't be in trouble, but it might help us to prevent something like this from happening again."

Jackie O turned to Alibi. "I asked Theresa if these windows were typically closed and locked before the fire. She told me they're supposed to be, but they have trouble keeping them secure. One was taped up. It had been broken into a couple of weeks ago. They're so busy here, with limited staff, that they hadn't gotten around to getting it fixed. Did I get that right, Theresa?"

The young woman said a very quiet, "Yes."

"Why don't you tell the lieutenant the rest? You can do it better than I could."

Theresa took a deep breath and kept her eyes on Jackie O, though Alibi understood her to be repeating the story for his benefit.

"I give him food sometimes, and it's been so cold. I thought it would be better if I let him . . ."

She paused and risked a look at Alibi, who didn't hide the compassion he felt for her. She'd been helping someone, and he was pretty sure he was about to hear how it had gone wrong—though Theresa might not know how terribly wrong yet.

"I know I shouldn't have, but the stuff in there is mostly junk. We throw it out. Anyway, I never saw him take anything. It was a place to stay warm and out of the rain."

"I understand," Alibi said. "When did you first start letting him sleep inside?"

"Just the two nights, Monday and Tuesday. But he would never have set a fire, I know he wouldn't. He was a nice old guy. I think he was sick or something. He lived by the river, or at least there's where I saw him come up."

"How long have you been giving him food?"

"Two weeks. No, three. Not every day, but when I could, I'd walk out here, and sometimes he'd be waiting. Over there." She pointed to a group of trees and bushes, then looked back at the wreckage of glass and charred wood from the fire. "He wouldn't do that," she said again.

Alibi did not want to have to tell her, but he felt it would be better for her to hear it from him than on the news tomorrow. "I don't believe the man you were so generously helping set the fire. But I do think there's a possibility he was inside when it happened."

Theresa looked uncomprehending. "What do you mean?"

"We think someone might have been inside who didn't make it out. We're looking into that now."

She burst into noisy tears, and Jackie O put both arms around her.

"I'll get the truck," Alibi said, wanting to leave Jackie O a few minutes with Theresa. He expected she'd try to calm the young woman down since she might not be ready to confide in her mother yet.

Alibi went back the way he'd come, and as he passed the front entrance, Irene waved to him. He got the impression she'd been watching for him. He went up the marked path, and she opened the door.

"Come in," Irene said. "I was thinking about it. I'd like to see the person caught who did this. If they've some grudge against us, if it wasn't just random kids, I don't want them to come back and set fire to the main building."

She led Alibi into the reception area and through the door Theresa had used. There was a short hall with a bathroom on the right and a small office, the door open, to his left. "If you're feeling tired, sit down over there." She gestured to a chair in front of the desk, on which sat an older-model computer. She'd raised her voice as though hoping someone might hear, though as far as Alibi knew, there was no one else around. Then she whispered, "Don't touch anything except to scroll down if you need to. Don't change screens. And don't use the printer. But if you look at the screen by accident while you're sitting there, taking a break, that can't be helped. An accident, you know, while I'm in the other room?" She spoke loudly again as she turned to go. "You just rest your feet, Officer. Thank you for your service. I'll be out here if you need me."

Well, look at you, Alibi thought. *Irene, super spy.*

He sat down and followed her directions.

He *accidentally* looked at the screen.

In the month of February, fourteen people had missed at least sixty days of payment at Clad Corp Ideal Storage, defaulting on their contracts. If they responded at all to the notices and calls, it was noted and their items were not seized. But zero responses evidently signaled to Irene that Ideal Storage was going to keep losing money if they didn't empty that unit and rent it to a paying customer.

Alibi had no need to scroll. It was alphabetical.

And Jonathan Hill was the fourth name on the list.

44

Matchbook Lane

T HE INTERACTION WITH Sid troubled Emma.

She'd always suspected him of trying to undermine her work, but finding him actively doing it, digging into files on the Community Fund of the tunnel project that she'd not yet seen, had been extremely disturbing.

Was he searching for an ethical breach that he hoped she might miss?

Malia had flagged oversight of contracts in the Community Fund as being inadequate, but Fran had steered Emma away from that, saying the small dollar amount meant it was a poor use of commission resources. Now, given Sid's interest in the matter, as evidenced by his having information on the Community Fund open on his screen, Emma felt justified in asking Malia to take another look. She might even look at it herself—Sid's attempt to catch her not doing enough had given her the cover she needed to do more.

On the family front, she hadn't heard from Atticus yet, despite having left him her laptop and the note taped to his door with her contact information. She'd never felt this nervous arriving at her own home before.

As she pulled the Mustang into the driveway, she was surprised Fox and Crash weren't at the window to greet her. Then she remembered she'd told Luke to keep them until Atticus had been properly introduced to Crash.

The first thing she did was check on the note she'd left for Atticus on his door. It was gone. He must have gotten it—that was good.

She knocked.

No answer. She knocked again. Same result.

She continued along the side of the house into the backyard. The drapes were drawn across the kitchen window to the studio. She didn't see light or movement inside.

She fought the sense of panic she felt at the thought that Atticus must have run away.

Again.

She returned to the garage studio door.

To Atticus's door.

But was it still his?

She stooped and felt for the key under the mat. It wasn't there. She thought that through. He'd commented on her lax security. So it made sense that he would prefer to have the key with him. Whether he was specifically afraid that the wine-throwing man from the gallery might use it to go inside while he was gone to lie in wait for him didn't bear thinking about.

Emma wished it hadn't come to mind.

She circled back to the front door and reached for her key beneath the planter.

It was also gone.

She took a breath.

Her note was no longer on the garage door. Atticus must have read it and come to retrieve the laptop waiting for him in the kitchen. To do that, he would have used the key under the planter. He was probably inside her house now. In fact, he likely had decided to sit down and use the laptop in there.

She tried her front door. The knob turned. It was unlocked.

As she pushed it open, she called, "Atticus?" to give him warning that it was her. She didn't want to startle him.

There was no response. When she stepped inside, she called out again.

"Atticus?"

She noticed a drawer on the small writing desk in the corner of the living room had been opened and not fully closed. If he wasn't here, he must have looked in the desk for pens and paper to leave her a note. To let her know where he'd gone. Still, she felt her heart rate climb.

It was deadly quiet.

"Atticus?" she called again as she walked into the kitchen. He wasn't there. There was no note for her. The laptop was gone, and several drawers were open in there too.

Does Atticus routinely forget to shut drawers? Is that a bad habit of his?

She didn't recall that happening when she was a kid. In fact, he'd been tidy and fairly exacting about how things were kept. She walked down the hall. She looked into her home office. More open drawers.

What could Atticus have been searching for? And where is he now?

Maybe he was in the en suite bathroom off her bedroom.

But that door was wide open, and the bathroom was empty.

Then she noticed the red velvet box on her nightstand next to her bed. The lid was off. Her mother's garnet-and-gold necklace was gone.

It struck her like a blow.

For twenty-two years, she'd kept it near her while she slept.

Under her pillow when she was younger, then next to her when she got older.

A chill passed through Emma.

A terrible thought occurred to her.

Would he have pocketed the necklace for his new wife? No. That was ridiculous. His art sold for $20,000 a pop. He had money. He could buy his second wife any jewelry she wanted.

Emma sat on the edge of the bed as she was struck with the worst thought yet. She investigated corruption, illegality, and unethical behavior. Suppose the $20,000 price tag on Atticus's drawing had been a scam?

Atticus could have inflated the value of the painting, then paid someone to ruin it when it was on display at the Blue Heron so that the gallery's insurance policy would cover it. Maybe Atticus was grifting and conning his way through life.

Maybe that's what he'd been doing for twenty-two years, and she was just one more stop on his petty path of crime. After opening every drawer in her house, having come across the only item of any real value—her mother's necklace—ignoring what it meant to her, he'd taken it and moved on to find his next mark.

Emma felt hollowed out. She'd lowered the barriers she'd spent nearly a lifetime building, and it had gotten her here. She lay down on top of the white eyelet cover on her bed, pulled her knees to her chest, and wrapped her arms tightly around them.

CHAPTER

45

Emma didn't know how much time had passed, but when she'd felt strong enough, she'd gone outside.

She sat on her front stoop.

She looked down at her favorite suit, at the sea-green knit with the ivory buttons, that she'd bought when she was promoted to investigator, when she'd achieved the professional independence she'd believed had meant abandonment could not touch her. She'd felt in charge of her own destiny.

She'd felt safe.

She wanted to feel that way again. She wanted her old life back. Her life before last night.

Her life before Atticus's return.

The sun was shining brightly. As Emma looked up, shading her eyes, she realized that if she didn't know better, she'd be thinking, *What a glorious spring day.*

But it was not glorious. Not at all. Not on Matchbook Lane. Not at her house. Not for her.

It was the epitome of anti-glorious.

Emma had never felt this angry.

Atticus had come back into her life, and in under twenty-four hours he'd left, taking with him her mother's necklace. She'd belatedly realized that unless her laptop was locked in the garage studio, he'd taken that as well. *Her personal laptop.* Most things on it were saved elsewhere, in the cloud or backed up. But not every-thing, and she didn't know what those things were that hadn't yet been saved.

Emma felt she fully understood for the first time the expression *consumed by anger*, because she was not at all sure what was going to be left of her when this rage burned itself out.

She thought of the twenty-foot-high wall of flames in the Clad Corp Ideal Storage warehouse and felt as though something every bit as reckless and destructive and dangerous was occurring inside her now.

Then she thought again of her laptop, and the fact that she'd left a note to Atticus inviting him to use it.

Maybe the problem with his phone wasn't simply a dead bat-tery; maybe it wouldn't be solved by a new charger. Perhaps it was broken and he'd kept the computer with him wherever he'd gone so he could contact her once he got there, until he had a replace-ment phone.

And suppose he wanted to do something wonderful with her mother's necklace for her? Have it cleaned? It was very old, and the gold had dimmed and the garnets no longer sparkled. Or perhaps he was having matching earrings made?

No.

No.

No.

Emma thought it, then she said it aloud. She wasn't going to do what she'd done the first time Atticus left—make excuses for him, come up with reasons for his despicable behavior where there were none.

Then something else hit her.

Where are the dogs?

She'd told Luke to keep them, but if they were at the duplex inside, they'd be barking at Kate's front window when they saw Emma sitting across the street. They must be shut in the backyard at Luke's. He wouldn't usually leave them outside for so long, not all day while he was at school and then at the commission. But maybe he'd forgotten.

Suddenly, Emma wanted nothing more than to have Fox and Crash with her.

Reliable, loving Fox and Crash.

They would never leave her.

She ran across the street, opened Luke and Kate's side gate, and enthusiastically called to them. "Fox, Crash. Here, boy. Here, puppy."

The response Emma got was not from Luke's yard.

It came from out front, down the street and far away. She recognized frantic barks of joy and excitement, one high-pitched and staccato, the other deep and barrel-chested.

Undeniably, that was Fox and Crash.

Emma rushed out to save them from the dangers of cars and dognappers. But when she ran into the middle of Matchbook Lane, where she was able to look down to the bottom of the cul-de-sac, she saw Atticus with a big grin on his face being pulled up the street behind the dogs, who were double leashed.

She put her hands on her hips and made no attempt to dim the murderous light in her eyes as she waited for Atticus to come to her. She didn't intend to take one step in that man's direction until he had fully explained himself. Although she did decide, after a moment's thought, to get out of the middle of the street.

She crossed to her front yard.

The dogs reached her, straining to the full length of their leashes. She knelt and hugged each of them around the neck, confusing Fox, who kept jumping even though Emma was now at her level, and concerning Crash, who recognized aberrant behavior from one of his humans when he saw it.

As Emma straightened up, she saw that while it may have taken Atticus longer to figure things out than Crash, he also knew something was wrong. His eyebrows were raised, and he was frowning. Emma stepped forward and took Fox's leash from him, and as she was about to snatch Crash's away too, she stopped.

"How did you get the dogs?" she said sharply to Atticus. "Why is Crash letting you walk him?"

Atticus looked puzzled. "From Luke. Across the street."

Fox was jumping again, so Emma turned and went through her side gate, ducked under the bougainvillea, and walked past the garage studio door and into the backyard. She heard Atticus following with Crash. She called coldly over her shoulder, "Shut that gate. Tightly."

Emma moved to the rattan table under the large maple tree in the far corner of her yard and sat down, unleashing Fox. She glared into the distance, away from Atticus. Because if looks could kill, she felt sure she'd be planning his funeral, and she couldn't be bothered.

Atticus cautiously joined her at the table, following her example and unleashing Crash. He took the chair farthest from her.

When he spoke, it was softly.

"Luke introduced me to Fox and Crash. Mostly to Crash." He looked toward the big dog, who was watching their interaction closely. "We hung out for a bit. They got to know me. Luke told me I was welcome to come back and spend time with them after he left. It seems to be a neighborhood thing, this open-door policy. Later, I did think it would be nice to get out and give them a walk. Luke had gone to school, or I think he might have said he had to be at work, but they seemed happy enough to go with me."

Emma cooled down a tiny bit.

From one hundred billion degrees to one hundred million.

There was still a lot to be explained, but the image of her father talking with Luke was really nice. It was something she'd hoped for.

"It's pleasant back here," Atticus said, looking up at the broad branches of the maple tree.

"How long were you gone?" Emma asked flatly, though the answer that popped into her head was twenty-two years. "Just now, with the dogs. How long were you out?"

"An hour, " Atticus said. "I followed the directions Luke gave me to the dog park. We stayed there a while. I met some interesting people."

"Did you have the key to the studio with you?"

"No, why? I left it in case you needed to get in."

Emma jumped up. She ran back around to the side of the house and flipped over the mat in front of Atticus's door. She searched the surrounding dirt.

"It's not here," she said. "Does that mean you don't have the main house key either?"

"What are you talking about?" he said. "Of course not."

Emma began to rethink everything.

"Did you take my laptop off the kitchen table into the studio?"

"Yes," he said, looking even more confused. "You said I could. I—"

"Wait here," she commanded as she ran out the side gate, pulling it roughly shut behind her, causing the dogs to let out a volley of barks in frustration at being left behind when there was clearly some good chasing to be done.

She was across the street in an instant, having retrieved the key to Kate and Luke's duplex from under a potted plant on their stoop. She let herself in and went into the kitchen to get the key to her front door, which was neatly labeled on a rack where Kate had all her keys organized, and then into Luke's room to look for his key to the garage studio. She hoped he didn't have it with him and after a quick search was relieved to find it on his desk in a nearly empty cereal bowl. Fortunately, it looked like the contents had been consumed without any milk.

She grabbed Luke's key, ran back across the street, burst through the side yard gate out of breath, and used it to open Atticus's door.

"Where is it?" she cried, seeing nothing on the table or on the kitchen counter or on the sofa.

"Where is what?" Atticus asked, coming in after her, crowded out by both dogs, Fox running around in circles and jumping on Emma while Crash put his nose to the floor catching some scent, sniffing furiously.

"My laptop. Where is it?"

Atticus turned slowly around, walked behind the couch, and shook his head. "I don't know. I left it on the table."

Emma's hair was flying in all directions, there was a pearly sheen of sweat on her forehead, and the top button of her jacket had fallen off somewhere.

"What is it? What's wrong?" he asked. "Sit down." He went to the kitchen and got a glass to pour her a drink of water.

"No," she said. "Come with me."

Atticus set the glass down and followed her to the front of the house, the dogs coming too, unleashed, with no interest in running off, since all the excitement was clearly happening here.

Emma stepped inside the front door, and when Atticus followed suit, she flung out an arm to keep him from going farther. "Look around. What do you see?" Then she realized she'd closed the drawer that had been open in the living room. "Never mind. This way." She took him to the small office, where the drawers were all still open. "Did you do this?" she demanded.

"What?" he asked.

"Did you open these drawers?"

"No," he said.

She marched to the bedroom, where the red velvet box sat empty on her nightstand.

"Did you take Mom's necklace?"

"What?" he asked, his voice breaking. "Your mother's necklace? What necklace?"

Emma's face fell.

He doesn't have it. He doesn't know where it is.

"The garnet one," she said, sitting down on the edge of the bed. Crash nosed his head onto her lap.

Atticus had a faraway look in his eyes. "I gave her that necklace for our tenth wedding anniversary."

Slowly, he seemed to come back to the present.

"It didn't cost much then. It's probably worth more now, since it's old and one of a kind." He scanned the room. "Was there any other jewelry visible in here?"

She frowned. "No. I don't wear much jewelry." She almost added that she'd never worn that necklace, but she was too tired for whatever that might make him feel.

"So it could just be a coincidence that it was your mother's," he said. "When someone took it. Maybe it was the only valuable or pretty thing here."

"Maybe," Emma said. "Come with me."

She stood slowly and shakily, her adrenaline depleted, and walked to the front door, pausing at the closet to take down her spare set of leashes for the dogs, since they'd left the others in the backyard. She handed Crash's to Atticus—the big dog seemed to have taken a liking to him—while she leashed Fox. She led her motley crew out onto the front step, where she sat down and called Alibi.

He answered on the first ring.

"I don't know if this qualifies as a major crime," she said. "Someone broke into my house and took two things, as far as I can tell. My personal laptop and a necklace my father gave to my mother. Oh, and the keys. They took the keys to the front house and the garage studio."

"Was anyone home when this happened?" Alibi asked.

"No," Emma said, losing energy. Almost losing interest.

Her mother's necklace was gone, and her father didn't have it.

"What about the dogs? Crash let someone in?" Alibi asked.

"No," Emma said. "They were out on a walk. With my dad."

Alibi was quiet for a beat. Then he said, "This is not a major crime. It sounds like it might be a routine burglary. Where were the keys?"

"Under the mat and in a planter," she said quietly, not looking at Atticus.

"Both outside and easy to find?" Alibi asked. There was no judgment in his voice. He'd used the front door key himself.

"I guess so," she said.

"Is your dad staying in the studio?"

"Yes."

Alibi knew about the studio. He'd seen it being built, even offered some design advice.

"Did they go in there, take anything? Does Luke still keep instruments in the studio? His performance sax is probably worth four grand, even hocked."

"Yes, Luke does, and no, they didn't take them," Emma said, though she was annoyed with herself for not having thought of it. "Whoever did this went in the garage studio. That's where my laptop was." Then something else occurred to her, and her stomach dropped. "They might have taken my khaki satchel too. I don't remember seeing it when I walked through the house just now. It had my work tablet in it." She privately thought the most important thing in that bag was her handwritten record of the tunnel investigation, which she wished she'd left in place on her office wall. But it had no value to anyone but her, so she didn't mention it. "I think I set it by the back door in the kitchen before I took the dogs out last night. Or maybe in my bedroom when I went to change." She tried to picture where she'd left it but couldn't. She'd been entirely preoccupied at the time with getting to San Francisco, to the jail to see Atticus.

"Okay, I'll ask burglary to send an officer to take your statement. I'd also like to come by, if that's okay. And I'd like to speak to your dad, if he can stick around."

That struck Emma as funny.

If he can stick around . . .

She wasn't going to lay odds on that.

All she said was, "Sure. We'll be here. Okay if we wait inside? I can check for my bag." She really wanted to know if the project notes were gone. The timetable of tasks would be a pain to recreate. The sooner she started that, the better.

"It's probably best if you don't," Alibi said.

"Okay, I've got a key to Kate's. We'll go over there, all of us, the dogs too. Will you let the officer know?"

After she rang off, as they crossed the street to Kate's, Emma said out loud, though really she was muttering to herself, "Too bad Crash wasn't at home. He'd never have let them in."

Atticus heard her and said, "Bad timing on my part."

"Like that's a surprise." Emma wasn't able to resist the dig, though she regretted the words as soon as they were out of her mouth.

But Atticus smiled.

She was suddenly glad he was there with her, that she wasn't going through this alone.

46

The River

LUKE LIKED ATTICUS after spending time with him and Crash and Fox in the backyard. He could see him fitting in, like a real part of the family. It'd be cool to have an old guy, like a grandpa, to talk to. Luke had a sort of grandma, Mrs. Cleveland, next door, but she was ninety and more like a great-grandma. He hadn't gotten around to talking to Atticus about his music. He didn't know his tastes, but maybe they could go to some local shows. Then it occurred to Luke he hadn't thought about whether he'd still be able to have band practice in the studio if Atticus was living there. He'd bet they could work it out.

He checked his phone and saw the time. He'd have to leave school for the commission in about ten minutes. He'd been surprised by how little he'd seen Aunt Emma there yesterday. He was on her team, but it seemed like she didn't see any of them more than once a day or so. Still, Nick and Malia were okay, Malia especially. Nick was moody, but Luke knew guys like that. It didn't bother him so much.

He checked his phone again. He couldn't help it. He hadn't heard from Daphne since they'd been interrupted midsentence when Atticus had shown up at the door and she'd slipped out the side gate and down the street. She'd been about to tell him what she wanted him to say to Fran for her, and he'd thought she'd let him know before he went to work. He guessed he could still check with Shaylene to see if she'd given Fran Daphne's contact information.

Luke really wanted to see Daphne again, though he was aware it was hard to figure out why when someone was as beautiful as she was—whether that was what was making him think she was great in other ways too. Like, Daphne seemed kind and funny and she liked his music, but he couldn't really say if those things about her were that different from the other girls he knew.

He'd thought about it a lot. He hadn't thought of much else, and he'd decided there wasn't really a risk to hanging out with Daphne because she didn't want anything from him except his help. She'd been in love with Johnny Hill, and it seemed like she still was. They'd been planning to get married. That wasn't something you got over right away.

So it wasn't like he could feel rejected or get his heart broken or anything.

Still, he didn't like lying to his mom and to Aunt Emma about Daphne. So he'd have to figure that out. But he just couldn't deal with their opinions about Daphne right now.

He didn't feel any of his anger when he was with her, and that was important to him. He'd bet his counselor would think it was important too. Maybe he'd tell her about Daphne. Maybe not.

He'd already gone to the school office and signed out for work. He was on his way to get his bike behind the gym when his phone buzzed. He didn't want to get his hopes up. Probably his mom making sure he hadn't forgotten he had to be at the commission today.

He froze when he saw it was Daphne. He felt as though his heart had dropped into his stomach.

Can you meet me now?
It's important.

Luke took no time to decide.

Yes.

She responded right away.

Do you know where the storage facility is? Where the fire was?

There's a path to the river right behind it. Meet me at the top of the path. Thank you Lucas. It's important.

She'd said it was important twice, and he liked how she'd used his name, though she didn't have to in a message.

He had to go see her.

It was the right thing to do, even though it meant missing work.

I can be there in 15 minutes.

A thumbs-up symbol appeared on his last message. Daphne had received it and agreed.

Luke looked in his contacts and found where he'd entered Hailey, Emma's assistant. Malia had said that was who he was supposed to tell if he'd be late to work or unable to come in.

Hailey, I'm sorry. I can't make it today. Please let Nick and Malia know. I'll be in tomorrow and can take work home then if it helps.
Luke Doyle (Intern)

He didn't wait to see if Hailey responded before tucking the phone in his pocket and putting his helmet on. It was getting harder to shove his hair under it, and in the summer it would be hot. He thought he might shave his head again. It made him look older. He hopped on his bike and pedaled hard. He intended to make it down to the river in record time.

When he got to the storage facility, the area was surrounded by caution tape. He didn't see any damage until he was across from the old building, where smoke had blackened the walls and the windows were all blown out. He hadn't thought about what it would look like after the fire. It was apocalyptic, like a worst-case video game scenario.

He biked along the bumpy gravel shoulder of the frontage road that he and Emma had used yesterday morning when he was driving the Mustang and they'd picked up the tables for his mom's party. Everything looked different in the daylight. The trees and bushes were less menacing. But the scent of the river was the same, and to him it smelled like fish. Luke didn't like it.

He didn't like fish to eat or as pets or anything that smelled like fish.

He saw only one path directly across from the storage facility. It wasn't the main river walk that bikers and joggers used. This one went straight down into the overgrown bushes. He wondered if there was poison ivy or poison oak. He was allergic.

Daphne had said to meet him at the top, though she wasn't there now. He took out his phone and messaged her. He got an "undeliverable" auto response. Maybe she'd turned her phone off. More likely, she just hadn't arrived and she was out of range somewhere. Though as he thought about it, the tone of her request had been urgent. It had sounded to him like she was already here. But maybe he'd gotten that wrong.

There was no place to sit and no shade. After five long minutes of batting away mosquitoes, Luke decided to check down the path. He thought it would be nicer to wait on the riverbank. It wasn't like you got away from the fish odor up here.

He tried walking his bike alongside him, but the path narrowed, and branches on each side scraped its already worn paint. After he checked to make sure none of the nearby bushes appeared likely to give him a rash, he dragged the Schwinn under a tight clump of plants and weeds until it was well hidden. He figured no one would come across it there and he'd hear them if they did.

His Converse skidded on the loose soil as he made his way down the increasingly nonexistent path. The bushes had multiplied, clinging to one another and giving no quarter to someone who wanted to pass. He'd begun to doubt she'd come this way when the quality of the light changed and he could glimpse the green-brown water about twenty feet away.

Something on the ground at the edge of the next turn shone bright in the dirt, like a piece of metal. He took another step and saw it was one of the buckles of Daphne's sandals reflecting the sun into his eyes. Her feet were comfortably crossed at the ankles.

He smiled. She must be lying down, getting some sun at the riverside, although given her pale skin, he figured she'd most likely be in the shade. He hoped she'd brought a towel or blanket. Even after the drought, it could get muddy close to the water's edge, especially after a big rain like last night's.

As he made the last turn out into the open, he thought to call her name so as not to startle her, but when Daphne came into view, Luke's voice caught in his throat.

At first he couldn't put together the pieces of what he was seeing.

She was lying on her back. That was right. It was as he'd imagined her from the way her ankles were crossed, heels down, the pale-pink polish on her toes visible as one foot rested atop the other. But her head was turned awkwardly toward the side, away from the river. She appeared to be looking down at the dirt around her, though from where he was standing, her face was in shadow.

Not shaded or hidden away were the several places where the bright-pink sweater and dark-blue tank top she'd worn when he saw her earlier were soaked with red-black splotches.

Like wine or paint . . . or blood.

Luke dropped to his knees and crawled alongside her to get close, staying on the riverside, instinctively shying away from seeing her face.

He didn't lean in to listen for Daphne's breath or to touch her neck or her unbandaged wrist to check for a pulse. He didn't have to.

He knew death. He'd seen it before.

47

Matchbook Lane

Luke's physician consulted with his counselor, and taking into account his existing PTSD they'd agreed it was best to give him a sedative so he could sleep, with the hope it might last until morning.

Kate had been cautioned to stay close in case he woke during the night—not that she would have considered doing anything else. It was important he not find himself alone.

Everyone else having gone, Kate and Emma sat at the table in Kate's living room, the door open to Luke's bedroom, where the dogs kept watch. Or at least Crash did. His large body was tense as he sat on guard between the bed and the door, his eyes on Luke, while puppy Fox slept with her head on Luke's chest.

Kate was in her Rainbow Alley work clothes—a black polo shirt with the multicolored rainbow logo on the back and black jeans. Emma was still wearing her sea-green suit, which she'd decided was now the unluckiest clothing ever. She couldn't wait to take it off and ritually burn it.

Both women were exhausted, and they looked it.

Emma had made mint tea for them. Their mugs sat untouched.

It had been more than two hours since Kate had gotten a message from Luke, which she now knew he'd sent moments after he found Daphne. He'd said only *I need you*, followed by a map marking his location across from the storage facility. Kate had raced there, not knowing what she would find.

Emma and Atticus had been with Alibi in Kate's house when Kate got Luke's message while at work.

The officer Alibi had called out on the burglary had gone, and Atticus was responding to a few informal questions Alibi had about the gallery incident.

"I was the target of a blackmail scheme years ago, and when the young man came up to me at the gallery, he identified himself as the son of one of the blackmailers. The best I can piece together, he must have overheard his mother saying something about blackmail when he was a kid, and she explained it away by telling him she was the victim rather than the perpetrator of that scheme, mentioning me by name. When she died, I'm not sure how, although I knew her boyfriend had been a violent man, her son blamed me and finally tracked me down."

Though Alibi seemed satisfied, Emma had her own follow-up questions to that.

Who was blackmailing my father and why?

But before she could ask, her phone had buzzed, and she opened the message and map from Luke, forwarded by Kate.

Emma was on her feet in seconds. She passed the phone wordlessly to Alibi, who, once he saw what it contained, jumped up and followed her. Emma had the Mustang in gear and was backing down the driveway while Alibi was still pulling the passenger door shut after him.

Atticus had stayed with the dogs while Emma and Alibi went to the scene.

When they got there, Luke was wrapped in a blanket, sitting stiffly in the back of an ambulance, its doors open. His skin was naturally fair, but he was paler than Emma had ever seen him.

Kate sat next to him, her arm tightly around Luke as he answered questions as best he could.

When Alibi got out of the Mustang, he went over and chatted with the detectives interviewing Luke, but he didn't interfere or take over—he was too close to the family to have his signature on any of this.

Later, when Emma was able to get him alone for a minute, she asked Alibi if Luke was a suspect in Daphne's death. He was reassuring, although he told her he could share with her only what the press would know soon. He said that while the person who found the body was always of interest, there was no evidence Luke had fired a gun recently, and cause of death for Daphne VerStrate was definitely several gunshot wounds to the chest, any of which could have been fatal.

Also, while he'd said he couldn't give details, Alibi noted there were things about the scene that indicated someone else besides Daphne and then Luke had been present. Whether that would turn out to be a witness or the killer, the most important thing was finding them.

Even in her blur of concern for Kate and Luke, Alibi had seemed to Emma to be taking Daphne's death hard, even personally, as though it was somehow his fault. She didn't see how that could be.

Since they'd gotten home, Kate hadn't mentioned Breno, but Emma assumed he must be up to his neck dealing with the media, who would be frantic to get information about the woman gunned down in broad daylight by the Sacramento River.

"I don't understand," Kate said quietly, lifting her mug and setting it down again without taking a drink. "How could this happen? Luke didn't know her. He'd never met her. How did he end up at the river with Daphne?"

Kate's eyes were dry, cried out for now, but they carried the pain of someone who had many more tears to shed.

Emma felt miserable.

She took a breath and began at the beginning, because like anyone bearing witness, she knew that would be the best way to give Kate the information she not only wanted but deserved.

"Yesterday . . ." she began, and stopped. Could it really only have been yesterday? She wanted to make sure she had it right. "Yesterday morning, I gave Daphne an informational interview. She had a lot of questions about my work at the commission, and she asked about my boss, Fran Hill."

Kate's face was listless and dull.

Though Emma wasn't sure she was getting through to her, she kept going. "The next time I saw Daphne was outside the Hayden Commission building before your party yesterday. She was hurt. That was the blood you saw on my jacket last night. It was hers.

Nothing too bad. I later learned it was from a gash on her arm. She told us she was almost run down by a car, that she didn't see who was driving. She seemed really scared, which I guess could be natural after that experience, but of course, now I wonder. She refused to let me take her to the hospital, and—"

Kate sat up straight. She leaned forward, and the laser focus Emma had seen so many times in her eyes had returned.

"Us? You said she told 'us'?"

Emma was sure Kate already knew the answer, but she gave it anyway. "Luke was with me. When I talked to Daphne yesterday afternoon. When she'd been injured."

"Why? Why was he with you? Why would you have him with you, with a woman who was scared, who was in danger?" Kate's gray-green eyes now blazed just like Luke's did when he was angry. "How could you? What is wrong with you?"

Emma made no attempt to defend herself. It didn't matter that there had been a reason Luke was with her, that she'd been about to drive him home from the commission after his first day as an intern. Kate's anger had to go somewhere. Worse than that, Emma knew she deserved blame for what had happened to Luke.

She hadn't told Kate that part of it yet, and she had to. Delay in the telling would only hurt Kate more.

"I went to get the car, the Mustang. Daphne was too injured to walk with me. I left Luke with her during that time to watch over her because she seemed like she could be in shock. She was shaking all over."

Emma left out how frustrated she'd been with Daphne and the fact that all she'd wanted was to get away from her, so much so that she'd not given any thought to what it would mean to leave a sixteen-year-old like Luke in the company of a gorgeous, even exotic woman from another country who clearly had problems and who herself felt unsafe. She wasn't hiding that from Kate—she'd tell her—but that was more about her own feelings and her own guilt, and she didn't want to burden Kate with it right now.

She owed it to Kate to keep the focus on Daphne and how Luke had ended up at the site of her murder.

"I don't know what Luke and Daphne said to each other while I went to get the car. I was gone for under ten minutes. But when

I came back, he had his phone out. She was speaking to him, and it looked like he was entering her number."

Kate folded her arms on the table and lay her head facedown on top of them. She wouldn't look up at Emma. Emma suspected it was because Kate didn't trust herself to show her anything other than hatred. But when Kate did raise her head, her eyes were not full of the fury Emma had expected. They were despondent and resigned, since there had been no accident here.

Her son had gone to meet this woman, and her best friend had let it happen.

Emma forced herself to continue the story. "Luke rode his bike here for your party, and I drove Daphne to her apartment to get her settled as best I could, since she had refused medical care. I didn't really give her another thought until I was here and you mentioned the blood on my jacket. I caught Luke's eye across the room, and I could tell by his worried expression that he'd not yet mentioned to you what had happened with Daphne. This is not a defense. Absolutely, it is not a defense. But I think neither Luke nor I wanted to ruin your engagement party with a story that we knew would upset you. And I don't think either of us thought it would go anywhere after that. We just thought it was over. But I'm the adult, not Luke. I should have known better."

Kate stood up. Both her hands were balled into fists. She turned her back on Emma, stared out the front window at nothing for seconds, and then whirled back around to face her. "That may be why you didn't say anything," she hissed at Emma. "But you know Luke didn't tell me because he didn't want me knowing he was caught up with this woman, that he was going to meet her, or at least talk to her. That must've been on his mind and on her mind when she gave him the number. And you knew—I don't know whether Luke did—that she was in college already. There's maybe only a year or two between them, but college and high school are two different worlds."

Having gotten that out, Kate let her shoulders slump. She sat down heavily in her seat. "Do you know how they ended up together today?" she asked quietly.

"I don't," Emma said, as she braced herself for the hardest part that she still had to tell.

"I did plan to talk to you about this when you got home from work tonight. Atticus told me that earlier when he came over to get the dogs to take them for a walk at about ten this morning, Luke came out to meet him on the front stoop. Atticus felt then that Luke might have been trying to stop him from going inside. He said he recognized the maneuver from his teenage years, keeping nosy old folks out of things that aren't their business. While Luke did that, Atticus glimpsed what he said was a very beautiful young woman slip out of your side gate and hurry down the sidewalk. Atticus said he didn't mention seeing her to Luke, but when I asked Atticus to describe her, I think there can be no doubt that it was Daphne."

Kate gave her head a tiny shake, as though it hurt to move it, but then surprised Emma when the hint of a smile showed on her lips. "That lad of mine," she said. "He doesn't know his own power. Those dark curls, these eyes. But it's not that, really. Those may open the door, but there's a goodness about him that draws people to him. This lassie wanted help. She knew Luke had the heart to try to give it to her. I can't fault her for seeing that in my son."

CHAPTER

48

Yesterday had seemed insane to Emma. First, pulling Daniel Baptiste out of the Clad Corp Ideal Storage warehouse as twenty-foot flames bore down on them. Then driving to San Francisco to bail Atticus out and getting home with him at three in the morning.

But clearly, today had topped that.

Before Emma left Kate's, she'd heard Fox whimpering and had gone into Luke's room to see the puppy pushing her cold nose against Luke's face, wanting him to get up, to come out and play, while Crash sat at attention solemnly nearby. The big dog had been at Luke's side for much of the last five years. Emma knew he would wait patiently as long as it took for his boy to be ready to walk with him again. But Fox lacked Crash's patience, and Emma couldn't have her pestering Luke, who needed his rest.

She had to produce several dog treats to lure Fox away from him . Once she had the puppy in the kitchen, she used a few more to get her outside so she could shut her in the backyard.

The pup protested bitterly. But minutes later, after Emma had washed the tea mugs and rinsed the kettle, Fox had quieted. Emma looked out the back window. The puppy had worn herself out and was curled up on the cushioned mat by the door, sound asleep.

When Emma peeked into Luke's room to say good-bye to Kate, knowing she'd not yet been forgiven but was still loved, Kate lay atop the covers on her side facing Luke, one hand on his arm. Kate's eyes were closed, but Emma knew every cell of her being was focused on healing Luke, body and soul.

Unable to locate Fox's leash, Emma went out back and picked up the unusually subdued puppy with the intention of carrying her across the street. But as she passed by the front door to the adjoining duplex, it opened, and Mrs. Cleveland stepped out on the shared front stoop using her cane and waved hello.

Ninety if she was a day, Mrs. Cleveland lived alone. Aside from a troublesome hip and difficulty hearing, she was in generally good health. She owned both duplexes, and Kate reported that Luke stopped in to see her often. Emma knew he helped her with things around the house, but she thought he might also find a measure of peace with Mrs. Cleveland, where all he had to be was "that nice boy next door" and not live up to anything his mom, his therapist, or even Emma might expect of him these days.

Fox wriggled and pushed and kicked until she'd broken loose from Emma's arms and ran to Mrs. Cleveland. Emma was afraid she'd start jumping and knock the older woman over, but to Emma's surprise, Fox sat as beautifully and patiently as Emma had ever known her to do.

"I saw Kate helping Luke out of her car," Mrs. Cleveland said, in a strong voice that belied her years. "Is he all right? He seemed hardly able to walk. He was wrapped in a blanket. Did he have an accident on that bike of his? I've been saying he needs a new one. I doubt those brakes are good anymore."

Emma managed a smile. "He's fine. He had a shock." She saw no reason to hide the hard facts from a woman who Emma thought it was fair to say was Luke's friend. "He found a young woman who'd been killed. He only knew her slightly, but it was a terrible shock."

Fox let out a single commanding bark, letting Mrs. Cleveland know she wasn't holding up her end of the bargain. Emma gathered that something good should have happened by now for a dog that sat that still.

"Oh my," Mrs. Cleveland said. "That is terrible. Where are you taking this little one?" she said, looking down at Fox. "She visits a lot, you know. She likes to lie on the couch next to me. We listen to audiobooks. She's a fan of Ellis Peters. There aren't many dogs in those stories, but there are horses."

Fox had not taken her eyes off Mrs. Cleveland, and her tail wagged steadily even as the rest of her body held remarkably still.

Emma had an idea.

"Do you think Fox might visit with you now? Kate and Luke are finally resting, and Fox looks far more content with you than she would be with me on her own without her buddy Crash."

Mrs. Cleveland smiled. "Of course. You'll let Luke know she's here so he can get her when he's ready? No rush." She opened her door wide. "C'mon, little lady. I've just started *The Sanctuary Sparrow*, Brother Cadfael book seven. I know you'll like it."

Emma felt relieved. She could use some time completely alone, and she suspected that in addition to the soothing sound of the audiobook and unrestricted access to Mrs. Cleveland's cushy sofa, there were likely treats involved for Fox too.

When she turned back to the street, Emma saw that Atticus was sitting on her front porch.

She was shocked to find he looked old to her.

Well, not old exactly, but not the father she remembered, the one from her childhood, from her memories and from her dreams.

This was a man on the cusp of sixty, with salt-and-pepper hair, his hand raised in a greeting that was tentative, his eyes squinting in the early-evening light, making the lines around them more pronounced.

I shouldn't be so hard on him, she thought.

Not one of us is perfect.

49

E MMA ASKED ATTICUS if he would like to come in for a cup of tea. He wiped his shoes on the mat. She noticed they were the same style he'd worn when she was a kid, classic brown suede Vans skate shoes. She was surprised she hadn't noticed them when she'd picked him up last night, though there'd been a lot going on.

"Would you like help?" he asked, as she put the kettle on and reached for the canister of mint tea.

"No, it's okay," she said.

He pulled a chair out and sat at the red-and-chrome dinette table.

She stayed standing, leaning against the kitchen counter. "Have you heard? About Luke?" she asked him.

He nodded, and she realized that was likely why he'd been waiting out on the front stoop. "How is he?"

"I guess about like you'd expect," Emma said. "It was the young woman you saw leaving Luke's house that was killed. I don't know if they've identified her or run photos in the news reports yet."

"No. I didn't know it was her." Atticus rubbed his eyes.

She set two mugs on the table, then carried the pot with the steeping tea and joined him. As she looked at her father sitting across from her, his hair falling forward on his forehead the same way Luke's did, she had an odd premonition of more difficult days to come.

She realized she had a question, among her many questions, that she hoped would seem ridiculous to him and produce an easy no in response. She had to ask him anyway.

"Did you know Daphne VerStrate?"

"What do you mean?"

"I mean the young woman who was with Luke who was murdered. Did you know her personally?"

"No," Atticus said without hesitation, once he understood what she meant.

Emma believed him. But as she poured them both tea, she decided it was time to stop holding anything back. "I'm concerned some of the weird things that have been happening might relate to where you've been and what you've been doing all this time. At least the break-in, and someone taking Mom's necklace. But maybe some of the other things too." She didn't see how the fire or Daphne's death could relate to her dad, but the timing put everything in question.

Atticus put his elbows on the table and spun his wedding ring on his left hand with the fingers of his right.

He was quiet as he did it, and Emma let him be.

She figured that with twenty-two years gone, there might be a lot to explain, and it was reasonable for him to want to organize his thoughts.

Atticus tried a sip of the tea but quickly put it down. "That's hot," he said.

Emma didn't respond.

No small talk. We'll sit here until you say something worth my response.

"As I told your friend Alibi, I never blackmailed or murdered anyone," Atticus said firmly. Then he seemed to think about it. "And while clearly that young man was under the mistaken impression that I did, I can assure you none of that has anything to do with the break-in here. There is nothing he would be looking for, and if he'd wanted to harm me, he would have brought a weapon to the gallery that was far more lethal than a glass of red wine."

Emma swallowed her tea wrong and started coughing.

"You okay?" he asked her.

She gave him a sarcastic half smirk, as in *Oh yes, definitely, I'm peachy keen.*

When she didn't answer, he continued, as though going down a mental list. "The break-in was most likely random, but it was frightening. I'm glad you made a police report so they can look for the person responsible and try to recover your lost property. Especially your mother's necklace. And you should stop leaving keys under welcome mats and beneath planters."

Emma didn't take the bait. She waited for him to continue.

He spun his ring some more, looked at her, and looked away. "As far as where I've been and why, it involves other people, who I have to talk to and get permission from to reveal it to you. These are not just my secrets to tell."

Emma nearly spit out her mouthful of tea in her rush to get the words out. "That's ridiculous. It doesn't matter what anyone else wants. I'm your daughter, and—"

"It does matter," he said quietly. He held up his hand and gestured toward the ring. "This matters." He set his hand down again. "It represents a promise and a commitment," he said gravely.

Emma had had enough. She got up and took his cup along with hers, without looking to see whether he had finished what was in it. With her back to him, rinsing them at the sink, she thought but did not say, *A commitment? A promise?*

I'll give you a broken promise.

I'll give you a broken commitment.

How about fathering two daughters, being their primary stay-at-home parent for a decade, and then walking away from them without a word?

"Emma," he began, speaking to her back.

She turned toward him and said, "Leave."

When he didn't move, hurt and confusion in his face, she said, "Now. Go to her." She pointed to his ring. "I don't ever want to see you again."

To her surprise, Atticus's expression cleared. Instead of looking more upset, he seemed to calm, to gain assurance. He straightened his back and lifted his chin. And when she saw him that way, exactly that way, she felt the strongest sense of déjà vu she'd had since he'd returned.

They'd had this conversation before.

When Atticus had overslept and Jasmine had missed her class field trip to the local children's theater performance of *Peter Pan*.

Jasmine loved that story with the dog as the nanny and hadn't been able to wait to see it live.

Emma had said the very same thing to him then, when he'd apologized for Jasmine missing the long-awaited show.

Atticus had made a simple, very human mistake. He hadn't set his alarm. And at ten years old, Emma had said to him, *"Leave. I don't ever want to see you again."*

Emma sat down now and stared at Atticus. She said nothing. Not because she was still angry, but because she was struck by the fact that she'd failed to ever consider Atticus's disappearance in the context of the central fact of her childhood: that the accepted and undisputed truth in their house had been that their mother couldn't help the things she did. She'd had an injury, she was in pain much of the time, and her medication was necessary.

So when Margaret had neglected to do the shopping or pack their lunches, when she'd yelled and screamed, or worst of all when Atticus had had to wrap his strong arms gently but firmly around his wife to keep her from striking her daughters again and again, Emma's mother had never been held responsible for it.

But Atticus had. Emma and Jasmine had made clear to their father nearly every day of their childhood that *he* had failed them. Was it really any wonder that when Margaret died, he'd thought they'd be better off with their grandma?

Was it really any wonder that their father had finally run away?

FRIDAY, MARCH 12

50

THE NEXT MORNING, Atticus made scrambled eggs and Emma sliced honeydew melon and cantaloupe. It was nice.

Emma decided to enjoy it.

She'd think more about her mother's behavior later and what it might mean for her future relationship with Atticus.

She'd spent time late last night online researching *opioid addiction*, *codependency*, and *psychological issues of adult children of addicts*.

None of it had been an easy read.

She'd set it aside for now.

Atticus had on a soft, dark-blue denim shirt of Luke's that Emma recognized, untucked over boot-cut black jeans that must also belong to Luke. It struck Emma as an appropriate enough outfit for a late-fifty-something artist.

Or for a cowboy of any age.

And it fit pretty well, considering Luke was a couple of inches taller and wider across the back and chest than Atticus. Her father hadn't made it to the city for his luggage yet. Emma imagined that after two days, it was nice for him to have something else to wear.

There was a knock at the front door, then the sound of it opening. Fox and Crash rushed into the kitchen. Atticus knelt and gave the dogs a warm welcome, which included scratches and treats.

Emma went into the living room, where she found Kate and Luke.

Without a word, Kate disappeared into the kitchen. She'd looked more sad than angry. Emma didn't know which would have been worse. Luke was very pale, but he was out of bed, a small victory under the circumstances.

"I'm not going to stay," he said, his eyes not meeting Emma's. "Mom wants to talk to you." He backed away—he was almost out the door already.

Emma wondered if he was upset that she'd told Kate the whole story about Daphne, including their having exchanged phone numbers. It seemed a small thing, given all that had happened, but in the face of feelings as raw as Luke's must be, who knew what felt important to him right now.

Emma heard murmuring she couldn't make out from the kitchen. Atticus appeared. "I thought I'd take these beasts for a walk. Luke, care to join me?"

Emma was surprised when Luke looked pleased, even giving Atticus a ghost of a smile. He retrieved the leashes from the front closet, and within a minute the two men were gone and the house was very quiet.

Emma found Kate filling a plate with scrambled eggs and fruit.

She joined her at the table with a cup of tea. "That seemed promising," she said. "Luke, up and about and going for a walk. How's he doing?"

Kate ate quickly without answering, then got up and scooped the last of the eggs from the frying pan onto her plate.

Emma gave her a disapproving look without meaning to—this was supposed to be the first meal she and Atticus had together in her home.

Kate smiled. "Oh, come on. These would be cold by the time they get back. Atticus will want to make a fresh batch."

Kate was right.

Even if she hadn't been, Emma was happy her friend was talking to her again.

Small as she is, she can really eat.

But when Kate returned to the table, she lifted her fork only to put it back down without taking a bite.

"Luke and I had a long talk early this morning," she said. "When I say early, I mean in the wee hours. He's off schedule, poor thing, from the drugs they gave him. He doesn't want to take any more." She poured herself tea, having put milk in the cup first. "It's been a lot for him. The problems of last summer, the trauma he's still dealing with from that, and now this bonnie lass. It's too much."

Emma watched Kate closely. She knew her well enough to be sure this was the warm-up for something important she wanted to say.

"I've decided he needs a fresh start. To get away and have everything be different. At least for a while. I'm taking him back to Ireland, Emma. It has to be done."

Emma felt her stomach clench. She couldn't believe it.

She didn't want to believe it.

"The thing about owning your own business is it makes money even if you're not there," Kate said, as though filling the space with more words might ease the sharpness of her news. "Rainbow Alley is doing well enough, and you know Jillian, the head teacher. She can handle everything."

"What about Luke's school?" Emma asked. "He's doing so well. And Vivian, what about Vivian?" Vivian was the governor's granddaughter, who Luke and Emma had saved from a kidnapping last August. Four years old now, she and Luke were an atypical but closely bonded pair of friends. He saw her frequently at Rainbow Alley, where she was enrolled in the preschool. Emma knew those encounters would happen less often now that Luke was interning at the commission, but she couldn't imagine the two not spending time together at all. "She'll miss him terribly," Emma said.

I'll miss him terribly. I'll miss you terribly was what Emma was really thinking, and she knew Kate knew it. But she fought to keep her tears at bay, and as quickly as she'd raised objections— and she had many more—she stopped.

Kate wouldn't do this on a whim.

Kate didn't do anything on a whim, ever. She wasn't impulsive like Emma was. If Kate had decided this was the best thing for Luke, it was because she had thought every element of it through, even in this short period of time.

"They have schools in Ireland too, you know. Good ones," Kate said. "He and Vivian will keep up with video chats and all the miracles of the virtual world." The heartiness in Kate's voice was forced when she added, "You and Luke will stay close that way too, Emma. We all will. Across the world isn't what it used to be."

Emma asked, "When will you go?"

"Today. Our flight's at six PM. We'll be leaving for the airport at two."

Emma was stunned. Taser-level 50,000-volt stunned. She pictured her body jerking and writhing from the force of it, though she knew the only outer evidence of the hit she'd taken was the color she felt draining from her face.

She hadn't wanted to argue, she wanted to be supportive, but she found her lips moving and words coming out against her will.

"Today? The tickets must cost a fortune. And what about Breno? What does he think of all this? He can't leave his job with the mayor."

Kate looked Emma squarely in the eyes. "Breno is one of the reasons I'm going, Emma. I didn't think of calling him to be with me yesterday in what was one of the worst moments of my life, when I feared for my boy's sanity, when I thought Luke's heart might be broken. I thought of you right away. I messaged you in real time. I didn't think of Breno."

A friendship built over seven years was a very high standard to hold a new relationship to, and Emma was about to say so when Kate said, "Breno's a good man. And I wanted so badly to have everything I thought I'd missed out on, having Luke when I was so young. A marriage, a second parent for him."

That stung a little. Emma thought she'd become that for Luke.

But she knew what Kate meant.

"You know this as well as I do. Those aren't the things that really matter. If I find them someday, I'll be happy, I will. But Breno and me? It's not right, Emma. It was good, but it wasn't right."

Emma nodded.

She guessed she'd known that.

"The tickets are from Torg. It doesn't cost him anything."

At first, it flashed through Emma's mind, though she had the good sense not to say it, that those tickets were a wedding gift or at least an engagement gift.

Weren't you supposed to return those things if the wedding was off?

Never having been engaged or married, Emma didn't know.

But when she took a moment, she felt sure—as an ethics investigator—that what mattered was whether the giver of the gift wanted it back. And Anthony wouldn't begrudge Kate taking her boy to give him a chance to breathe after he'd found a murdered young woman he'd hoped to get to know. Emma couldn't swear Anthony Torgetti was a romantic, but based on the several hours she'd spent with him in commission interviews, he seemed a decent sort, and this was as much about decency as it was about anything else.

She heard the door open again, then Atticus helping to get the dogs in before telling Luke he was going back to the studio. Kate stood and busied herself rinsing the dishes.

Emma went into the living room. Luke was on his knees, his face buried in Crash's fur. Emma remembered him doing just that when the big dog had first appeared as a stray on her doorstep and Luke had begged Kate to keep him.

When he looked up and saw Emma, Luke rose and wrapped her in his arms, in the same tight hug. She could feel his tears damp on her neck. When he finally let go and stepped back, his face looked so young.

She didn't think he had any idea what he wanted. The idea of escape must be both appealing and terrifying to him.

The adult in the room, she reminded herself. *You have to be the adult in the room.*

"I'll visit," she said, keeping her voice steady if not upbeat. "No, it will be more than a visit. I'll come stay for a while."

She heard footsteps from the kitchen.

Kate went around Emma to Luke's side.

The three of them stood in silence until Emma broke it.

"Love lasts," was all she could think to say to them.

But as she looked at the two most important people in her life and knew they were preparing to leave her, Emma wondered if it really did. And if it didn't, whether she could survive this.

51

Second Chance Café

JACKIE O HADN'T arrived yet, so Alibi ordered for both of them.
"That's a large black coffee, a bottle of ginger kombucha, and two maple scones," the barista confirmed.

Alibi nodded.

"Name?" she asked.

"Al," Alibi said.

"Like Al Franken?" she asked.

"Sure."

Not the reference he would have chosen. He tried to think of another well-known Al that someone in their twenties would have heard of. He couldn't come up with one. He'd have to work on that. He'd given up using his name, since repeating "Alibi" over and over again, spelling it, and saying, "No, it's not a joke," had gotten tiresome.

He grabbed a table outside near the door so he would be easy to spot. Their order had been delivered, and he'd just taken his first sip of coffee when Jackie O appeared. Her hair fell in soft waves around her face. Her eyes were clear and bright. Some days she made Alibi feel remarkably old and tired at forty-three.

"I ordered for you to save us time," he said. He knew she liked kombucha. It was the scone that was the risk—they were out of blueberry.

"Thank you. I appreciate your making good on our bet." Jackie O smiled. "You look tired."

Alibi shrugged. He wasn't thrilled to hear he looked as bad as he felt. Still, he supposed failing to save a young woman from murder had that effect on him. "I overdid the coffee yesterday, so I didn't sleep well."

She eyed the large mug in front of him. "Hair of the dog?"

"Something like that." He took another sip and decided to get down to work. "I'm speaking with Clive Carter over in arson later today and will check whether he has any objections to our getting a sketch artist to meet with Theresa at the storage facility to help us identify our possible victim."

Jackie O set down her bottle of kombucha. "That might not be necessary. I have a friend, Gerry, on the county homeless out-reach team. Based on the location and the description, he's pretty sure he knows the guy."

"Does he have a photo we can take to Theresa to confirm?"

"No photo, but he says there's no encampment down there, so there's not much chance of a mix-up over who it is. Name he gave is William Bowers. Bowers is a veteran, fifty-two years old. No history of violence, no drug issues. He's got PTSD and gets claustrophobic, so he avoids the shelters. Gerry says Bowers would have accepted get-ting inside somewhere warm at night if he could be alone."

"What do you think?" Alibi asked. "Bowers was in the wrong place at the wrong time? An accidental death?"

Jackie O had just taken her first bite of maple scone. After swallowing it, she said, "It's good. A nice change from blueberry. As for Bowers, there doesn't seem to be a reason for anyone to have targeted him. No drugs, no gangs. Nothing."

"Could he be our arsonist?" Alibi asked.

"At fifty-two, with no priors? Seems unlikely. Why set fire to the place that had kept him warm for two nights?"

Alibi nodded. She might not realize it, but Jackie O sounded more like a homicide detective every day. He followed her example and tried his scone. He concluded that making anything with real maple flavor was a good idea.

"Does arson have a motive in mind for the property damage, if that's all this is?" Jackie O asked.

"Vandalism tops Clive's list. He says in all probability it was a rank amateur—a beer bottle filled with gasoline isn't exactly state-of-the-art. And based on our interview with Theresa, no forced entry was required, since there was a broken window—easy enough to light the bottle and toss it in. A twelve-year-old could have done it." Although Alibi hoped one hadn't.

"What about ecoterrorism?" Jackie O asked. "I saw something about that online. I gather the storage franchise is part of the Clad Corp corporate empire."

"Clive passed it over to the FBI. They said no group or individual made threats or took credit related to this fire. That was good enough for Clive."

Having quickly finished his scone—they weren't very big—Alibi decided to get Jackie O's thoughts on Emma's theory for a motive in the fire.

"Items that are seized for nonpayment of storage fees at the Clad Corp facility are kept in the basement warehouse to be sorted for disposal or sale. What if one of the people who lost access to their property due to nonpayment wanted to be sure no one else saw it? Maybe they were storing something illegal or evidence of illegal activity and they didn't want it to go through the assessment-for-value process. Might they set a fire to destroy their own stuff?"

Jackie O looked thoughtful. "That makes sense."

"Here's a twist to it." Alibi paused and looked around. All the surrounding tables were full. "Let's check Marie's office, see if it's vacant."

He picked up his coffee. Jackie O brought her items and followed him around to the back of the café. Marie and her son, Jeff, were at the picnic table marked RESERVED in the back that she used as her office. Alibi started to turn around, but Marie saw them and waved them over.

"Hi, Alibi, Jackie O. My boy and I just finished our management meeting. The office is all yours." Marie stood, smiling, and Jeff did too.

Good people, Alibi thought, as he and Jackie O took over their seats.

Now that they had some privacy, Alibi picked up where he'd left off. "While you were busy with Theresa, I was able to take a quick look at the list of folks who've defaulted on their storage unit payments over the last sixty days."

"You didn't need a court order of some kind?" Jackie O asked.

"It was an accident," Alibi said, thinking of Irene, Clad Corp Ideal Storage facility manager by day, super spy by night. "One name was recognizable. Johnny Hill had missed a payment the month before he died, and then one the month after, which caused his property to be seized so they could rent his storage unit to someone who would pay."

Jackie O had picked up her scone again but put it back down. "So Johnny's stored items were destroyed in the fire Wednesday morning?"

"Yep. The contents were moved to the warehouse last Friday, and nothing had been removed by management for sale or to junk since then."

Alibi waited. He knew Jackie O would see the problem with the timeline relative to the motive Emma had put forth.

He didn't have to wait long.

"Johnny Hill was dead when the fire was set," Jackie O said. "That doesn't fit the scenario you've proposed." She thought for a beat. "Though he could have had a partner, still alive, who destroyed the incriminating property. Or Johnny might be the good guy in all this. Perhaps he'd gathered evidence on someone else, which motivated the arson. That could also be why Johnny was killed, because his brain was like another storage unit."

Alibi smiled. "I don't know that I would have put it that way, but yes, it would fit to have someone kill him and destroy his storage unit contents if Johnny had something on them."

"What are the next steps?" Jackie O asked, still neglecting her scone.

"Clive's biggest fear is a serial arsonist. Each day that goes by where there's not another fire with a similar MO, the better he feels. With Theresa's statement and the ID you have from your friend, Bowers' death was almost certainly accidental—there was no homicide. So it will be Clive's call regarding whether the Clad Corp case stays open." He considered what they might need to find out to convince Clive there was more to it. "Who had keys to

Johnny's unit? Irene at Ideal Storage told me every tenant is issued two keys. Did Johnny have a girlfriend or boyfriend? Did his mother have a key? We need to think about who might have known what was in that unit before Johnny's property was seized. And we can't forget, we may find that others on that list have criminal histories when we run it, which makes them look better for the arson than Johnny or anyone he knew. Coincidences are hard to accept, but they do happen."

Alibi stopped talking, since Jackie O had stopped listening. She was smiling broadly, looking past him over his shoulder.

"Look who's here," she said.

Alibi turned and saw Detective Carlos Sifuentes in jeans and a T-shirt, a day's growth of dark stubble on his face, holding a cardboard cup tray with four tall cups in one hand and a white pastry bag in the other, coming toward them from the front of the café.

"Good to see you," Carlos said. "Marie told me you were hard at work back here. This is Marc's favorite place. He swears the maple scones will give him strength to get through another sleepless night."

Alibi could see the wisdom in that.

"Are you giving the babies coffee?" Jackie O asked, her eyes on the four cups in Carlos's cardboard carrier. "I think that's frowned upon."

"What? Oh no, two cups for each of us, one for now and one for later," Carlos said, grinning. "The Second Chance brew is much better than what we have at home." He set the bag and the carrier on the table and took his phone from his pocket. "Here they are."

Alibi looked at the two apple-cheeked, smiling, toothless faces, framed by black curls, on Carlos's phone screen.

Cute.

"This is Rosa, named for my abuelita, my grandmother, and this is Ruthie, named for Marc's nanna. Our daughters have their own birth names as their middle names. Meet Rosa Dolly and Ruthie Jolene."

Alibi really liked those names. He thought it would almost be worth having twins to give them those names.

He couldn't tell if Rosa Dolly and Ruthie Jolene were identical or not. He decided not to ask, because Carlos's monologue in response would almost certainly take the time Alibi still needed to talk to Jackie O.

Jackie O asked Carlos, "How does Donnie like having baby sisters?"

Donnie was Carlos and Marc's very busy three-year-old.

"He thinks they're great. It's better than TV. The two of them keep him entertained. Even when they cry, he runs around trying to think of things to cheer them up and makes funny faces."

"I hope you and Marc will bring them to the office soon. I have a baby gift waiting," Alibi said, by way of closing the impromptu visit. Although he did have gifts to give. He'd bought two bright-yellow toddler-size sweaters, one with a lamb on the front and the other with a bunny, from Bubble Belly in nearby Davis. The owner had told him it was best to give the little ones room to grow.

"Definitely," Carlos said. "I better get back. Marc says I have to spend as much time with our girls now that I can so they won't forget me when my paternity leave is up." He waved and walked briskly away.

No strolling for that guy. Alibi thought he could use some of that energy. He lifted his coffee cup to find it empty, but intent upon a good night's sleep tonight, he resisted the temptation to go back for a refill.

"You were saying?" Jackie O said.

Alibi collected his thoughts—he wished he had a whiteboard. "Let's suppose Johnny Hill was murdered, which our witness, Bee, gives us reason to at least consider. We know from the Clad Corp records that Johnny Hill had a storage unit, the contents of which were destroyed in a suspicious fire. The murder came first by more than a month. What might be the trail that gets us from one to the other?"

Jackie O was quiet.

"Until we have an answer, we'll want to keep all the balls in play," he said, hoping to encourage her to think as far afield and as creatively as she could.

"What about the young woman who was shot yesterday?" Jackie O asked. "Didn't that take place near the storage facility? Do we have access to her things to see if she had a unit there, perhaps a key?"

Alibi felt another strong pang of regret for not having pre-vented Daphne's death. "I don't know. I think forensics has been to her apartment. Let's see if they're ready for visitors." He made a call. "Tomorrow morning," he told Jackie O. "First thing. We can meet there at nine AM if you're up for an early-morning city bike ride. Daphne was subletting a short-term rental at a condo com-plex in Midtown."

52

Matchbook Lane

WHEN KATE AND Luke left to prepare for their departure, Emma decided to do the only thing she thought a sane and reasonable adult could do under the circumstances: go back to bed. She'd asked Atticus to take the dogs to the studio so she could grieve in peace, but he'd protested that given the break-in yesterday, it didn't make sense for her to stay by herself in the main house. He had a point, and she appreciated his concern, so the dogs stayed with her.

Crash refused to leave the front window.

When Luke had returned to pick up the trunk Emma was contributing to his luggage needs for Ireland, the big dog had howled piteously, producing a sound Emma had never heard him make. He seemed as concerned as Emma about being permanently abandoned by the teen.

Fox was upset because she took her cues regarding the state of the world from Crash, though there might have been more to it. Luke had always been the least likely to push her off him when she was having a lapdog moment. The puppy alternated between lying on the floor next to Crash and whimpering and jumping on Emma's bed, where she was not allowed.

Whether Emma would have been able to fall asleep absent Fox's gymnastics was doubtful, but she certainly couldn't under the circumstances. She got up and made more tea. Dr. Branco would have been proud of her post-smoke-inhalation fluid intake. That might be the only thing she was going to get right today.

Her laptop and tablet both having been taken in the break-in, the sole internet access Emma had was via her phone. But when she brought it to the kitchen table with the intention of finding something silly and entertaining to numb her pain, she remembered that her handwritten notes on the tunnel project were also gone.

Recreating the concise record she'd had on her wall of the key elements of that investigation might not have made most people's *This is what I'll do to feel better* top-ten list, but it was appealing to Emma.

She would largely be retreading old ground, so she wouldn't need to be creative, just attentive, and diverting her attention from Kate and Luke's move was the best she could hope for right now.

She started with reviewing the files on the Community Fund, since that had garnered Sid's interest, and Sid's knowledge of contract fraud and corruption, given his years at the IRS, dwarfed hers. She might as well let him point the way to where she should start rebuilding her outline.

Instead of going through the commission's server with its multiple interfaces as she would have done if she'd had her work tablet, on her phone she had to navigate directly to the Community Fund's own streamlined site. On its home page were images of each of the three train stations that had benefited from upgrades paid for by the Community Fund account—Oakland, San Francisco, and Sacramento.

Emma clicked on Sacramento and was immediately rewarded with the identical thumbnail images she'd seen in Sid's office on his computer.

There was accompanying text she'd not been able to read before Sid closed the window down.

LHD Designs has been awarded $1 million from the Trans-Bay Tunnel Community Fund to remodel and revamp Patio Station, a popular historic outdoor café and restaurant at the Sacramento Train Station that had fallen into disrepair. While preserving the original surrounding angled stone wall

*that makes the Station Patio a unique and architecturally
dynamic space, the upgrade includes new natural slate floor-
ing, drought-resistant plantings to shade and beautify the setting, and custom-made furnishings. The work on Patio
Station is well under way and will be completed in time for
the celebration of the new station's opening on March 15th!*

Emma sat back in her chair.

She'd gone with Fran to Patio Station only two months ago,
and Fran had said how sad she was that it wouldn't be open much
longer. Fran had frequented the spot for years, enabling her to get
away from capitol insiders, since Patio Station's clientele was largely
tourists. According to Fran, it was slated to close because it was at
the opposite end of the rail yards from the new terminal and lacked
convenient parking. Even before that, its business had taken a nose
dive when the cleanup of the Clad Corp toxic site, located only a
fifteen-minute walk from Patio Station, had been made public.

No one wanted invisible chemical waste, real or imagined,
blowing over their burgers. The café had been nearly deserted the
day Fran and she were there.

Emma tried to put the information from her visit with Fran
together with what she'd just read on the Community Fund site,
where it stated that the renovation and remodel of Patio Station
was "well under way."

How far under way could the remodel be if it hadn't begun
two months ago? And how could Fran, who was a regular there,
be under the mistaken assumption the restaurant was closing forever? Wouldn't Patio Station management have hung banners and
shouted from the rooftops that their business was getting new life?

Speaking of new life, Emma's energy returned, and she leapt
into action. One of the reasons she was so good at her job as an
ethics investigator was that she genuinely enjoyed puzzling
through real-life problems to protect taxpayer money from misuse
and abuse.

She messaged Hailey and asked her to set up a video meeting
with Nick and Malia as soon as they were available, preferably
now.

Then Emma went to her bedroom, pulled off the T-shirt she'd
slept in, and put on a sky-blue suit jacket.

From there, she hurried to her home office, where she sat in the location she used for her professional Zoom calls, in front of a bookcase filled with policy tomes and a few favorite novels, with flattering lighting from above.

She set the phone in a hands-free holder, making sure it was angled so she was visible only from the waist up, since she was still wearing her *Go Cal Bears* college sweatpants.

She completed her preparations just in time, as Malia's and Nick's faces came into view on the screen from the second-floor bullpen at commission headquarters.

"Good morning," Emma said. "Malia, the oversight issues you flagged with the Community Fund have me concerned about a specific project. I want to know what work has been completed on it and what, if any, funds have been paid out to the contractor to date. It's the Patio Station upgrade for the old terminal at the Sacramento station. The designated recipient is . . ." Emma paused. She couldn't navigate back to that screen without taking her phone out of the holder. "You'll be able to find it. I want a deep dive into this. Any questions?"

Malia said, "I know the contract you're talking about. It's LHD Designs."

Nick said, "I can look into that company. I'm sure all the relevant information is accessible online."

"Excellent," Emma said. "Thank you, Nick, and would you let Sid know what you're looking for? If we find any hints of contract fraud, Sid will know how to get to the bottom of it quickly and thoroughly." She didn't think it necessary to tell Nick and Malia she'd been snooping in Sid's office, peering over his shoulder at his monitor, so she knew he was already curious about the Community Fund. "I'd like you to make this a top priority," she said, employing her *We're wrapping up now* tone.

Malia asked, "Is Monday okay for a report?" Half of her face was out of view. The screen was filled mostly by her frizzy hair, but Emma could hear her clearly.

"Monday's fine. I'll go to the site today. That's going to be the easiest way to see what we're dealing with."

Then she thought of Kate and Luke's six PM flight.

She wanted to be available to help with any last-minute preparations, if Kate would let her. And if Kate was having doubts about her decision to go, Emma wanted to be able to talk it through with her. She didn't believe that was likely, but neither could she foreclose the slim chance of it happening.

"Amend that. I'll do a site visit to Patio Station tomorrow morning. If you find out anything that will help me to prepare, please shoot it over tonight or early tomorrow. My commission tablet and my personal laptop were stolen in a break-in at my home yesterday, so I'm available by phone only."

"That's terrible," Nick said. "Are the police on top of it?" His voice had risen, and his face was flushed. The half of Malia's face that Emma could see also appeared shocked.

"I've made a police report. Malia, would you ask Hailey to get started on getting me a replacement tablet? Nick, don't forget to tell Sid we're looking at Patio Station and I'd like his urgent help. If he's out of the office, ask Hailey. She'll give you his cell to call him. I want him on this in real time."

If it had been Malia, she wouldn't have given the reminder, but Nick was new, and good as he seemed to be, she was still unsure of him.

Sharp staccato barks on the other side of her home office door let Emma know Fox was calling the meeting to a close.

"That's it. Thank you both," she said.

Nick said, "Have a nice weekend. I hope you're doing something fun."

That annoyed Emma. She wasn't sure why. Maybe it was because she felt Nick shouldn't offer his opinion about how she should spend her weekend, not even a vague and generic one. Though she knew it was far more likely that her annoyance stemmed from the fact that, with Kate and Luke leaving, "fun" was definitely not on the agenda anytime soon.

EMMA DIDN'T THINK she had ever felt this alone. It was seven in the evening, and the high she'd experienced from initiating an investigation into the Patio Station remodel had long since worn off. She'd made herself yet another cup of mint tea and sat at her kitchen table with no intention of drinking it.

She avoided the living room, where Crash sat stoically and heartbreakingly at the front window, watching for Luke. Even Fox had quieted, the duration of Crash's change in mood apparently having impressed upon the puppy the gravity of their situation.

Atticus had gone to San Francisco to finally get his things from the hotel. Emma hadn't had it in her to make good on her offer to drive him—just getting out of a chair was an effort. But before she could say anything, he'd told her that he'd bought a train ticket, knowing she would want to be at home and available for Kate and Luke, since they might need her before they left.

Emma wished that had turned out to be the case. But Kate, as though to ward off the possibility that Emma might show up on the doorstep to the duplex to offer help, had messaged Emma to let her know, though not in so many words, that one good-bye had been enough. She'd told Emma it would be too hard for Luke to see her again before they left. But knowing her best friend as well as she did, Emma thought Kate was worried she wouldn't follow through on moving halfway across the world if Emma had an opportunity to dissuade her.

Emma didn't believe she would have done that. She'd decided to respect Kate's choice, which she knew must be difficult enough as it was. Still, for Emma, one good-bye had not been enough.

Not nearly enough.

She inventoried her losses. First and foremost, Kate and Luke. Next, her laptop, her computer tablet, and her notes from the tunnel project, all of which were making her work life more difficult. Then the garnet-and-gold necklace, the only keepsake she'd had of her mother's. And finally, a sense of loss that Emma wouldn't have expected, since Daphne VerStrate had been a disturbing presence when alive, stemmed from that young woman's death. Emma recalled the photo of Johnny Hill and wondered whether Daphne might have already lived a magical "year and a day" with him—she hoped so—or whether both Johnny and Daphne had lost the wonderful year they'd thought was yet to come.

Emma was contemplating that when Crash's booming bark and Fox's accompanying yelps filled the room, followed by a knock on the front door.

Alibi stood on the stoop with a white paper bag in one hand and a bottle of red wine in the other. "I came to drop these off," he said loudly, to make himself heard over the chorus of barks. "Breno told me about Kate and Luke leaving."

Emma hadn't thought of Breno since Kate had said he was "a good guy, but not the right guy." She asked, "How is he?"

Alibi didn't attempt to be heard over Crash's welcome. He handed Emma the bag and the wine. She started toward the kitchen so the dogs would follow and let Alibi enter unimpeded. But when she reached the swinging door, she looked back and saw Alibi hadn't moved.

"I should go," he said. "I just wanted to make sure you had some good food."

"And alcohol?" Emma asked, with a smile she knew was sad. She was doing her best.

He shrugged and looked uncomfortable.

"No, really. Come in," she said.

He hesitated and then followed her into the kitchen. She set the bag on the counter and peeked inside.

"It's from Delicious Island Fare," he said. "All vegetarian choices."

"No Chicken Katsu?" she asked. "You really weren't planning on staying to eat. Why don't you open the wine?" she said.

He did. It was a screw top, no wine opener needed. He took two glasses from the cabinet, poured barely an inch of wine in one, and then held the bottle over the other glass with an inquiring look at Emma.

"I'll have the same as you're having," she said. "Going slow on your beverage of choice tonight?" She found her smile came a little more easily this time. But she wasn't hungry. She closed the bag, picked up her glass, and sat down.

Alibi stayed standing and said, "I'm driving."

She observed his posture.

He's going to leave. He's going to drink that one swallow of wine and walk out the door.

Emma was suddenly overwhelmed by loss. She couldn't take one more. She didn't say the words out loud, but she felt them.

Don't do it. Don't drive. Don't go.

Then without thinking—because when had doing something without thinking ever caused her a problem—she crossed to Alibi, took his face in both her hands, and kissed him with everything she had. With every ounce of desire and longing and desperation for connection pulsing through her as she felt his lips on hers, this time not lightly.

No holding back. None at all!

Not until she realized that Alibi might not be responding.

That Alibi definitely was not responding.

She stepped away from him. She felt her face flush bright red.

"It's a good idea," Alibi said gently. "For another night."

He reached for her hands, but she pulled them behind her back and took a second step away.

"I have a rule—" he began.

She interrupted him.

"Don't."

She knew he was about to say something chivalrous and upstanding like *I won't screw a woman who just lost her best friend.*

She didn't want to hear it.

She didn't want to be "a woman" to whom *any* rule applied.
He said, "Got it," and turned to go.
His face had been unreadable.
Emma wondered if there was any way to salvage this.
She couldn't think of one.

SATURDAY, MARCH 13

54

The Station

THE MAN HAD been lucky. He knew that.

Getting the call yesterday to let him know his work was being scrutinized had given him time to come here and set things up. Others might have been too tired at this hour, but it was no hardship for him. He wouldn't have gone to sleep yet regardless.

He was fortunate to have found exactly what he needed.

He circled the trailer a second time.

It was a bonus that this site had been deemed too toxic from the waste left behind by Clad Corp to put the new terminal here. The big, bright skull-and-crossbones poison signs that had not yet been taken away, despite the completion of the cleanup, would surely deter any witnesses. Yet it was walking distance from the Patio Station restaurant.

Perfect.

People liked simple stories where the pieces fit together, and this would give them that. He stashed the backpack behind an identifiable tree, one with striations on the bark near the bottom that he couldn't miss when he returned later that morning.

* * *

Matchbook Lane

Emma had overslept. It was almost eight AM. She'd planned to be at Patio Station by nine.

But why rush?

No one would be waiting for her.

At least she'd already walked the dogs. Afterward, she'd put them in the yard, and they weren't complaining. Crash was probably hoping Luke would show up to take him across the street, which he often did. She wondered if the big dog would ever stop waiting.

As she passed her home office, she saw the printer had a new document in the tray. Emma had never received anything external on that machine. Malia must have gotten creative and found a fax application that worked to send it there, knowing Emma had neither her laptop nor her tablet. She took the five-page printout with her to the kitchen and set it on the table next to her tea, which was steeping. She selected a peach yogurt from the refrigerator, got a spoon, and sat down to take a look.

Malia had sent an excerpt from the LHD Designs contract for the remodel of Patio Station. She'd circled the payment schedule: $250,000 due to LHD last June, another $250,000 last October, and the third and final payment of $500,000 due and payable today. Payments were to be mailed to a PO box in Sacramento. Malia had written in the margin that the first two checks had been sent and cashed. All of which meant that when Emma arrived at Patio Station today, a fabulous, fully completed, newly hardscaped, landscaped, and furnished outdoor restaurant should await her.

Why then did she have the horrible feeling that was not going to be the case, and that the $500,000 already paid might have been funneled to a bogus company that never existed, ultimately disappearing into an offshore account somewhere?

She was making several leaps to get to that disastrous conclusion, but she didn't think they were unduly large.

First, a June-to-March payment cycle meant the Patio Station upgrade was intended to be a nine-month project, an ambitious timeline. Yet no visible work had been done on the Patio Station two months ago when Fran and Emma were there.

Second, Malia had flagged concerns that consultants were overseeing other consultants on the Community Fund projects. State oversight would have meant timely and frequent site visits, but what might a consultant in that role have done? Cut corners, possibly accepted electronic transmission of "documentation" of progress, mocked up and photoshopped, showing work that had never been done?

Emma vaguely remembered Sid having held forth at one of their staff meetings regarding the prevalence of virtual company scams when he'd been at the IRS. He'd said something about there being so many, that the "smaller" thefts were written off as a loss rather than pursued, given the resources required to investigate, track, and recover any money and the dismal success rate. Would $1 million be considered a "smaller" theft? In the context of the $30 billion tunnel fund, it might.

She wished she'd listened to Sid more carefully, at least that once.

It would be helpful if Nick was able to find information on LHD Designs' corporate structure as quickly as Malia had located the contract information. Because if there was sufficient evidence of fraud and they wanted to stop payment on the final $500,000 check on the contract, they'd have to do it today.

If not, and if Emma's suspicions were correct, those funds could follow the first $500,000 out of the country via wire transfer in no time at all.

Most importantly, she hoped Nick had called Sid right away when she'd stressed to him how important it was that he do that. Because having Sid on this now, whether she liked it or not, was likely the single best chance she had of understanding whether anything unethical, corrupt, or even illegal was going on.

A drip of yogurt fell from her spoon. Emma looked down to see where it had landed. It had missed her sky-blue jacket and hit the leg of her *Go Cal Bears* sweatpants.

The yogurt stain became less of a concern to her when she realized she was still in the clothes she'd put on for her video meeting nearly twenty-four hours ago.

She'd fallen asleep in them last night.

Classy.

What was worse, it was what she'd been wearing when Alibi had shown up. No wonder she'd been irresistible to him. (*Not.*) But she found that when she thought about last night now, it didn't seem quite as bad as it had at the time, when the word *debacle* had come to mind.

Alibi had arrived planning not to stay. Not even to come inside. He'd made that clear on the doorstep. Before she'd done *anything*, he'd already decided that giving her space was the right thing to do.

When she looked at his actions in that context, it seemed that in Alibi's mind, the return of her father together with Kate's departure had left her in a fragile and vulnerable state. One that, no matter how great his desire for her, he did not want to exploit.

No Matter How Great His Desire For Her.

Emma liked that headline. Though there was a chance it was "fake news," she decided to permit herself a little hope, at least enough so that she would get up and change her clothes.

55

EMMA HAD JUST gotten out of the shower and was standing in panties and a camisole, deciding what to wear, when her phone let out a blaring sound like a foghorn. It took her a minute to remember that when she'd been promoted to investigator, she'd chosen that ringtone for Fran. Her intent had been to ensure she never missed a call from her boss.

She scrambled to pick up. "Hello, Fran?"

"Emma, thank goodness. I didn't know if I would reach you. I need to see you. Are you able to meet me now?"

"What?" Emma said. Though not impressive, it was Emma's go-to response when she wasn't sure what was happening.

"I have concerns," Fran said.

"I—" Emma said.

Before she could say anything more, Fran said, "I need to speak to you. I have information for the police. I don't want to take it to just anyone. You're close with that senior police officer with the strange name. Felony Moonbeam, something like that? Anyway, I'll speak to him. But I want to talk to you first and get your sense of how best to proceed. I appreciate your quick thinking and your integrity."

How did Fran know she was close to Alibi? Maybe through Breno?

Emma supposed that was the least important thing right now. "Of course," she said. "I can be at the office in—"

"No. Do not go to the office under any circumstances," Fran said.

"Okay," Emma said. "I was headed to Patio Station this morning to do a site visit. When you and I were there a few months ago, you may remember, you told me it was closing. That's not the case. Or maybe it is the case. Anyway, I can explain when we get there. It's something I planned to talk to you about."

Dead air.

"Fran? Are you there? Patio Station—"

"Fine. How long will it take you to get there?" Fran asked.

Her voice was flat. It didn't sound like Fran to Emma. Maybe it was a bad connection.

Emma did a quick calculation. She'd showered. She could put on jeans and a blazer and look professional enough for a Saturday. She couldn't tell if this was a work meeting, but Fran was her boss. Figuring in the short drive and parking, she told Fran she could be there in forty-five minutes.

"Does nine fifteen work?" Emma asked.

"Good," Fran said, and hung up.

Emma got dressed and was glad she had, because when she passed through the living room to get to the kitchen, she first saw Crash by the window, then Atticus sitting on the couch, making a drawing of the big dog, Fox curled up next to him. He probably had knocked and then come in while the foghorn phone was blaring.

She didn't think it worth telling him the puppy wasn't allowed up on the furniture.

Nothing was as it should be around here anymore.

"How was your trip to San Francisco?" she asked. "Did you get your things?"

Atticus didn't break his concentration on the sketchbook in front of him. She called over her shoulder as she pushed open the kitchen door, en route to making sure the kettle was off, "I have to go to the train station to meet my boss. I'll be back in an hour or two."

A minute later, Atticus came in. "Could I tag along? I won't disrupt your meeting. I'd like to do some sketches of the Sacramento train station to add to a series I'm working on. I completed one using online sources, but it would be great to see it in person."

"I'll be right back," Emma said. She hurried to her room and returned with one of the postcards she'd bought at the gallery. "Is it this one?" she asked, handing Atticus a drawing of his with the faint image of a group of diners in the foreground and, in bolder strokes, his trademark train streaking past in the distance.

"Yes. That's the old terminal, the Patio Station café. I found a photo of it in the 1960s and used it as the model."

Emma stared at it. She hadn't noticed the light outline of the Patio Station's unusual stone wall jutting out at an angle. Atticus's drawings were always more conceptual than realistic, and she'd missed it the first time. But there was no mistaking it now.

She picked up the papers Malia had sent her and flipped through to the section of the application with the images.

Emma was a midcentury furniture buff, and when she focused on the faint dining area in Atticus's drawing on the postcard, she could see the classic 1960s silhouettes and curved legs of the chairs. When she compared those to the Patio Station upgrade proposal that Malia had sent, the difference was dramatic.

The new chairs and tables were to have deep-red-painted wood frames with gold trim and seats upholstered in a distressed brown.

Her sharp intake of breath was so sudden that Atticus asked her, "Are you all right? What is it?"

Emma was having trouble accepting what she could see with her own eyes. They were Johnny's designs. Almost identical to the furnishings he'd done as prototypes for Fran's office. Just like Atticus had a style that was easy for Breno to spot, Johnny's work was distinctive too.

"Is something wrong?" Atticus asked again.

Emma managed to mumble, "It's work-related," as her mind raced through the possibilities.

The Patio Station award had been given based on Johnny Hill's designs. Would Fran have noticed Johnny's chairs in the far background of the small, busy image on the Community Fund's site? Unless she'd been specifically examining the furniture, as Emma had done, Emma thought it highly unlikely.

And what, if anything, might this have to do with Daphne, who almost certainly had been Johnny's girlfriend, and had appeared in the United States before the final $500,000 payment on that contract was due, only to be murdered days before the payment was made?

Emma tried to slow down. She was getting ahead of herself. She knew she shouldn't jump to conclusions.

A good investigator worked on facts.

And there might not be fraud here at all.

It could be that the payments for the Patio Station upgrade had occurred before the work was done for good reason. Many government funds had a ticking clock, a date at which they "expired" and if not spent were returned to the state. To avoid that kind of forfeiture, if the work was planned in good faith, lump-sum payments in advance of fund expiration were not uncommon.

To follow the money, she would need to speak to the consultants responsible for oversight of the Patio Station contract as well as representatives of LHD Designs.

It might all be innocent.

A lot would turn on what Nick was able to find out about LHD.

She'd been lost in her thoughts when she realized Atticus was still looking at her with concern.

"Is there a reason you don't want me to come with you?" he asked.

She'd completely forgotten about his request.

She thought for a beat. Fran had sounded agitated, but Atticus didn't need to sit with them. He'd be off somewhere sketching.

"It would be nice if you came," she told him. And she meant it. She was terrible at this whole "work-life balance" thing. Maybe that was one of the reasons she hadn't been able to keep Kate and Luke here, because as much as she loved them, she had often (always?) put her work first. She had to do better.

"But we need to leave soon," she told him.

"Right away," Atticus said. "Just let me get my sketch pad and charcoal. I bought replacement supplies yesterday."

56

The Station

T HE MAN WAS pleased that a corporation accused of crimes against the world's climate would be at the center of the news coverage of the events today. Just yesterday he'd seen a great blue heron at the edge of the river. Four feet tall with bright-yellow eyes, it had stabbed a steelhead bass with its sharp beak and then shook the fish to break its spine, making it easier to swallow.

By drawing attention to those who ruined the great bird's habitat, even if it was only a side benefit on the way to his ultimate goal, he would be doing his part to keep the cycle of life and death on earth in balance.

Time was on his side. He would finish it all today.

Eliminating the girl had been difficult emotionally.

Though it had made him appreciate the value of firearms.

He'd never been one for guns. He hadn't understood the attraction. Not until he'd discovered, firsthand, that if a target was close, extensive gun-handling experience was not required to have a successful outcome. Of course, watching a few instructional videos on YouTube and familiarizing himself with the weapon had increased his odds of a good result significantly.

The man wore a plain black T-shirt, a brown eighties-style thrift shop blazer with big pockets, and unattractive shiny blue dress pants, along with an oversized black ball cap without a logo, pulled down low on his forehead. He had on his own running shoes—he might require speed, so he'd opted to skip the false flair in his footwear.

The finishing touch would be a pair of large black women's sunglasses. He didn't need those yet, not here among the trees.

They said clothes made the man, but in this case he was counting on them to unmake him. It might not be true that his own mother wouldn't recognize him in this getup, but Emma Lawson, the woman who mattered now even more than his mother, wouldn't know him until it was too late.

He pulled out his pocket binoculars and waited.

* * *

By any definition, Emma had a lot on her mind. But with the top down on the Mustang, the mild, cool weather, and the morning breeze, she was reminded that she lived in a beautiful place where good things could and would happen.

Although maybe not today.

She didn't want to be overly optimistic.

Atticus had closed his eyes. She didn't know if he was asleep or just resting them. She smiled when she thought of their drive back from San Francisco only three nights ago. He'd fallen asleep then. This car seemed to have that effect on him. Fortunately, the cloudless blue sky above showed no signs of repeating its performance of waking him with lightning and buckets of rain.

As she rounded the turn on Fifth Street, she found she was glad not to have to make conversation. Though she'd wanted to hold off on analyzing the Patio Station contract until she'd gotten the facts that were easily obtainable at the site, a new wrinkle, a potentially serious one, had occurred to her.

If there was corruption and fraud in this project, and if Johnny had been a willing participant, was it possible Fran had been too? Had she partnered with him somehow?

She looked at it from a few angles and felt able to dismiss that possibility quickly. Because the only gain in this scam was money. A total of $1 million.

And Fran's extensive wealth was public knowledge. She'd shared her tax returns openly as a senator and again as mayor.

She came from money, and she'd never lost it. She'd made smart investments and been cautious with her spending. She owned several expensive homes.

Fran Hill's net worth was estimated at $22 million.

As important as the fact that the money wouldn't be life changing for her—far from it—was that the risk of losing everything she had worked for would have been crushing and real. Fran had devoted her life to building her personal and political power. Being associated with having defrauded the government, even on a relatively small scale, would destroy all that, beginning with killing her chances for a congressional seat.

Emma pulled into the recently opened new parking garage for the station, and Atticus opened his eyes.

"We're there already?" he said, smiling in a guileless way that almost made her ready to trust him again.

"Yes. Although we're in the garage connected to the new terminal. We'll have a fair walk to get to Patio Station, if you're coming with me to that end."

They emerged in the open air to a vibrant scene of commuters, tourists, and local residents ambling and strolling and racing to and from trains, the new food court, and a posh indoor restaurant that the sign said was serving "a fabulous brunch" at this hour.

Atticus carried a large backpack.

"What's in there?" she asked him.

"You know," he said. "Sketch pads, a foldable easel, drawing supplies."

She noticed he was wearing different clothes, and she'd bet they weren't Luke's. Not that they had an old-man vibe, but they were classic rather than current: a plain brown V-neck sweater over a white dress shirt and dark-blue jeans that were just the right length for his Vans skate shoes.

It looked like he really had gone to the hotel to get his things.

The crowd thinned out noticeably the farther they walked.

They still had a ways to go, but Emma could see that once they got through the last scattered cyclists, pedestrians, and dog walkers passing the old terminal, it was deserted at the end where Patio Station stood.

Atticus asked her, "Have you heard anything from the police about your missing property?"

Emma said, "No."

"I found it terrifying that you might have been home during that break-in," Atticus said.

Emma wasn't used to having someone feel protective toward her.

Unless she counted Alibi thinking not making love to her last night had been protective in some way.

Emma decided now was as good a time as any to raise with Atticus the difficult topic she'd had on her mind. Or at least one of them. "Last night, I was reading about addiction. Opioid addiction."

Atticus stiffened, or maybe that was her imagination.

"I thought about Mom. I don't know what I might be remembering wrong or what I might have missed, since I was just a kid when she died. But was she addicted to her prescription drugs? It seems like her behaviors, the extreme ups and downs, sometimes had an almost desperate quality, which might not only have been the pain."

Atticus didn't look at her when he answered, but his voice was clear and unwavering. "Yes, your mother was addicted to drugs."

Emma's stomach dropped. He had just expanded the possibilities, and she could only assume he'd done that intentionally. She looked overhead to make sure the sky was still blue and the sun was still shining.

"Not only prescription drugs?" she asked, her voice small.

"Not only," he said.

Emma flashed back on that last day before Atticus left. When she hadn't known he was going. She'd said she wanted to see her mother's "final resting place." She'd heard that phrase, and she wanted to be able to think of her mother as asleep and peaceful. Not just gone.

There'd been no trip to the hospital after Emma had found Margaret on the kitchen floor, in great pain but alive. There'd been no funeral and no memorial, just a rushed cremation that only Atticus had attended.

Emma had seen it in the movies, kids going to visit a grave or reverentially touching the silver urn where their parent's ashes were kept. But the only memory she had of her mother's death was how sad Atticus had looked.

Now she wondered.

Sad or something else? Guilty?

They were almost to the end of the old terminal.

Emma saw a couple and a man at the outdoor café, but she didn't see Fran. She stopped walking and looked Atticus square in the eyes—eyes so like the ones she'd inherited from him.

"Did Mom die of a drug overdose, not a heart attack?" she asked him.

"No," he said. "This is a longer conversation than we can have right now."

"Do you promise you'll have that conversation with me?" she asked. "Before you leave?"

His eyes filled with tears, and he looked away.

She couldn't remember ever having seen him cry. Not even when Margaret had died.

But Emma was not letting him off the hook.

She'd waited twenty-two years, and who knew how long she'd have to wait again if she didn't get the answers to her questions now? "Tomorrow?" she asked. "Can we talk about where you've been and why you left? Tomorrow?"

CHAPTER

57

"T OMORROW?" EMMA ASKED again.

"Yes," was all Atticus said.

But he held her gaze after that one word, and she knew it was as good as a signed and sealed promise.

Tomorrow we will talk.

They stood together silently until Emma spotted Fran at a table at the edge along the back of the patio. She must have arrived while Emma was focused on her conversation with Atticus.

Emma turned her attention to the task at hand. She'd always been good at compartmentalizing, walling herself off into work when it served to keep her steady. To keep her sane.

Patio Station was bigger than she remembered it, or maybe the partial images she'd been viewing had caused her to forget its actual size. It would clearly seat more than fifty when full, but there were few tables set up in the broad expanse of space now, and only three were occupied.

Emma looked at her watch, and the thought of Kate wearing her matching BFF timepiece in Dublin as she made her way cross-country to the coast of Galway with Luke was almost too much for Emma to bear.

She turned to Atticus. "That's my boss," she said, pointing her out.

Atticus had unzipped his backpack and appeared to be check-ing his supplies. It looked like his mind was already on his art. He seemed to Emma to have come to terms more easily with the date they'd made with the truth than she had.

She decided that was likely good.

It could mean the things he'd tell her wouldn't be that bad.

He zipped up his bag and said, pointing, "I'll walk down there, along the old tracks. It should provide a good perspective of the two terminals that will make for some interesting lines in charcoal." He squinted in the distance. "There are a lot of signs. Is it accessible?"

Emma followed his gaze. "Yes. Those mark a toxic clean-up site."

Atticus took a step back, as though the toxins, whatever they were, might reach him where they stood.

"The cleanup has been completed," she clarified. "It looks like they haven't formally opened it yet for public access, but I'm sure it's safe. Reviewing it was part of my work at the commission. My guess is they'll take any construction equipment and the signs away before the governor's VIP event next Tuesday, even though that's being held at the opposite end, where we started, at the new terminal."

The site where Atticus planned to draw was about a fifteen-minute walk from Patio Station.

"Did you ever get a charger for your phone?" Emma asked him.

"What do you mean, ever?" he asked. "I've only been here three days. The answer is no to the charger, but I do have a working phone. I bought a burner, I think they call them. A prepaid phone where you can add minutes. Do you want the number?"

"No, I'm about to be late," Emma said. "Fran's not a patient person. I'll walk over and find you when Fran and I are done. If you're going to leave the toxic site"—she stopped and smiled at him—"come by and let me know."

When Emma reached Fran, she saw that she looked no better than she had when Emma met with her on Wednesday in her office. But her silver hair gleamed in the morning sun, and the genuine smile she gave Emma brightened her tired features. She wore a black lightweight sweater and black pants that flattered her thin figure.

"I want to do this quickly," Fran said.

She seemed very nervous. She had nothing to eat or drink in front of her.

"Should I get us coffee or herbal tea?" Emma asked, thinking Fran could use a dose of chamomile. "It's counter service inside, isn't it?"

"No, it's okay. They won't bother us. It's not busy on this end of the terminal anymore. I wanted the privacy."

Well, you got that.

There were a total of six people at Patio Station, counting them. One elderly couple sat far to their left with a young adult with them who looked like he might be their son; they had similar coloring and body types. Another man sat alone near the back wall to their right. The threesome had plates in front of them that looked nearly empty. The man had only coffee.

Fran picked up a large brown leather bag from next to her feet, put it on her lap, and removed a folder from it.

So this is work.

But seeing how worn and stressed Fran looked and thinking about the older couple she'd just observed with their grown child, Emma suddenly had a terrible thought.

Fran would not have been motivated by money to defraud the Community Fund. The cost to her reputation if she were found out would be much too high. *But what might Fran have done to cover up that fraud if she thought it could be linked to her through her son?*

Emma flashed on the Clad Corp storage unit key with Johnny's name on it in Daphne VerStrate's backpack. If Johnny had failed to make his payments—and of course he had; *he was dead*—and if Fran knew of the Patio Storage fraud and of Johnny's designs at the heart of it, she had the motivation that she and Alibi had discussed: to destroy whatever it was in Johnny's storage unit that implicated him in the fraud and, by extension, if discovered, would ruin Fran politically.

Emma looked at the folder Fran set on the table between them and at Fran's narrowed, crystal-blue eyes, which struck her as both defensive and calculating.

In that moment, Emma knew she was right.

Fran had called to meet her today, had said she needed her help, not because Fran had committed fraud.

But because Fran had committed arson.

58

O NCE EMMA HAD landed on it, it was the only thing that made sense. Fran would not have wanted the press or the public to know her only son had committed a million dollars' worth of government fraud, especially not fraud on a project that Fran's commission was investigating. At a minimum, it would cost her her job, and it would most likely end her political career.

For that, Emma could see Fran committing property destruction in a heartbeat.

She sat fascinated and appalled as Fran took two bottled waters from her bag.

Fran unscrewed the cap of one of the bottles and put it in front of Emma. Emma found herself considering whether it might be poisoned. Then Fran pulled the open bottle back toward her and took a long drink.

So, not poisoned.

Still, Emma realized she had to determine whether she was in danger with Fran, since Fran must have called her here because she knew she'd been found out. Most likely, Sid, wanting brownie points, or Nick or Malia had revealed to her that Emma's team was looking into the Patio Station project.

Yet even with her crime about to be an open secret between them, Fran did not shy away from eye contact. Emma could feel her watching her as she weighed the facts and the odds.

Fran had been in the public eye for nearly two decades. She had no history of violence of any kind. Emma had known Fran in the workplace for four years, first as an analyst and then as an investigator. She'd spent hundreds of hours with her. And it wasn't an overstatement to say that Emma owed Fran her career.

But would she stake her life on Fran not being a killer?

Emma gave it a moment and decided that she would. She stayed in her seat. "Tell me what you've come to say," she said.

Fran nodded and began to talk in what sounded like a prepared speech, rehearsed so she would get the words right.

"Johnny was talented." She opened the folder, and the same image Emma had been looking at from so many angles came into view. The Patio Station remodel, but blown up to full size.

Fran didn't look down at it. She looked at Emma, and when she saw no surprise registered there, she continued. "I got to an age where I wanted a child, or at least thought I should want a child. That was more common in my generation than it is in yours. I made use of a sperm bank—only the best—had Johnny, and continued to pursue my political career as I always had. Giving him whatever he needed, except for time with me. You likely have seen some stories criticizing me for my parenting, linking that to depressive incidents Johnny had in high school."

Fran seemed suddenly smaller. Emma had compassion for her, but it didn't extend very far, and it wouldn't until she knew exactly what Fran had done.

Fran lifted Johnny's design page from the top of the folder and moved it to the bottom, revealing a sheet dense with text. It was the information Malia had prepared with her questions about the Community Fund. Emma had given the document to Fran twice, once last week and again on Wednesday. Each time Fran had shown a distinct lack of interest.

"You have a smart team, Emma. Especially Malia. She was quite right that the oversight of the thirty million in the Community Fund was woefully inadequate. With three different stations to upgrade, Sacramento, San Francisco, and Oakland, and a goal of involving as many community organizations as possible, the selection process and the monitoring of results were shoddy. Consultants were overseeing other consultants, and the usual state contracting rules that help to make things transparent and ethical were not followed. In this appendix you gave me were several interesting projects. When I saw one to remodel and redesign this very outdoor seating area, I was curious, since I've been coming here for years. There was an IT glitch, so I couldn't get to the Patio Station application from the commission server, but I was able to go in directly to that site." Fran again pulled out the one page with Johnny's designs and set it next to Malia's memo. "This is what I found, which I recognized as being drawn by my son. I read through the signed contract and discovered that five hundred thousand had been paid to LHD Designs with another five hundred thousand due at the close of the project, which interestingly enough, is today." Fran looked around. "Yet as you can see, no work has been done." She folded her hands atop the stack of papers. "This is a fraudulent project start to finish, and had Malia dug a little deeper, she would have unearthed the rot at the core of it. There is no LHD Designs firm in real life. Someone created a virtual company that did virtual work but got real money for it."

Fran had just admitted that Johnny had committed a million-dollar fraud before his death. She'd been dispassionate about it.

Emma thought it hadn't been all that hard for Fran because the part that mattered was yet to come.

The part where Fran would get to talk about how it had affected her.

CHAPTER

59

EMMA CONSIDERED RISKING a drink from the other water bottle, still closed, but decided against it. She didn't believe Fran was a killer, but she also saw no reason to test that theory personally.

"While I'm not clear on all of the machinations that produced this fraud, I do know that the million-dollar award would not have been made possible without my Johnny's designs." Fran was unable to hide her pride in her son's talent, even in the context of a criminal enterprise. "I didn't know about it, of course, when he died. I didn't know any of it until you gave me Malia's report last week, which just scratched the surface, but which led me to the application and the contract and to my conclusion that my son had been a criminal." She took a long gulp of her water. "As you know, I have aspirations. Political ambition is a better way to put it. I had plans to run for Congress. Think of how it would look if the mother of a man who had defrauded the government of a million dollars in a program that she was responsible for investigating wanted to be put in a position of responsibility in Congress. My campaign would have been over before it started." Fran spoke faster. She was getting to the heart of it. "So when I saw Malia had found shoddy oversight and followed it through to discover my son's designs and a big payout, I panicked. The first thing I did was steer you away from the Community Fund and toward

Anthony Torgetti's naming contract. By the way, Torgetti is clean; you'll find nothing there. I know this because he gave me the flash drive when you wouldn't take it. Important side note? He'll be our governor someday. Make friends in high places, and keep them. That's my advice to you."

Emma heard a bit of the old Fran in that last statement, but she knew that despite her boss's bravado, this couldn't be easy to tell.

"I'm getting away from why I called you. Last week when I uncovered the fraud, I searched Johnny's room thoroughly. I turned it upside down. I didn't know what evidence there might be of his plans for his theft of government funds. Perhaps the initial sketches, a budget, how he intended to disguise the payments. I knew he kept physical journals, he had since he was in college, and they weren't there. But I did find a Clad Corp Ideal Storage key card. I'd been unaware until then that he had a storage unit. I figured that's where he kept anything he wouldn't want me to see, including his journals. On Tuesday, I went there with the intention of getting his things back and found that because he'd stopped paying, they'd moved his possessions into the basement warehouse a week ago. I said I would pay to retrieve the items, but they said I couldn't. I wasn't a signer on his account and he was an adult. The manager there told me there was an appeals process that takes up to six weeks. I couldn't risk it. It would take only one of their employees putting together who I am and who Johnny was. They could make a lot selling whatever was in those boxes to the tabloids."

Fran looked down. At last, she wouldn't meet Emma's eyes.

"I didn't know there was anyone in the warehouse. I never would have—"

"You set that fire?" Emma said quietly, wanting to get Fran to admit it, to get past the hardest part.

"You have to understand, I thought my political career was at stake," Fran said. "And there wasn't supposed to be any fire. I'd walked around the building and had seen the broken window. I'd looked inside and saw the sprinklers all along the ceiling. And most of all, I saw flimsy cardboard boxes with Johnny's name on them. They were along the wall near the window. I thought if I came back and threw something flammable in there, anything that would create enough smoke or heat to set off the sprinklers, they'd go off and the water damage would cause staff there to throw out Johnny's boxes. They'd never open them to see what was inside. It seems crazy now, but it was such a simple solution."

"Until the sprinklers didn't work and illegally stored household propane canisters were there," Emma said. Both those things had recently been reported on the news.

Emma kept her tone neutral, even as she relived the twenty-foot-high wall of flames, Daniel Baptiste collapsed on the floor, her chest hurting and her eyes burning. And worst of all, in that room had been someone who, when Fran had thrown the fire starter through the window, had been blown apart so completely that they didn't have body pieces to make an identification.

Emma felt sick.

"So while I didn't mean it, and I had only intended to cause water damage, I committed arson, and I killed someone," Fran said. "I have an attorney, we've been in conversation, and I want to turn myself in. I know my political career is over, and I may do some time, accident or not. But not so much, and perhaps I might just get a fine. My attorney is the best, and I didn't mean to kill anyone." The last came out as a plea.

"I understand," Emma said.

Though she didn't really.

She was bothered by the calculating way that Fran had put herself first and was still putting herself first—even when Johnny had been alive, it had always been about her.

And to think I wanted to model my life on yours.

60

Midtown Condo

WHEN ALIBI AND Jackie O entered Daphne's short-term rental in the Midtown condominium complex, there wasn't much for them to look at. It wasn't a crime scene. Daphne Ver-Strate had been shot and killed where she was found by the river.

The young officer who let them in was impressed when he viewed Alibi's identification as head of major crimes. He apologized that they hadn't been told in advance that what evidence had been found in the flat had already all been bagged and taken downtown.

While Alibi knew the reports would eventually be available for review online, he didn't want to wait. "Who was leading the forensics unit here? I'd like to expedite seeing any photos that were taken of the evidence."

The young officer smiled, happy to be able to help. "That's Amelia Zed."

Alibi thanked him and immediately messaged Zed, requesting urgent access to the raw evidence files.

Daphne's killer was still out there, and Alibi wasn't in the mood to jump through bureaucratic hoops.

"We could have saved a trip, since there was nothing here," Jackie O remarked as they exited the building. "Though it was a nice morning for a bike ride."

"I think it was good to see where Daphne was living," Alibi said.

His phone pinged.

Amelia Zed had come through.

Alibi texted the link to Jackie O, reasoning it would be easier to view the images on her tablet than on his phone.

Jackie O asked, "How about here?"

They'd come upon a bench at a bus stop.

They sat down, and she and Alibi put their heads together—literally—to look at the images of items from Daphne's apartment that they'd just received.

First up was a Clad Corp Ideal Storage key card with Johnny Hill's name written on the back. They already knew Johnny had a unit there and that the items in it had been destroyed through an act of arson. But this gave them a link from Johnny's storage unit back to Daphne. Alibi wasn't sure yet how the dots connected up, but they were there.

Then there was the photo of Johnny smiling happily while in Denmark, the one featured in many of the news reports after his death. But on the reverse side of this one, *One year and one day* was written in pencil. Definitely something to follow up on.

Finally, there was a thin notebook or journal found in the main compartment of Daphne's backpack. It was new—only four pages had writing on them. But though each page had been photographed separately and Daphne's handwriting was crisp and clear, Jackie O and Alibi couldn't make anything of most of it, since it wasn't in English. Alibi assumed it was Dutch. Still, he kept scanning the pages. There was something important there. He could feel it.

Suddenly, a single phrase jumped out at him.

J's moordenaar werkt Hayden Commission.

It was easy enough to translate, assuming *J* stood for *Johnny*: *Johnny's murderer works at the Hayden Commission.*

Alibi felt a sharp pain in his chest.

He struggled to get to his feet from the bench and pulled his phone from his pocket.

Jackie O watched him, wide-eyed. "Are you—" she began, but he shook his head.

He listened as Emma's number rang. And rang.

The pressure in his chest worsened.

He considered whether he might actually be having a heart attack and dismissed the thought. He didn't have time for it, even if he was.

Emma finally picked up. Her tone was formal—he must have caught her in a meeting or at work. "Alibi? Thank you for calling. I did have an issue that—"

He interrupted her. His voice was strained as he pushed through the pain. "I've just come from Daphne VerStrate's flat. We were able to view her journal. Johnny Hill's murderer, and I'm guessing her own, is an employee of the Hayden Commission. Are you in the office? If you are, get out now."

In the back of his mind, Alibi wondered why he wasn't feeling better. He'd reached Emma. He was following the signs.

"No, I'm not," Emma said, "Are you okay? I—"

A feeling like an acid wash, stinging and searing, was spreading through Alibi's arms and legs.

"I have to go," Emma said abruptly. "I'll call you later."

"Wait, where are you?" he gasped.

She'd hung up.

Alibi tossed his phone to Jackie O. "I want a trace on that last call," he spit out. "A location for Emma Lawson."

Without waiting for her acknowledgment, he took off running. Or something like running.

He felt as though he were carrying a hundred-pound pack on his chest and was knee deep in snow, every stride meeting resistance, his movements jerky and uneven.

He couldn't understand why he'd found no relief physically when he'd told Emma to stay away from the office.

Unless that didn't make her any safer.

He kept pushing. So long as he didn't stop, he'd get to Emma's house faster if he went there directly on foot than if he circled back in the other direction for his truck. She'd sounded like she was working. Maybe she was in her home office.

It was still the best plan, and the only one he had.

* * *

The Station

Emma put down her phone and said to Fran, "Do you have your tablet?"

She needed it to access the internal commission server. She couldn't do it from her phone.

Fran took it out of her bag.

"Open the commission site," Emma said.

Fran did as she was told. She must have seen the steely look in Emma's eyes.

"Go through the link from the commission site to the Community Fund site. Locate Johnny's designs."

Fran clicked and scrolled. She made a face. "I can get to the Community Fund site, but I don't see Johnny's designs. The image isn't there. The Patio Station project isn't there. This happened to me last time I tried from the commission site."

Exactly, Emma thought.

The links had been redirected so that commission staff wouldn't be able to see the Patio Station project or Johnny's designs.

It wouldn't have worked for long. That didn't matter.

Today was the last payment.

Time is on his side.

Emma knew of only one person who could manipulate the internal commission website that way.

Only one person who had known all along that the Patio Station project was fake.

Only one person who had silenced Johnny so that he couldn't blow the whistle on the Community Fund contract for which he'd created the designs.

Only one person, who would clearly go to any lengths to steal a million dollars and get away scot-free.

And that one person had just pulled up a chair and was sitting across from her now.

* * *

Twenty minutes earlier, Atticus had found a place he was happy with. It was just inside the tree line, about halfway between the outdoor patio where Emma and her boss were seated and the site where construction had been halted due to toxic soil contaminants. He liked the relative privacy and the shade of the towering eucalyptus trees overhead and all around him, yet he had a good view in both directions.

He'd dragged a couple of open wood crates over from the construction site, one to sit on and one on which to put his mini easel, and had started sketching when he saw a man dressed strangely for the day. He had a cap pulled low over his eyes, which were hidden behind huge dark glasses. He wore a shirt and blazer that were too big for him, cheap-looking dress pants, and modern running shoes.

Kind of a warped eighties Miami Vice *look.*

Like Atticus, the man seemed to be seeking the shade and privacy of the trees.

Atticus had just about forgotten about him when he saw the man walk toward the patio where Emma and her boss were sitting.

He didn't pass right by Atticus—he was on the other side of the unused tracks. But Atticus was able to keep him in sight. The man's hands were shoved into the pockets of his blazer. It looked like he might have made fists with his hands. Either that or the pockets were very full. Something was distorting their shape.

As Atticus watched the man head toward the patio where his daughter sat, he thought about the break-in at her house and set his charcoal down, paying close attention.

The man stepped onto the patio, sat down, and pulled something from one of his bulging pockets. It looked like a cardboard cup you'd get coffee in if you ordered it to go. It must have been empty or it would have spilled inside his pocket and gotten his jacket wet, but the man appeared to be pretending to take occasional sips from it.

Very weird. Still, he didn't seem to be bothering anyone.

A few minutes went by, and Atticus, knowing there were strange people in the world, had reminded himself it was no use worrying about every single one when the man he'd been watching got up and, one hand still firmly stuffed in a front pocket, went over to Emma and her boss, pulled up a chair, and sat down at their table.

* * *

Emma had looked up to see the man she now knew beyond a shadow of a doubt was a killer dressed in a ridiculous way, in an oversized cap pulled down on his forehead, huge sunglasses, his face barely visible, and wearing clothing much too big for him so it disguised his body type.

He'd taken Fran's tablet from her hand and picked up Emma's phone. "I'll need these," he said. "Fran, I'd like your phone too."

Fran was staring at him. Emma didn't know if she'd recognized his voice. She hadn't spent as much time with him as Emma had.

Emma had noticed his hand in his pocket shoved up against the edge of the table, the shape of what could be a gun pushed against the fabric. She said to Fran, "He would like your phone. I would give it to him." Emma avoided saying his name, hoping he might let Fran go if he didn't think she knew who he was behind those ridiculous huge glasses and under the cap.

Though Emma knew that was a long shot, since Nick Lillard had proven himself to be someone who would not let anyone go.

Not Johnny.

Not Daphne.

Right now, he looked like the cat that had swallowed the canary, barely able to contain his smile. He turned his attention to Fran, and tipped his glasses down so she could see his eyes.

Fran gasped.

So she didn't know.

"Ah, Fran. I recognized Johnny's talent back when we were in college. I was certain we could win the million-dollar contract to remodel this space if Johnny did the designs." He gave her a moment to take that in before continuing. "That's why I paid him a fair fee, ten thousand dollars, for his efforts. But I hope you understand why I had to mislead him and say we didn't get the money. I did the high-level entrepreneurial and financial work, creating a bogus company, setting up a series of bank accounts and the PO box, creatively constructed so the cash would be clean for my own personal use. I didn't want Johnny to get confused and think some of that money was his or, worse yet, decide I shouldn't have it at all."

While Nick was holding forth on his accomplishments, Emma, having recovered from her shock at seeing him, considered how best to get her and Fran out of what she was certain was soon going to deteriorate from a "polite chat" about Nick's criminal genius to something darker and much more dangerous.

She didn't like the way he kept his hand in his pocket resting on the edge of the table. It could be a gun, no question, though she hoped it wasn't.

If it was, it was at point-blank range and gave her very few degrees of freedom in terms of available actions.

Still, it looked like she had a little time, since Nick seemed to be enjoying being in charge of the two women who at the commission had been in charge of him.

"It was too bad that Johnny came out here when he did," Nick continued. "I was supposed to be long gone before he figured out the project was a sham, and Fran, if it hadn't been highlighted on the commission website, which he saw when he was curious about your work before I realized I had to remove that link, he might have never known. And he would still be alive."

Fran stifled a cry, her eyes wide as a child's upon waking from a nightmare.

It looked like Nick found that rewarding.

In fact, Emma realized he was entirely focused on Fran.

At the commission, Fran was at the very top, and Nick was near the bottom. It seemed to matter to him to have skipped all those rungs today so that he was not only sitting with Fran; he was in the boss's chair. Emma hoped Nick's interest in impressing upon Fran how smart he was would give her the opening she needed.

But when Emma started to stand, Nick said, "Uh-uh," and after looking around and finding the rest of the patio still empty, he lifted the gun Emma had hoped he didn't have and poked it out just enough so she could see it pointed at her stomach above the level of the table.

"Let's take a walk." Despite his polite tone, he gave Emma a calculating look that made her catch her breath. He motioned with the gun for them both to get up and then looped one arm through Fran's, pushing the barrel of the weapon into her side.

The few people passing were on the sidewalk twenty feet away on their way to the new terminal and the new restaurants. Holding Fran so close, Nick could shoot her multiple times before Emma could get them any help.

Still, there had to be something she could do.

Then Nick called to her. "Emma, I'd like you where I can see you better. Come up here. Just in front of Fran. So I can shoot both of you if it becomes necessary." He spoke clinically, as though he were thinking through one of his IT problems. How to keep two windows in a program open at the same time.

Emma had no choice. She moved to the spot he'd indicated, and Nick guided them off the patio and down to the far side of the tracks.

They were headed toward the old construction site, the one that had been abandoned by Clad Corp due to toxic contamination. The warning signs were still up. Nick was one of the few people besides Emma who knew the area was perfectly safe now, thanks to a five-month cleanup project, which the commission had reviewed.

Nick had worked on it.

As they got closer, Emma could see there were a few items at the site besides the signs still to be taken away—pallets and crates and an aluminum double-wide trailer that likely served as the headquarters for the contractor's team.

Between here and there were only the deserted old tracks.

Emma thought hard about what her next moves might be. She was scanning the area for a possible weapon when she saw Atticus across the unused tracks, sitting just inside the tree line, apparently absorbed in a sketch he was making.

She didn't know whether she wanted him to see them or not.

If he knew they were in danger, he could use his phone and call for help. But he couldn't see the gun in Fran's side from where he sat, and given how strange Nick looked in that getup, Atticus might decide to come over and find out what was going on.

She remembered how protective he'd been of her after the break-in at her house.

Better for Atticus not to notice, Emma decided. Because whatever Nick had in mind for her and Fran, he couldn't possibly want a witness.

She turned her head away from the trees where Atticus sat, as though if she couldn't see him, that might keep her father from seeing her.

Ridiculous, but she couldn't help herself.

They were well past Atticus and he hadn't moved. Emma was both disappointed and relieved.

Nick seemed preoccupied. Perhaps he'd said all he'd felt he needed to say back on the patio. Or it might be that his preferred audience, Fran, was no longer capable of listening. She moved like a sleepwalker. She didn't cry or shake. She just shuffled her feet in her Sarah Flint leopard-print loafers.

Emma hadn't noticed Fran's shoes when they were sitting down. She was pleased to see they were flats, in case they had an opportunity to run for their lives. Though Emma thought shoe style was going to be the least of her problems in getting Fran moving.

When they arrived at the trailer, Nick said, "Turn slowly and look at me, both of you. Stand close together. Closer, shoulder to shoulder. No gap between you, with your backs to the trailer. To the left of the door. That's good."

He seemed calm enough, which Emma liked, since it made it less likely he would fire the gun in a panic or out of rage. On the other hand, what Nick was doing should not come naturally to anyone. His hands should shake, he should look nervously about. Nick did none of those things.

She recognized from work his problem-solving mode.

He was singularly focused on getting this right, whatever "this" was, and that seemed to trump any other feelings he might be having.

Emma gauged the distance. He stood less than a foot from her and Fran. She decided her best, perhaps her only play was to throw herself at him, aiming to knock his gun-holding hand to one side and with her body weight bring him to the ground.

Nick wouldn't be able to get a shot off at Fran that way, and hopefully he wouldn't manage to pull the trigger and shoot her before she'd changed the trajectory of the bullet.

It didn't feel great to go toward rather than away from what she assumed was a loaded gun.

But Emma didn't see any other move.

She had to risk it.

He literally had their backs against the wall.

She had just tensed her muscles, ready to charge, when Nick said, "Step further to the left. You're in my way." He used the gun for motivation, pointing it squarely at Fran's chest as he said again, "Step left. Away from the door. It won't open if you stay where you are."

His aim looked true, and Emma couldn't chance it. She slid to the left as instructed, slipping her arm through Fran's and pulling her with her.

The new problem for Emma was that this put Nick at least another foot away from her, maybe two.

Which made her plan much harder to execute.

She could no longer throw herself at him. She'd have to run a few steps to cover the distance, which would give him time to shoot. While Emma was thinking this through, Nick transferred the gun to his left hand and raised it so that it pointed at the center of Fran's forehead.

CHAPTER

61

E MMA HAD SUPERVISED Nick Lillard for the last three weeks. She'd spoken to him at least once, often more than once, on most days. Yet she had not seen this coming. Not even close. Her biggest concern regarding Nick had been that he might have a crush on her. She knew it was due to fear and hysteria, but she was having a hard time keeping from laughing out loud at her own stupidity.

With the gun still aimed at Fran's forehead, his hand steady, Nick said, "Don't worry. Don't be frightened. If you do exactly what I say, everything will be fine. Can I get a yes to that?"

Hearing his voice, remembering the gun, Emma didn't feel like laughing anymore.

"Yes," she said, firmly and clearly. Fran said nothing.

"I have a final payment of five hundred thousand to collect from my post office box today. Fran, are you listening?"

Emma was not surprised when Fran again said nothing.

Emma could feel her trembling.

Having no other functioning audience, Nick directed his next comments to Emma. "When Fran hired me, I volunteered to upgrade the commission's website and was given an administrator's account privileges. It was my motivation for taking this job. When I found out the commission was investigating the tunnel project, I knew if I didn't act, it was only a matter of time until

Fran saw Johnny's designs as one of the awardees in the Community Fund. It was child's play to change the information she and you could access through links on our site. I simply deleted that award."

Nick was back in his *Aren't I the cleverest?* mode.

Emma watched for any point of weakness on his part. But so far the gun had remained trained on Fran's head with Nick's finger on the trigger.

"Then Daphne came along and took the whole thing off-line. Into the real world. With secret meetings by the river. Such a shame—we were all so close to getting out of this with no one else getting hurt."

Abruptly, Nick closed the distance between him and Fran and shoved the cold barrel of the gun against her head in the center right above her eyes.

This seemed to go against his earlier *Don't be frightened* admonition.

Emma thought she could see the struggle Nick was having between wanting to be a respected professional, politely conversing with his peers, and the headiness of the power he had with that weapon in his hand.

Fran hadn't made a sound when he made contact between the gun and her head, but she'd turned so white that Emma thought she might faint.

Emma wouldn't blame her if she did.

Then Nick played a wild card.

"I want to lay out for you, while I have your full attention, what needs to happen next. You're going to go inside this trailer and stay there until Monday. I'll gag you so you don't call out, and bind your hands so you don't take off each other's gags. There is a bathroom in there, since Clad Corp thought of everything for the convenience of their construction crew. You'll be reasonably comfortable."

Keeping the gun trained on Fran, Nick lifted the unlocked latch on the door to the trailer and opened it. He waved the gun to indicate they should enter first.

As Emma passed through the door, she noticed it had a mail slot near the bottom. Not a skinny one for just envelopes; it was sized to receive small packages. Emma was glad to see it. It might prove useful later.

Because right now she was all about believing there would be a *later*.

The trailer had a desk in the far left corner, a bookshelf along the right-hand wall filled with books, several large open boxes of printer paper on the floor, and two oversized recycling bins, also full of paper. There was a closed door in the far corner on the right, which Emma assumed led to the bathroom. So maybe he wasn't lying about that? There were no windows. There was no phone or computer equipment.

This may have been how the Clad Corp people had left it the last day on the site, but from how comfortable Nick seemed, Emma thought it likely he'd been here earlier to make sure things were the way he wanted them.

That was confirmed when he had the two of them sit on the edge of the front of the desk, Emma helping Fran up, while he kept the gun trained on Fran and went around to the other side, where there were precut lengths of duct tape adhered to the back of the desk.

He directed Emma to firmly tape Fran's mouth and then to put Fran's palms together and tightly wind tape all the way from her wrists to the top of her fingers, immobilizing her hands. He somewhat awkwardly did the same to Emma's mouth and hands one handed while pointing the gun at Emma instead of Fran, who had appeared to be no threat even before she was bound. She'd slid down on the floor and was sitting against the wall, unmoving, her eyes closed.

Finished, Nick examined his handiwork and told Emma to sit on the floor next to Fran, who hadn't moved since she'd taken that position.

Once she'd complied, he pulled a large padlock from one of his jacket pockets, presumably the one that had not held the gun. Backing toward the exit, Nick said softly, as though they shared a secret, "No one works at this site anymore. But I have it on good authority they are coming to take this trailer away on Monday. I know you'll be a little hungry, but what a story you'll have to tell."

Still facing them, he dragged the two boxes of loose printer paper next to the door and crumpled a few pieces on top. He pushed the recycling bins next to those boxes.

After that, Nick went out the door.

There was a moment's silence.

Then Emma heard the latch slide securely into place and the click of the padlock closing.

CHAPTER

62

THE FIRST THING Atticus had done after Emma and her boss
had passed by on the far side of the tracks with the strange
man was to reach for his new burner phone in his backpack.

Only to find it wasn't there.

He hadn't remembered to put it in.

He had no doubt the man was taking them somewhere against
their will. Emma had turned her head away from him, a sure signal that she was concerned he might call out or come to her, which
led Atticus to believe the man had a weapon, probably a gun. He
certainly had the pockets for it.

Since he didn't have a phone, Atticus thought his best plan B
was to sneak back toward the patio to get someone there to call the
police. But just as he ventured out from the tree line, he saw the
man point his gun, now clearly visible, at Emma's boss's forehead.

Atticus had to face the fact that he didn't have time to go get
help, though he did hope someone would happen to come along. It
was daylight, and they were only a fifteen-minute walk from the
terminal, where there were lots of people. On the other hand, it did
work against the likelihood of a random visitor that there were signs
all around saying KEEP OUT! DANGEROUS! TOXIC CHEMICALS.

Based on what Emma had told him, the place had already
been cleaned up and those signs were out-of-date. But Atticus
couldn't expect other people to know that.

He quickly inventoried what he had on hand.

Charcoal, pencils, a sketch pad, a water bottle, and a yogurt.

He'd seen pencils used in movies as effective weapons, usually when poked straight through an eye. He didn't see how he'd get close enough to the guy to do that.

Atticus was looking around for a brick or a stone when he saw the man, Emma, and her boss all go inside the trailer.

Atticus expected to hear the terrifying blast of multiple gunshots.

It was quiet.

He decided to use the opportunity to sneak closer, going back a little farther into the tree line. But he'd barely gotten a few feet nearer to the trailer—still a good fifteen feet away—when the man came back out, shut the trailer door, and padlocked it securely.

That seemed good.

It appeared the man was keeping Emma and her boss hostage rather than killing them, at least if his gun was going to be his weapon of choice. Atticus didn't want to think about whether Emma could have already been harmed in some other way.

He wished he could remember Emma's boss's name. It would make it easier to keep track of things in his head in a crisis situation. He'd heard it only once, and it hadn't seemed important at the time.

He decided he would call her Shirley.

Just for now. He figured she wouldn't mind.

So he was thinking how best to get Emma and Shirley out of the trailer when the man came out of the trees.

Atticus had missed seeing him go in there while he was studying the trailer door.

Now he had something different in his hand, not a gun. It looked like it might be a rolled-up rag. He took it to the front of the trailer, used a cigarette lighter that he produced from one of those big pockets of his, set fire to the rag, then quickly opened a wide mail slot in the bottom of the door and shoved it inside.

After that, the man took off.

He was a fast runner. He looked back only once and, apparently satisfied with what he'd seen or hadn't seen, kept running. He turned left into the trees.

If Atticus had to guess, he had a bike back there, but he might have just kept running.

Atticus didn't wait one second more. He raced to the trailer and yelled and pounded on the door. "Emma, we've got to get you out of there. Emma, can you hear me?"

Nothing.

He tried the padlock. It was securely closed.

Atticus knelt down, lifted the letter slot, and looked through. What he saw made him sick and furious. One big box of paper was nearly consumed by flames, and the one next to it had also caught fire. Dark smoke was billowing upward to the ceiling of the trailer. Through it, Atticus could just make out both women on the far wall, gagged, their hands bound, but their legs were free.

Emma was helping Shirley up onto a desk in the corner.

The rag turned out to have been soaked with something flammable. It smelled like gasoline, which had started the fire in the boxes of paper and was now spreading rapidly to some recycling bins, also densely filled with paper.

That worried him, because the longer those things burned, the more smoke there would be in that small enclosed space. It looked like all that paper had been put right next to the mail slot for that purpose.

Atticus ran around the trailer to see if there was a back door or some kind of emergency exit. There wasn't one. But there was a small window high up in the back. It looked big enough for the women, one at a time, to possibly squeeze through. But he couldn't reach it, and it didn't look as though it was meant to be opened.

Still, it seemed his only hope.

He went back to where he'd found the shipping crates to sit on and dragged them two at a time until he had all of them. There were ten. He stacked them two by two against the wall of the trailer under the window until he ran out. He had four on top of each other right next to six on top of each other. They were made of wood slats, not solid, but they seemed fairly strong.

His concern was how steady the tower he'd built would be.

Just then, two kids rode their bikes across the unused tracks, maybe fifteen feet away. They were staying just outside the area marked with the TOXIC signs. They paused to goggle at Atticus's shipping-crate tower.

The smaller boy looked six or seven years old; the bigger one might be ten.

Atticus called to them, "Do you have a phone? Either of you have a phone?"

They walked their bikes a little closer. The bigger boy nodded. "It doesn't have internet or anything. It's just to call my parents if I have an emergency."

Atticus wondered what the response time was for the fire department out here on the edge of the city. He had no idea where the closest station was. *Five minutes? Eight?* Emma and Shirley had already been cooped up in that tin can breathing smoke for two or three minutes. With no open windows.

They couldn't wait.

Atticus said, "Good. This is an emergency, so use your emergency phone. Call 911, tell them there's a fire and two women are trapped in a trailer. But first, quick, which of you is the better climber?"

The smaller child raised his hand, while the bigger child pointed at the smaller child. "Okay, we're agreed. What's your name?" Atticus asked the little guy.

"Trey."

"Okay, Trey, you afraid of heights?"

He shook his head no.

"What's your name?" he asked the bigger boy.

"Henry."

"Henry, you make that phone call right now. Make sure they know this isn't a prank. It's hard to be a kid sometimes. People don't always believe you. But make them believe you, Henry, okay? Oh, and find me something that can break a window. A rock, a brick, anything."

Henry nodded. He dropped his bike and began searching the area for something that would work.

Atticus said, "Henry, make the call first. Trey, I'm going to hold these boxes steady for you. I want you to climb up the stack of four here and then hoist yourself up the last two to the top of that stack of six. You'll be almost level with the window. When you stand up, you will be. Think you can do that?"

Trey grinned. "Easy."

"Okay, go."

Atticus figured the trailer was maybe twelve feet tall, no more. If the crates could take his weight, Atticus would be up there already. But he didn't know if they would.

And the kid could do this. He had faith.

Trey started climbing.

Atticus still hadn't heard anything from inside.

When he'd seen Emma and Shirley, they had been in the process of getting up on the desk in the farthest corner from the door. It didn't seem a terrible plan, getting away from the source of the fire. But it wouldn't save them from the smoke—in a double-wide trailer, one end to the other wasn't far enough.

Henry returned with a chunk of broken concrete the size of a large brick, carrying it in both hands. "I got this over there." He pointed to a pile with more like it.

"Perfect," Atticus said.

"Trey, I'm going to throw this up to you. It's heavy. Watch your face. I want you to use it to crack the window, okay?"

"No," Trey said.

"No, what?" Atticus said, working to convey calm, which was definitely not how he felt with two kids not out of grade school as his crew.

Trey lay flat on the top crate and stretched his arms down as far as they would reach, opening both hands wide. "Henry, bring that here," he yelled.

Henry jogged over with the concrete, then climbed with less dexterity than Trey but just as much determination up the smaller stack of four boxes.

Trey could just reach the concrete when Henry handed it to him.

"That was a good idea," Atticus said.

Trey was no longer listening. He was on his knees, his small left hand flat on the trailer wall for balance, turning his head away, closing his eyes, bringing his right arm back and forth so that the chunk of concrete slammed like a hammer head onto the center of the window.

There was a crack in the glass, but it didn't break open.

"Good. Again," Atticus yelled.

Trey kept at it until there was a shattering noise as the square of glass fell out and busted apart on the floor.

Atticus was getting ready to issue his next set of instructions when he saw Trey put his head inside the opening where the window had been, checking for something. Then, without warning, Trey sat on the edge of the frame, his thin, short legs dangling inside the trailer, and he jumped.

Out of sight.

Atticus heard a loud thump and a yelp of pain.

63

Emma hadn't believed it at first when she'd heard Atticus yelling outside the front of the trailer. She would have pounded on the door with her bound fists to let him know they were in there, that they were alive, but she couldn't get anywhere close to the door because that's where the fire was. And the duct tape gag was doing its job well; she couldn't make a sound.

The two bins of recycled paper were burning. It was still a pretty small fire, certainly tiny when compared to the one at Ideal Storage, and the walls of the trailer were steel or aluminum. It wasn't like the whole thing would go up in flames. But in one way, this situation was a hundred times more terrifying because they didn't have an escape route. There was no open door behind them like she'd had in the storage warehouse.

Emma had pulled Fran up on the desk, thinking that was their best bet. Then she remembered the small door in the back was a bathroom, if Nick had been telling the truth and it wasn't a closet.

She didn't know if there was only a toilet in there or also a sink, but if there was any water and towels, they should be able to soak them and block the gap between the door and the floor to keep the smoke from coming in there, at least for a little while. And Atticus would have called for help. Thank goodness he'd bought that phone.

Still, as the flames grew in the small space and the smoke billowed, she knew the time they had was very limited, verging on microscopic. She'd just been treated for smoke inhalation. She knew it needed only minutes to kill.

When she'd called for emergency help at the storage facility, the fire engines hadn't been slow in getting there, but they couldn't fly, and as she watched the thickening smoke climb the trailer walls, she pictured it gobbling up the oxygen she and Fran needed to survive.

She slid off the desk and pointed with her bound hands to the bathroom door and motioned for Fran to follow her there, to move with her to a safer place.

But Fran wasn't going anywhere, for any reason. She might be in shock, she might be catatonic—Emma didn't know what word best described it, but Fran was not functioning.

With difficulty, Emma hoisted herself back onto the desk. At least up close, she could see Fran's eyes move, tracking the flames over her shoulder. She was conscious. Nonetheless, getting off the desk didn't seem to be something Fran had any interest in.

Fran was on her knees or Emma would have held Fran's ankles together and pulled her by her legs or feet. But Emma's attempts to yank on one of Fran's arms with her bound hands as the single point of leverage had been a complete failure.

Fran had inertia on her side. And without the ability to speak, Emma's powers of persuasion were limited.

She was getting desperate.

She knew she could buy herself time if she went into the bathroom and closed the door with a rolled, wet towel jammed at the bottom. But she couldn't get Fran to go with her, and that meant Fran would die out here if the firefighters didn't arrive within minutes.

Emma really didn't want to die with her.

She hated the fact that if their positions were reversed, she was pretty sure Fran would already have hightailed it into the bathroom and let Emma become human kindling for the fire, which was not small anymore. It had reached the bookshelf on the side of the trailer, and the heat was immense. Forget the smoke, it was so hot, Emma could picture the soles of her feet blistering.

By not moving, she was making a decision, she knew that.

She was staying with Fran, and she wasn't happy about it.

But then the bathroom door opened and a small face peered around it.

"Hello? Ma'am, hello?"

At first, Emma thought she was hallucinating. Then she could tell she was not, because something besides the fire had finally gotten Fran's attention. Her wide eyes focused on the child, and she was moving stiffly toward the edge of the desk.

She was calling out something, a muffled sound, nearly unintelligible, though Emma had tried not to seal the tape on Fran's mouth tightly.

Then she realized Fran was looking at the boy and saying, "Johnny?" and then, "Johnny, is that you?"

It was eerie and horrible and sad, but Emma decided she would deal with those emotions later. Besides, Alibi had taught her the dead appeared in all kinds of ways. Maybe this boy did carry something of Johnny in him. Enough that he wouldn't let his mother die.

Emma helped Fran down and hustled her as best she could into the tiny bathroom with the boy. She closed the door behind them, which gave some relief from the heat, though smoke had gotten there before them. It was a tight fit even without a shower or bath. There was a toilet and also a sink set in a cabinet for storage.

When Emma saw all the broken glass on the ground, she looked up and noticed the boy's bloodied hands.

He had tousled dark curly hair and stick-thin arms and legs. He couldn't be more than six, maybe seven years old. He was staring at her and Fran, his eyes round and alarmed.

What must he think, seeing two women with duct-taped mouths and wrists?

Then Atticus's face appeared, as though he were flying, peering through a hole in the wall above her, a glimpse of blue sky behind him.

"C'mon," he yelled. "Let's get you three out of there."

64

Atticus yelled, "You've got to get up here. Come on, I'll pull you through. One at a time."

The boy would go first, but they'd need their hands free to follow him, and it would help if they could give and take directions. So Emma knelt and gestured to the boy to rip the tape off her mouth.

He shook his head no. Evidently, he was not afraid of leaping from great heights into a pool of broken glass, but he knew what it felt like to have a Band-Aid ripped off, and he wanted no part of this larger version of that.

Emma understood and tried to use the tips of her fingers to get beneath the edge of the tape on her mouth, to do it herself. She had no luck.

The boy watched her struggle. Then he took a deep breath, stepped close, and reached up to her face. His hands were so small.

He pushed her hands aside in an oddly gentle motion and then without hesitation ripped the tape off.

Emma grimaced but managed not to yell or curse, at least not out loud.

Then she offered him her wrists. That took a few attempts but didn't hurt as much. Next, Emma pulled the tape off Fran's mouth and hands.

She could feel the heat though the bathroom door. There were no big towels, just washcloths, and the gap at the bottom of the door was just a sliver, so Emma decided time was better spent getting them out of here.

She asked the boy his name.

"Trey."

"Nice to meet you, Trey. I'm Emma. This is Fran. You climb up on the sink, and I'll make a stirrup for you with my hands and boost you the rest of the way up to the window."

"I'll help you from up here," Atticus called, but as Emma was moving to help the boy, there was a crash and a loud, deep yell.

The kid looked at her with a matter-of-fact expression.

"I think the tower he built fell."

Emma was horrified, certain Atticus had broken his back or his neck.

But Atticus called out, "I'm okay."

There was the sound of boxes being shoved and lifted, and within a minute instead of Atticus there was a new face at the window, this one a boy bigger than Trey. Still, he couldn't be more than ten.

He yelled to Trey, his arms outstretched. "C'mon, I'll help you."

As Emma boosted Trey up to his friend, she concluded the tower could support the weight of a boy but not Atticus.

It was getting hotter in the small space, and she saw tendrils of black smoke snaking under and around the door.

She said to Fran, "You're next."

Fran nodded and climbed up onto the sink.

Emma had noticed before how fit and strong Fran's arms were.

She figured Fran, nearly sixty, must be as obsessive about exercise as Kate, and decided she might increase her own workout if she got out of this alive.

Emma did the same maneuver she had with Trey, offering Fran her hands laced as a stirrup, although this time Emma climbed up onto the closed toilet and leaned against the wall to better brace herself and take Fran's weight. Fran was slim, but still, a grown woman was more difficult to boost than a child.

Fran called to the kid above, "I think it's better if you get down and let me pull myself up on the window frame so the tower doesn't have to hold both of us."

He nodded, and his head disappeared from view.

Emma looked up and considered the metal frame of the window. The glass hadn't come out cleanly; there must be shards and slivers all around the edges. She reached down, grabbed two washcloths, and handed them to Fran.

"Wrap these around your hands."

"No, I won't be able to get a grip," Fran said.

Emma picked up the discarded duct tape and placed a piece flat against each of Fran's palms, pressing them down. They were sticky enough to stay put.

"That should do it," Fran said, her fear apparently gone now that she saw a clear path for this to end for her.

Emma boosted her. Fran went up and pulled herself through the window. There was another tumbling crash and a scream, higher-pitched.

Fran's.

This time, Emma knew what had happened.

Atticus's voice floated up through the window. "It's packed dirt on this side. They've pulled all the concrete up. It's not a bad fall. It's the price of admission. Come on, let's go."

Emma guessed he might think she was hesitating out of fear, but that was only because he didn't know her. She was trying to figure out how she was going to reach the window with no one left to boost her.

Her eyes burned and she was finding it seriously hard to breathe. She realized the one window wasn't enough to combat the amount of smoke that had worked its way in and around the bathroom. She had to get out. *Now.* She climbed up, but even on tiptoes, she was inches too short.

"Dad, can you get a rope? I can't reach."

She heard muffled conversation. What seemed like two long minutes passed. She felt faint. Emma feared she was going to lose consciousness. Then Atticus's head appeared again.

"Grab this," he said, holding on to one end of what looked like a broken bicycle chain.

This is going to hurt, Emma thought, as she wrapped both hands around the bumpy metal, then used the last of her strength to jump at the same time that Atticus pulled until she could free one hand and grab the edge of the window. She felt the glass pierce her palm but didn't let go.

As she pushed herself through and landed next to Atticus, there was a wobbling and a shaking and then the sound of the crack of the top crate splitting beneath them. They tumbled through the air onto the ground, just as Emma heard the first siren in the distance, growing louder.

SUNDAY, MARCH 14

65

Matchbook Lane

I T WAS ANOTHER beautiful spring day in Sacramento. Emma and Atticus sat in the backyard of her bungalow on Matchbook Lane, the dogs at their feet, tired out after Trey and Henry had biked over and played with them. The boys had thrown sticks, chased each other and the dogs, and wrestled with puppy Fox, which Crash found undignified.

Atticus paid them each twenty dollars and made an agreement for them to come back next week, since neither Emma nor Atticus would be up to much exercise for a while.

Atticus had cracked a rib. Emma had countless glass-related injuries, from slivers to cuts that had needed stitches; a sprained ankle that required crutches; and another case of smoke inhalation, this one a bit rougher to come back from.

Nick had not made his flight to Morocco, where he had hoped to disappear with his million dollars. He was smart, but there was a difference between smart and clever, and he wasn't anywhere near as clever as he thought he was.

After Emma and Fran had made their escape and told the authorities, Nick was quickly found and taken into custody for Johnny's murder, Daphne's murder, the break-in at Emma's house, and attempted murder of Emma and Fran.

Alibi had mentioned someone named Bee who would be a key witness, able to place Nick at the scene with Johnny when Johnny died.

Bee and Nick evidently looked somewhat alike, both having short-cropped blond hair and a slim build. In fact, that similarity had caused Alibi to include Bee in his list of suspects. Alibi had told Emma that sometimes killers wanted so badly to be on the inside of an investigation that they posed as a witness. But it turned out Bee was exactly what he'd said he was—an innocent bystander with a cat—and Nick, who had so dearly wanted to be one of a kind, was going to be brought down by the testimony of someone he might have been mistaken for in a crowd. There seemed some justice in that.

As to Daphne's brutal killing, Nick had held on to the gun. It was the same one he'd used to force Emma and Fran into the trailer. While firearms might make killing easy, they also provided extremely compelling evidence. And to add to Nick's troubles, Sid was already hard at work helping the government with their case against him for his attempt to steal $1 million of state funds.

In Sid's first day investigating Nick, he'd found out the kid came from money. Lots of money. He had trust accounts that would have set him up for life. But there were strings attached, and Nick was done playing that game, so he'd made up a game of his own. Unfortunately, it was an immoral and deadly one.

Emma was pleased California no longer had the death penalty. She didn't want anyone killed on her behalf, and she knew Luke wouldn't want it for Daphne. Instead, Nick was going to be an involuntary guest of the state in less-than-luxury accommodations for a long, long time.

Fran would pay a price for the arson, certainly a fine and possibly some prison time, regardless of whether she'd thought it would be water damage instead of flames. She had put in motion the events that had led to the death of William Bowers, who had only wanted to get out of the cold.

She was already working on rehabilitating her political image, having put out a press release stating that she would establish the William Bowers Foundation with $1 million of her own money to help the homeless. Emma supposed there were worse ways for the rich to try to right an unrightable wrong. In any case, Fran's lifelong punishment was that in Emma's family, she'd forever be known as Shirley.

Meanwhile, in Emma's life, the biggest news was that it was Sunday, five minutes to noon. She and Atticus had agreed this was the hour at which he'd make good on his promise to tell her where he'd been these many years and why.

"I'LL BEGIN THIS at the beginning . . ."

Atticus's storytelling voice was as familiar to Emma as her own.

"Your mother was a drug addict. Addicted to opioids prescribed to her for her back," he said, starting in the place Emma had expected. "She needed increasing amounts of opioids, first to find relief from her pain, but later she needed the drug for the drug's sake. As a public health nurse, she was afraid she'd lose her job if she admitted her problem and sought treatment. You'll recall I earned no money. Your mother's paycheck meant everything for you kids. Food, shelter, books, and toys. All that was from your mom. She wouldn't risk it. So when she couldn't get the drugs she needed from her doctor and she'd exhausted her doctor-shopping options, she started obtaining them illegally through a clerk at the clinic. That woman's boyfriend was a dealer and a very bad guy. He sold drugs to respectable people like your mom and then blackmailed them to stay quiet with their employers and their families."

He paused and asked, "Are you okay?"

As long as they broadly defined *okay*, Emma figured they could keep going, so she nodded.

"It was that woman's son, now grown, who came to see me at the gallery. I'm making some educated guesses here, piecing together his drunken rant, but he must have uncovered some evidence of the blackmailing she and her boyfriend were doing, and she spun a story that she was the one being victimized by your mother and me. Then she died—possibly was murdered—and he believed I was the cause, directly or indirectly."

"Did you leave because of the blackmail? Why didn't you take us with you?" Emma asked.

"It's complicated," he said. "Your mother was doubly trapped, by the drugs and by her dealer. The day you found her on the floor and I sent you off to your grandmother's and later told you your mother had died of a heart attack—"

Emma couldn't stand waiting for the words she knew were coming. She had to say them first.

"It wasn't a heart attack. She died of a drug overdose."

"No," Atticus said. "Though your mother did overdose. More than once. But not that day. That day, I learned about the extent of the trouble and the danger she was in. Because it wasn't only drugs that day. Her dealer had beaten Margaret up in places it wouldn't show. I know cracked ribs," he said, moving gingerly and grimacing, "in part because that man had cracked hers."

Emma shook her head. It didn't make sense.

"Stay with me, Emma. I want you to know what really happened. Okay?"

She took a breath and gave a slight nod.

There's no way out but through.

Had her mother said that? Atticus? Kate?

"I decided then that I had to get Margaret completely away from the life she'd fallen into or she wouldn't survive. And I couldn't let you and Jasmine live in a home where violence was one hit and one missed payment away. So I spoke with your grandmother and made arrangements for her to raise you girls. I know now that she had her own problems, which I turned a blind eye to for too long, but she wanted to make a home for you. A safe home, away from the drugs and the violence."

Emma felt confused.

Not a heart attack? Not a drug overdose?

"What did she die of?" she asked.

Her dad was spinning the wedding ring on his left hand with the fingers of his right, faster and faster. "She didn't," Atticus said.

"She would have died if I'd not taken her away, completely away. And she would have put you in danger with a man like that coming into our home."

Emma looked stubbornly at him, like he'd better come up with a different lie for why he'd left and where he'd been, because this one was not acceptable.

"I didn't know how long it would be for," Atticus said. "She relapsed many times. We lived rough at times because she couldn't work and I couldn't earn much. Turns out I'm not a good waiter or salesperson or just about anything you can do to earn a living. Plus, when I'd leave her alone so I could work, your mother would find a way to get drugs again."

Emma wasn't listening anymore. She had latched on to what he had said earlier.

The part she'd heard as a lie.

But he hadn't withdrawn it.

"Mom's not dead?" Emma asked.

"She's not dead," Atticus said.

THREE WEEKS LATER
SUNDAY, APRIL 4

67

E MMA SAT ON her front stoop alone. She watched as Henry and Trey made their second loop of the cul-de-sac with the dogs. Crash stayed protectively by seven-year-old Trey's side, just as he had with Luke when he was little, while Fox tested the limits with ten-year-old Henry, demanding another tummy rub before permitting any additional forward motion.

Though her sprained ankle was nearly healed, Emma still wasn't up for dog walking. Besides, she enjoyed having the boys around and had convinced their parents to let them come twice a week, on Sunday afternoons and again on Wednesdays after school, when Emma left work early to meet them and they stayed for dinner. Mrs. Cleveland, across the street, often joined them, to Fox's delight.

She checked the time. When Emma looked at the watch Kate had given her, she felt the familiar pang of loss that was never far away. They messaged every day, often several times a day, and video chatted most evenings—Kate had been right about that. The virtual connections helped. But it wasn't the same. And they stayed away from the topic of whether and when Kate and Luke might come back.

Emma was somewhat comforted by the fact that Mrs. Cleveland had set up Kate and Luke's now-vacant duplex, with Emma's help, for short-time rentals through Airbnb. At least that meant they had a home to return to, if they decided they wanted to.

It was two fifteen pm, and like clockwork, Alibi's Chevy pickup rounded the corner at the bottom of the street. The old brown truck rumbled as he pulled up to the curb, and moments later he was out with a small takeout bag in one hand and a cardboard drinks carrier in the other, both from Second Chance.

"Where are the boys?" he asked, sitting on the stoop and placing his offerings between them.

"Across the street," Emma said.

There was no one staying at Kate and Luke's yet, so Mrs. Cleveland let Henry and Luke and Crash and Fox play in the backyard. She served them cookies and dog treats, after which the boys would make another few circuits of the cul-de-sac before returning the tired dogs to Emma's care. It was all part of Emma's new Sunday routine, which also included Alibi's Second Chance deliveries.

She and Alibi hadn't revisited their one-sided steamy kiss that had occurred the night of the day Kate and Luke had left. Nor had they talked about what, if anything, their renewed friendship might mean or evolve into. For now, Emma was just happy she could count on Alibi's reliable presence every Sunday—having him with her, his tall and steady form, his black hair grazing his shoulders, his dark eyes at times alight with humor, at others warm with affection or intent upon hers with concern or compassion.

He conveyed so much while saying very little that was personal, and she'd discovered that was exactly what she needed right now.

She picked up the iced herbal tea he'd brought her, removed the top, and took a sip—it was delightful. Spring had arrived in earnest in Sacramento, with temperatures in the midseventies, and the cool drink was refreshing. Alibi was drinking his coffee, black and hot, as he did in all seasons at any time of day.

"I brought you something," he said, reaching into the pocket of his sports coat. That was another thing that didn't vary—what Alibi wore, at work or at play.

But Emma wasn't prepared for what he produced for her wrapped in soft white tissue paper: her mother's necklace.

"I couldn't get your laptop or tablet released yet. They're in the queue to be scoured for evidence in one or more of the many charges against Nick. But photos of the necklace will do, so they let me have this."

"Thank you," she said, without enthusiasm.

She made no move to accept it. She felt she owed Alibi an explanation, though she wasn't sure she could put what she felt into words. After a beat, she tried.

"The last time I saw that necklace, my mother was dead. Or I thought she was. And for twenty-two years, it was my only connection to her. When I was little, I imagined it held some part of her spirit, that my mother was near me so long as I had it. As I got older, I never quite shook that feeling, and when the necklace was taken, it was as though I'd lost her."

Emma's voice cracked. She felt her eyes fill with tears.

Alibi's expression remained open and calm.

"It's like the necklace lied to me. It should have found a way to convey that my mother wasn't inside it in some ethereal, other-worldly sense. That she was living in Edmund, Oklahoma, with my father." At that, Emma smiled. "Atticus wasn't in La Réunion, France, and Margaret wasn't dancing with the angels. I blame that necklace for not having made that clear."

She looked again at the delicate gold chain and the pendant ringed in garnets that lay in the crumpled tissue paper in Alibi's hand. "Would you keep it for me? Until I'm ready? Maybe after I've seen her?"

It wasn't that there'd been no physical opportunity for Emma to see Margaret, because it wasn't just Atticus's luggage that had been at the hotel in San Francisco when Emma had picked him up at the jail. Margaret had been there too. But it was only after the fire in the trailer that Atticus had finally revealed that the last two decades had been a lie. Not one perpetrated by an inanimate necklace but by her parents together, in collaboration.

To shield Emma? To protect her?

Whatever the reason, given the fragility Atticus had asserted Margaret would always bear—the relapse into drug use that was around every corner—he and Emma had decided that both she and Margaret would do better to take some time before an in-person visit.

They'd had several video calls after Atticus and Margaret had returned to their midwestern home, and Emma had been shocked by how much her mother had aged. At fifty-six, Margaret looked ten years older than Atticus, her once-long thick auburn hair cut short in a cap of thinning white curls, her eyes a faded blue, her skin lined beyond her years.

The drugs had not been kind to her body or her mind.

Emma's anger had softened toward both of them as she saw the toll her mother's addiction had taken on her and realized how extraordinary it was that her father had stood by her mother through it all.

Having read about codependency now, Emma understood that perhaps it hadn't all been out of love and altruism for Atticus. But whatever terms one wanted to use, he hadn't run away from anything.

Instead, her father had run toward decades of care and sacrifice.

"Sure," Alibi said, tucking the wrapped necklace back in his pocket and pulling out a well-worn deck of cards. "You ready? Are you tired of losing yet?"

He smiled, and she felt her shoulders relax.

"You sure those aren't marked?" Emma asked, only half kidding, as she pushed the bag of scones and drinks aside to clear a space for their weekly poker game.

She hadn't beaten him yet.

Today just might be the day.

ACKNOWLEDGMENTS

ACKNOWLEDGMENTS ARE THE most difficult part of writing a book for me. I did not feel safe in my own home as a child. When someone did show me kindness, I wanted to keep it a secret. I believed if I said it aloud, it might be taken from me or, worse yet, the person who provided it might disappear. The fact that my imagination was a scary place (reflecting my reality) is likely the reason I didn't attempt to write fiction until I was nearly sixty years old. Instead, I read others' books, two to three a week, delighting in adventure stories that weren't too violent and where children weren't harmed, in which I got to see "the good guys" win.

When I finally decided to write a story, at first it was only for me. I guess I was afraid—as with the kindnesses of my child-hood—to expose it to the light. It took many supportive people—friends, family, colleagues, and yes, mental health providers—to bring me to the place that I am now, where I could not imagine going a day without the joy of telling stories. So I'm going to endeavor to put "thank yous" to paper. If I miss you, please know it's due to my shortcomings. A glitch in my wiring. If you helped me in any way, you are in my heart.

(Caution: This contains vague spoilers . . .)

My editor at Crooked Lane Books, Terri Bischoff, is a legend in the mystery/suspense/thriller genres. I wanted to work with Terri as soon as I began writing. My sincere thanks to everyone at

Crooked Lane Books, including Madeline Rathle, Rebecca Nelson, and Melissa Rechter.

I provided an early draft of this book to my agent, Abby Saul at The Lark Group. She suggested dropping two subplots that related to the protagonist Emma's personal life and focusing more on the crimes. I agreed in principle, but when I saw it would require cutting thirty thousand words and replacing them with something new, I balked. Abby said simply, "You can do this." I am so fortunate to partner with an unfailingly kind and whip-smart, effective agent.

My daughter, Erin, is my extraordinarily knowledgeable and compassionate go-to resource on criminal justice issues. My son Matt provided the initial idea for the nonprofit contract fraud in this story and is my expert on all things related to public service and politics. I wrote *Under a Broken Sky* during the pandemic, and my youngest son, Nate, was my rock throughout that time. Nate was also my sounding board for numerous plot twists, and the idea for the blackmail spin was his.

Having come to writing fiction late in life, I've been fortunate that the professionals I've worked with are top-notch. Developmental editors Eileen Rendahl, Trey Geisman, Amelia Geser, and Hailey Council-Galper Kerschen all provided important insights and positive guidance. Copy editor Rachel Keith not only did a careful review for errors but also identified and gently offered options that improved the manuscript. Joseph Borden created beautiful, compelling ads and graphics. I received invaluable input from Addie Conway (@bookcrazyblogger on IG) on addiction issues, which I used in developing a central character. (All errors, of course, are my own.)

I've had the pleasure of meeting with many welcoming Rotary Clubs and book clubs. I want to especially thank my dear friend Mieke Kramer of the Epsilon Book Club, the entire club, and club member Sharon Lefler. Sharon generously read the final draft of *Under a Broken Sky* on a tight timeline to give me a careful "reader's perspective" on anything I might have missed.

I'm amazed by how many established and talented authors are willing to give of their valuable time and wisdom to those of us starting out. In master classes and workshops with Meg Gardiner,

Lee Child, John Lescroart, Gayle Lynds, and Robert Dugoni, I've gained craft skills that I've done my best to incorporate into my work.

The following authors, all of whom I admire, have repeatedly provided timely encouragement and support: Lisa Alber, Eric Beetner, Mysti Berry, Sarah M. Chen, Joe Clifford, Matt Coyle, Chris Holm, Dietrich Kalteis, James L'Etoile, Jess Lourey, Rob Pierce, Tom Pitts, Lisa Preston, Kirk Russell, Laura Jensen Walker, Mark Wheaton, Naomi Williams, and Tony Wirt. Then there's "The Gang," as we refer to ourselves, of local writers and partners in (fictional) crime who always come through for one another: John Lescroart (again), Catriona McPherson, Eileen Rendahl, Tamsen Schultz Bhachech, Lisa Nalbone, and Spring Warren. Public libraries and independent bookstores across the country are my favorite stops on any trip—thank you, librarians, library volunteers, booksellers, and bookshop staff! The Capitol Crimes Sacramento Chapter of Sisters in Crime has been a great resource, as has local independent bookstore Capital Books on K.

Thank you to my work colleagues at the American Academy of Pediatrics in California and nationally (many of whom have become lifelong friends), and to my family, especially the next generation, my nieces and nephews. Julie Roberts Sanders, LMFT, has provided me with a safe space through caring, compassionate, and steady therapy. And not yet mentioned above, to Kathy and Lori, there's no "thank you" that would be enough.

Finally, I am deeply grateful to every reader who has given my stories a chance. It is only through you that they come to life.

Kris Calvin

December 2021